FINDING TIME

FINDING TIME

12 METICULOUSLY CRAFTED TIME TRAVEL STORIES

ROBERT J. MCCARTER

LITTLE HUMMINGBIRD PUBLISHING

Time is relative; its only worth depends upon what we do as it is passing.

ALBERT EINSTEIN

The distinction between the past, present and future is only a stubbornly persistent illusion.

ALBERT EINSTEIN

CONTENTS

INTRODUCTION

I think a fiction writer has some very important duties when it comes to telling stories. We are, after all, lying to tell the truth.

I think that's what good fiction does. It lies to you, over and over, but it does so in an entertaining way that illuminates some truth about us humans. At its best, fiction illuminates truths that are otherwise hard to see. Stories aren't nearly as messy and chaotic as real life and they are great tools to transmit knowledge. In fact, our brains are hardwired to receive information via story.

That's why when it comes to time travel, I think a writer has an even more important responsibility and the bar should be set high.

Why?

Well, to me time travel is, plot-wise, a really big gun—or, to put it another way, a really big lie. You can do amazing things with time travel, get at some of those human truths through this particular "lie," but you can also create a huge mess.

When you are dealing with things like time travel with its causal loops, its ability to rewrite the past or the future, and, frankly, with its ability to confuse the hell out of the reader, it's really important to get it right, to play fair, to use the power of time travel wisely, and to have it all make sense in the end.

The twelve stories in this collection are my attempt to do justice to the idea of time travel, to play fair with the plots, to entertain, and to, hopefully, illuminate.

There is not just one type of time travel in these stories, there are many. Some are more sci-fi, some are more fantasy—" My Love's Past" features a telepathic Corgi, so, yeah, that's fantasy—and one, "With Light Years Between Us," you could call hard science fiction given that the time travel involved is based on Einstein's theory of special relativity.

We've got causal loops in "The Travelers," "My Love's Past," and a few others. One-way time travel into the past with "The Pearce Shootout" and "Butterfly in Training" (both of those feature the same protagonist and take place in the same fictional world). One-way into the future with "Jump in Time" and "Kelli Who Prays to Kali." Choosing between two timelines in "Fold. Shift. Goodbye." And even time travel where you can't change anything, future or past, in "Goodbye Mrs. Hopkins." And finally a brand-new story that insisted on coming out while I was putting this collection together with "Which Came First: The Chicken or the Time Traveling Egg?"

As always, I'll tell you a little bit about each story, after the story, so I don't have to worry about spoiling anything.

I think the title of this book "Finding Time" is appropriate. Time is the single most valuable thing to us mortal human beings. We only get so much of it and how we spend it is important. I spent some of mine writing these stories so I hope your precious time is well spent reading these stories.

Robert J. McCarter

Flagstaff, AZ

April 2024

PART 1

WITH LIGHT YEARS BETWEEN US

WITH LIGHT YEARS BETWEEN US

The butterflies in Henry's stomach went from a hearty protest to full on rioting the moment he saw Melody. She stood on the edge of the concourse, her brown eyes searching the crowd. She wore the blue uniform of an International Space Alliance (ISA) officer, and her curly black hair was pulled back into a ponytail.

She looked... young, too young, and beautiful. She looked just the same as she had fifty-eight years ago when she had left for the mission to Gliese 667 C.

He paused, gripping his cane, wanting to turn around, but she meant too much to him. His first love. His first wife. He brushed at his white hair, suddenly feeling self-conscious about something he was usually proud of.

He stepped forward and walked resolutely towards her, his cane in hand, tapping on the concourse tile. When she saw him, she stared, her eyes wide and her jaw slack, her hand coming to her mouth.

"Well, what did you expect?" Henry asked, a sour look on his wrinkled face, his hand brushing at his white hair again. "It's not like we didn't exchange vids the last year when your damn ship got close enough to make it reasonable. You knew what I looked like."

Melody's nostrils flared as she took a breath and opened her mouth to speak. Her lips moved, but no words formed.

Henry blinked as people flowed around them in the Denver Beanstalk Terminal. They ignored Melody in her ISA uniform, but many openly stared at the stooped form of Henry Fischer. He was dressed in an archaic way, in cotton-based shirt and pants in muted earth tones, which stood out among the bright tunics and leggings that were the norm. He gripped a gnarled wooden cane in his left hand, the only gray-haired person in sight.

"I..." Melody began, her sad eyes continuing to look him over. "I'm... I'm so sorry."

Henry shrugged, wishing he could run and not sure exactly what she was sorry for.

He saw a young girl pass close to him, staring with eyes wide. He needed a distraction, so he feinted a step towards her and laughed when she ran away, grabbing her mother. "Ha!" Henry called. "Respect your elders, missy."

"Why did you do that?" Melody asked, her hands clenched.

He wasn't going to tell her it was because of him being a nervous fool. He took a deep breath to say something rude, but stopped when he caught a whiff of her scent. It was a shock, so strange yet so familiar. Among the smells of the busy concourse, a jangle of food, perfumes, and sweat, her smell was just a whisper, a bit sweet and a bit musky. His brain struggled with what to do with it, a smell so old and yet so familiar, a smell with a complex web of emotions attached.

He shook his head and sighed. "That one's probably never seen a proper old man. Just the fake ones running around these days that pretend to be fifty when they're a hundred-fifty, not a gray hair on their heads." He looked at the retreating girl, who kept looking back, resisting the urge to shake his cane at her, not wanting to look too silly.

"Henry."

"What?" he said, turning to face the tall, elegant woman, her dark skin smooth, looking ageless like all the other adults on the concourse.

"This isn't... this isn't what I wanted after so long. I—"

He snorted, his nervousness twisting towards anger. "Were we to fall into each other's arms and start kissing after fifty-eight years?"

"No. I..."

"Spit it out, Mrs. Fischer." When she didn't answer quickly, he pointed to her left hand and the simple gold band there, the butterflies gone and his heart beating hard. "Did you just put it on when you left your fancy ship and said goodbye to all your handsome explorers?"

Her jaw bunched, and she took a breath before answering. "That's not fair, Henry. I was gone for..." She trailed off. Henry knew she didn't want to highlight the difference in how many years each had experienced since they parted.

His eyes returned to hers, and he nodded. "Sorry. You are right. But it wasn't fair of you to spend twenty-eight years gallivanting off to Gliese 667, taking your great lap around the galactic neighborhood, while us earthlings aged almost twice that."

"Jesus, Henry! You agreed to this. You know what this meant to me."

Henry exhaled, his shoulders slumping as he slowly nodded. "We were so young. How could we know...? Can we try this again?" he asked, smiling shyly.

She nodded warily.

Henry walked ten meters down the crowded concourse,

stopped, took a deep breath, and tried to get his bitterness and anger under control. He walked back to Melody. "My God, darling," he said, his voice less gruff, "you look fabulous. You do." He took her hand and squeezed it and felt the anger mounting again. She was so young. He was so old. "Relativistic speeds and modern medicine have been so very kind to your complexion. I hope you're ready to settle down, restart our marriage contract, and get to having our baby."

She pulled her hand away from him and crossed her arms.

"My God, Melody!" he said loudly, unable to stop himself, his cheeks flushed and his breath coming fast. He raised his cane in the air, attracting stares. "You are so beautiful. I could do you right here and now. Get that uniform off, woman. I must have you!"

Her jaw locked, she brushed past him and marched down the concourse without him.

<hr>

A HALF AN HOUR LATER, AFTER PACING THE CONCOURSE and calming himself down, Henry found Melody sitting outside the terminal, her face to the sun, the cool breeze playing with her curly black hair.

"I'm a little shit," he said, slumping onto the bench next to her, taking in the view of the distant Rocky Mountains hunched on the horizon. The anger was gone, as were the butterflies—he just felt drained.

"You could act your age, you know," she said, not looking at him.

He snorted. "I'm not going to do that. Ninety-three is a boring age. Besides, when did I ever act my age when I didn't have to?"

She took a deep breath and slowly let it out. "I missed clean air, real air. And the sun, I missed the sun." She turned and looked at him, her brown eyes serious. "And I missed you too, Henry."

He nodded, feeling his face flush. He took her hand and smiled, breathing in her scent and welcoming it this time. "I missed you too. And you are beautiful. As beautiful as the day we met on Jupiter Station."

She looked at him, her eyes slowly scanning his face, tracing the lines there. "Why?" she asked.

"The wrinkles?"

She nodded.

He took a deep breath and pursed his lips, his eyes distant. "I have no real objection to aging. The world is more afraid of death now than when we lasted eighty years instead of a hundred-twenty. I don't know." He shrugged and squeezed her hand again. "I just don't want to look at a perfectly smooth face in the mirror the day I die. Doesn't seem right."

She nodded and squeezed back. "But you've got decades left. Why?"

He sighed, she still knew him, there was more to it. "I... I'm special this way. And..." He ended in a weak shrug.

She nodded. "And the cane?"

He grinned, leaped up, his stoop disappearing, and did an awkward tap dance in front of her, drawing more looks from the people walking from the terminal to the waiting cars. "I'm not stupid," he said, shaking the cane in the air. "I got the nanites. A few years with arthritis and I said, bring them little anti-inflammatory machines on. The cane just completes the costume and makes it easy to mess with the kids."

Melody laughed, delicate wrinkles forming around her eyes as she stood and drew him into a hug. "I did miss you," she whispered, his heart pounding and his nose filling with her sweet/sharp smell. He didn't know how much he had missed it.

He nodded. "Want to go home now?"

"Yes."

The hug ended awkwardly, and Henry stood there staring at her. He appeared to be so old and she appeared to be so young. He didn't know if he should kiss her, and surprisingly, he didn't know if he wanted to kiss her.

"IT'S NOT MUCH," HENRY SAID, POINTING AT THE OLD BRICK house with his cane. "Spent the last decade gutting her and rebuilding her; two hundred years old, but good bones. It's small, just two bedrooms, but there's room for a garden in back."

Melody stood on the sidewalk, staring.

The ride from the terminal had been awkwardly silent, the butterflies taking hold again in Henry's stomach. The car that had brought them had just driven away.

"Grass," she whispered.

"Hardy stuff, too. Barely needs a drop of water. Thought you might..."

And then she was on the grass, her fingers digging into it, her face finding the sun again, a laugh escaping her. "I love it, Henry. I love it. Did you... did you do this for me? Knowing after all the years in space I would need some grass to sit on."

Henry leaned on his cane and smiled, but didn't answer. He had, but for some reason he felt embarrassed about it.

"Come," she said, patting the grass next to her. "Come sit with me."

"Don't you want to see the inside? I've been—"

"Henry. Please."

He nodded and walked over the lawn and sat down gracefully next to her. She leaned close and whispered, "Do you feel it?"

He shrugged, her closeness stirring things in him again, long forgotten things.

"The breeze, it's cool, and the grass... it smells like... like the color green. And the sun, do you feel it radiating us with its warmth, like it's feeding you and me in the same way it's feeding the grass? Come on, Henry. Do you feel it?"

He smiled and nodded, although he knew he didn't feel it like she did. He hadn't spent over twenty years on a spaceship and couldn't imagine what that had been like. They were so different now. "What are we doing, Melody?" He stared at the grass and picked at it.

She sniffed and took a deep breath. "We had an agreement," she said.

He nodded. "When we met, I was seven years older than you. I was twenty-six, working as a teacher on Jupiter Station; you were a tourist, all of nineteen. Remember how big that gap seemed then?"

She nodded, stiffening next to him.

"We were different people then, when you decided to join the mission to Gliese. It was ten years after our meeting, we were still silly in love, and time didn't seem to hold sway over us." He shook his head. "I'm thirty-seven years older than you now. What are we doing?"

Henry remembered that young woman he met, with the curious brown eyes and the insatiable love of space. He remembered how he felt the first time he saw her eyes wide as she stared at Jupiter's swirling storms far below. He remembered their passion as they traveled to the asteroid belt, to the moon, and finally landed on Earth to build a life before the need for space had taken her away.

He opened his mouth to speak, but caught sight of a girl peeking out from behind the hedge that bordered his yard.

"Young lady," he said, getting up, his voice deep and serious. "What did I tell you about today? I can see you, Nina."

The girl, seven years of age, stepped from behind the hedge. "You told me I was to stay away and give my new Gran time to accli... acclimate."

Henry walked slowly over to her and, when he was close, reached out and grabbed her, lifting her up and twirling her around, Nina's long blond hair flying. She laughed as Henry's fingers found her ribs.

He carried her over on his shoulder and then set her down in front of Melody. "Melody Fischer, may I present my granddaughter, Nina Powell. Nina, this is Melody, your new gran."

Nina slowly held out her hand and Melody stared. Henry had told her this part, sent her the vids and pictures, told her everything, but the reality was proving to be different than either of them expected.

Melody took the girl's hand in hers and shook it. "Glad to meet you, Nina."

Nina paused, licked her lips, and then asked, "What is Gliese 667 C like? How is the colony? Do you have any vids I can see that you took? A virt would be so much better. I've seen all the official documentation, but you know, they don't give you a real look at it. Are the domes there really over two kilometers in diameter? Will the atmosphere ever be breathable? Where do you think—"

"Now, now, Nina," Henry said, grabbing the girl and hoisting her into the air again. "You've got to give her some time to answer." He looked at Melody. "This one wants to follow in your footsteps."

"Yes!" Nina said from Henry's embrace. "Yes, please! I want to work for the ISA like you. I want to travel at over 90 percent the speed of light. I want to step onto another world. I want to—"

"You want to go home now," Henry said, walking to the sidewalk and setting her down and pointing her in the direction she came. He looked back at Melody's wide eyes. "We have to let her adjust some. She's been in space a very long time and is still getting used to the feeling of the earth beneath her."

Nina nodded seriously at Henry and then gave Melody a bright wave before skipping down the sidewalk.

Henry sighed and walked back onto the grass, sitting down next to Melody. "I guess we should talk about this. About my other family."

She nodded, biting her lip.

THE BACKYARD WAS MODEST, WITH A ROUND LATTICEWORK table and two chairs sitting on a covered patio, more grass, and some raised beds that had no plants in them. Henry took her through the side gate, not ready to let her see the inside of the house yet.

"For you," he said to Melody, pointing to the planters. "No soil in there yet, I know you'll want to prepare it yourself." He paused. "Or maybe you're sick of plants, a couple of decades working in hydroponics could do that. I just thought that maybe you'd like it."

Melody walked into the yard and sat on the grass with a sigh. Henry stood there, his arms crossed, staring at her, his stomach clenched like a fist. His body and mind were at war. His body recognized her, wanted to go sit next to her, breathe her in and devour her with his eyes, but his mind was holding on to anger. She had left. Physics had intervened, and fifty-eight years had passed for him and only twenty-eight for her. And what of it? Would twenty-eight years make this any better? Well, at least they would be closer in age then.

"Oh," he said, recovering from his reverie. "Here." He took

the bottle off the table and the two short glasses and walked over and sat down, putting the bottle and glasses between them.

"The Glenlivet," she said, a small smile playing on her lips. "I had completely forgotten about it. We bought that after our last dinner. Bought it for tonight."

Henry nodded and broke the seal. The bottle had sat on the hearth next to her portrait, a promise of her return. "The extra years won't make it any better, but..." He shrugged and poured a little in each glass and handed her one. "Remember when we bought it?"

She nodded, taking a small sip, her eyes widening. "Yeah. We ate Italian, we were living in Austin then, and you pulled me into a little liquor store on the walk home. You said we were going to need it when I got back."

"To homecomings," he said, and they clinked glasses and sipped more.

"So..." she offered. "You ready to talk?"

"Let me finish my drink first," he said, his voice sounding rough again. He had grieved Melody's departure. He had moved on. And now she was back—which he knew would happen, and yet he wasn't ready to have this conversation.

"My second wife, her name is Fiona," he said after he finished his scotch, but refrained from pouring more even though he wanted to. He felt the alcohol, warm in his stomach, relaxing him, but he didn't want to take it too far. "We have one child, Elena, and she has one child, Nina, whom you just met. Our marriage contract was for thirty years. We didn't renew." He shrugged. "It was amicable. I see her all the time, we just... Well, you know all this."

She nodded, pouring the amber liquid in both of their glasses, pouring much more than Henry had. She took a swallow and said, "Yeah. But knowing and... and meeting your granddaughter, my—what is she?—step-granddaughter. Well..." She took another drink.

"She wants you to be her gran more than anything."

Melody swirled the scotch in her glass and then asked, "You and Fiona. Did you only have one child because of... because of me?"

"ZPG, you know, can't have more than two kids. Before you left, we agreed to all this." He took a big drink and sighed. "God, we were young."

She laughed, the sharp smell of the alcohol mixing with her musky scent. "Enough with that, Henry! No one is old enough to make the decision we made, and no one is old enough for this conversation." She drained her glass, laughed, and then eyed his glass pointedly.

"I'll drink to that," he said, throwing back the rest of his drink and then coughing hard and then laughing. They sat and drank and talked until the sun went down and the air got cold.

"Holy shit..." Melody said when she stumbled into the living room. "Henry... what the hell?"

Henry watched from the kitchen, peering through the entryway. Her eyes went from painting to painting to painting. Jupiter Station against the colorful swirls of the Great Red Spot, two young people staring out a window as they held hands. A painting of a thin arrow of a spaceship with a habitat ring and a shield glowing at the front. Its engines were alight with fire as it shot towards a galaxy in the distance. A man and a woman on top of a mountain, the wind tugging their hair, the land all around them. And a portrait of Melody in her dress whites, the tight curls of her black hair a halo around her head slowly transforming into a starfield.

"Henry!" she said, stamping her foot, stumbling and then laughing. "Get in here. Now!"

Henry walked in slowly, his head down, his heart pounding from the scotch, from Melody being back, and from her seeing this. He put all the paintings away this morning but got mad at himself and put them back out before going to get her.

"When did you become such a romantic?" she asked.

His shaggy eyebrows danced above his eyes as emotions played on his face: uncertainty, fear, curiosity. "I... I..." he began.

"You can paint. These are good." She went around the simple living room with its couch, two comfortable chairs, and prominent media wall. She stopped in front of the large canvases, lingering for a moment in front of all of them but the portrait. She ended in front of Henry. "When did you learn how to paint? These are oil paintings. That's not easy."

He licked his lips and shrugged. "I started after Fiona and I ended. Fifteen years ago. I still teach history a bit, but..." He shrugged again. "I like this."

"You never told me." Melody walked around the room again, her bare feet soft on the carpet, still wearing her uniform, but the tunic unbuttoned at the neck. She stopped in front of the fireplace and the large portrait of her. "And this?"

Henry walked up next to her, breathing deeply, trying to ignore her scent. "I just... as your ship got closer, I wanted to feel you close, so..."

She took his hand and he closed his eyes, remembering that enthusiastic young woman on Jupiter Station and the young man he had been, before marriages and a child and a grandchild and age had settled in on him.

"Sometimes I feel like this," he said, his eyes still closed as he swayed slightly.

"What?" she whispered.

"Sometimes I feel like I look. I feel old. Even if I had all the extension treatments and not just the ones that let me stay active, I think I would still feel old." He opened his eyes and she was staring at him. "You're still young. I don't know that I'm the partner you need right now." He let go of her hand and walked out the front door into the cool Colorado night.

HENRY SLOWLY SWUNG ON THE SWING SET AT THE playground down the street, the Milky Way a bright line of stars arching in the dark sky above. He didn't speak when Melody walked down the street to the park, tossed him a jacket, and got in the swing next to his.

He put the jacket on and they swung gently as the stars executed their imperceptibly slow dance above them.

"You've been out there," he whispered after some minutes. "So far away, with light years between us for so long. What can I offer you down here?"

She sniffed and nodded. "Henry..."

"No. You left me for the stars. Do you even want to stay?" She opened her mouth to speak, but he continued. "Don't answer that. You've been on the ground ten minutes. You can't know."

They swung a little more, and she said, "And, Henry, you can't know if you want me to stay. Those paintings, they're amazing, as was our time together. But... I can't live up to what you've painted. I can't be the woman you painted."

The thoughts whirled through his head of who they had been, who they were, what they wanted to be. His anger was gone, the butterflies had been drowned by the scotch, and he felt tired and wrung out.

"I made up the master bedroom for you," he said, getting up.

She nodded and Henry walked over the park's lawn and

toward the street. She caught up to him and took his hand. This time, Henry was content to hold hands as they walked back home.

***

"Real eggs, sunny-side up," Melody said after Henry set the plate down in front of her. "And cantaloupe and toast and coffee. My God, Henry, this is perfect."

He had gotten up early and moved the iron latticework table onto the grass so Melody could enjoy breakfast in the open air. The sun wasn't on the yard yet, but she had the sky above.

He sat across from her and said, "Sorry for the theatrics at the terminal yesterday."

She shrugged, her long hair cascading down past her shoulders. Henry thought she looked odd in the normal synthetic tunics everyone wore these days. Hers was a deep purple and looked good on her. She ummed and ahhed over her first bite. "With this, all is forgiven."

Henry didn't touch his food and just stared at her, sipping at his strong, black coffee. During the night, he had lain awake for hours thinking about those paintings and what she had said. He had awaited her return for too long. He had put too many expectations on her, and the haze of age had romanticized their younger years together. He had been too long alone waiting for her.

When she was done with her plate, while she still chewed the last mouthful, she pointed at his plate with her fork. "If you don't want that..."

He smiled and handed it over. "But don't touch my coffee, woman, not if you want things to remain civil."

She eyed him for a moment, making sure he wasn't serious, and then smiled and started in on his plate.

When she was done, he said, "I've been thinking…"

Her eyebrow arched, but she didn't say anything, taking a sip of her coffee.

A smile played on his lips and he swallowed hard. "What if I catch the next ship to Gliese, go gallivanting twenty-two light years away, and you stay here. Get married. Start a family. And when I get back, we'll both be the same age."

"You are a shit, you know that," she said and threw her napkin at him.

He held his hands up. "A joke. Just a joke."

She bit her lip and nodded. "But your point is well taken, Henry. We didn't know what this would be like. We couldn't."

"So… can we… you know…?" He sighed and his shoulders fell as his butterflies put on their riot gear.

"One day at a time?" she asked, her voice gentle.

He nodded. "I took the portrait of you down. I'm giving it to Nina. She'll pee herself, she'll be so happy."

They heard a muffled squeal from around the side of the house. Henry shook his head and stood up. "Over here, young lady," he said sternly.

Nina peeked around the edge of the house. "I still get the painting of Gran with the stars in her hair, right?"

Henry smiled. "Yes."

Nina ran to the table, a wide smile on her young face. She looked at Melody. "And you're going to be my gran, right?"

Melody bit her lip, her eyes finding Henry's.

"Oh, no," Nina said, folding her arms across her chest and rolling her eyes. "Adult stuff." She shook her head. "Is it really that complicated? Because I don't think it has to be." She went to Henry, took him by the hand, and pulled him to Melody. She took Melody's hand and pulled her up and then joined their hands and stood in front of them. "See. Just hold hands. The rest doesn't matter so much. You just need to get to know each other."

Henry looked into the deep brown of Melody's eyes, his face flush and his stomach tight. "You can have the master bedroom," he said. "We can... you know... do things together. No rush. Just... see."

Melody smiled as tears formed in her eyes. She bit her lip and nodded.

"Okay, Papa," Nina said, separating their hands and looking at Melody. "Gran has to tell me all 'bout Gliese 667 C now, right?"

Melody looked at the blond-haired girl, paused, and then shook her head. "Do you really want to join the ISA?"

Nina nodded enthusiastically.

"Well then, you must learn to take orders and work as part of a team."

Nina's eyes widened.

"So today, we are going to do something together, all three of us." She took Nina's hand and smiled at Henry. "We're going to build a garden. I'm going to start teaching you an important skill that got me into the ISA. And then, if you are an excellent helper, I will tell you a story, one story, but it's a good one. Is that acceptable, Ensign Nina?"

The girl nodded, her eyes wide.

Henry smiled. He didn't know what would happen, but for today, for right now, it felt like family.

BACKSTORY—WITH LIGHT YEARS BETWEEN US

Genre: Hard Science Fiction
Type of Time Travel: Forward only
Nature of Time Travel: Einstein's theory of special relativity

Just like "Jump in Time" this story was part of my 2017 "Short Story Marathon" (you can find out more about it at *RobertJMc Carter.com/category/story-marathon/*).

It was inspired by another short story that used Einstein's theory of special relativity as a plot device. I loved the idea of that story but not the execution of it, so being a writer, I wrote a very different story using the same hard sci-fi idea of time travel.

This story was originally published in *Pulphouse Fiction Magazine, Issue #8* and reprinted in *Destination Tomorrow or Yesterday: Stories from Pulphouse.*

This story received an honorable mention in the Writers of the Future contest.

PART 2
KELLI WHO PRAYS TO KALI

KELLI WHO PRAYS TO KALI

"Just a decade or two," Kelli told me before she did her magic. "That will be enough. There will be a cure." Her big blue eyes and tentative smile told another story. She kissed me, her sandalwood scent filling my nose, her lips still hungry after all these years.

She stood back and raised her arms. Her hands stopped shaking as they formed mudras framed against her loose-fitting, tangerine-colored sari. The world—what I could see of it—went fuzzy and she disappeared, and I was left there alone, deep in a cave in the Rocky Mountains watching the years spin by on a monitor.

Kelli prays to Hindu Goddess Kali. Kelli has azure blue eyes the color of Kali's skin. Kelli sent me spinning forth in time with an oxygen tank at my feet—to keep the air breathable—and a longing in my heart that her desperate plan would work.

I WAS TWENTY-FIVE YEARS OLD WHEN I MET DR. KELLI Lata. She was a veterinarian famed for her surgical skills and her ability to clean the teeth of dogs that were allergic to anesthesia. Reilly was a hyperactive Doberman mix that wasn't all that sensitive to anesthesia, I just couldn't handle the twenty-four hours of pitiful groans while he recovered.

I brought him to see Dr. Lata. She, most oddly, worked alone in a historic nineteenth-century home. It was a two-story Victorian with metal tile on the ceiling and wainscoting on the walls. On seeing her, I became a bumbling idiot. She had beautiful brown skin and piercing blue eyes, dressed in a traditional sari, she spoke with an English accent.

She smiled, more with her eyes than her lips, told me she would take good care of Reilly, and gently guided him into the back. I had forgotten to tell her about his penicillin allergy—this one was real—and walked into the back room a few minutes later.

And there was Reilly sitting on a gleaming metal table frozen like a statue, his mouth open. Above him was a painting of a four-armed warrior goddess—Kali. Reilly looked fuzzy, like he was out of focus. Dr. Lata was working away at his teeth with a little metal pick.

The beautiful Dr. Lata slowly turned, a grim look on her face, and said, "I pray to Kali." She nodded to the painting. "She lends me her power so I can do this work."

She was so calm. I was not. My heart beat out a Caribbean rhythm from fear for Reilly and from the closeness of this strange and beautiful creature.

"Sit," she said. "Watch. Your Reilly is fine."

I had just discovered her secret and yet she was as calm as if she were ordering breakfast. I sat and I watched as she carefully cleaned my boy's teeth. Afterwards she chanted a prayer in Sanskrit as her hands danced through a series of mudras. Reilly came back, no longer out of focus, as fine and rambunctious as when I had handed him over.

Then I knew. There could be no other woman in the world this amazing. This beautiful. This special.

Kelli cast her eyes down and shook her head when I first asked her out. This was the day after she froze Reilly and cleaned his teeth. I brought flowers and chocolate. "I am sorry," she mumbled.

But I would not be swayed. Several times a week I would bring her gifts. Little things like a cupcake or coffee. I was working as a freelance writer, pounding out blog posts for people who put their names on what I wrote. And while that took a lot of time, it left me with some flexibility.

I stopped asking her out after the first few times and just started showing up at that lovely Victorian house that sat in an older section of Colorado Springs. Sometimes I would bring Reilly. "Hi, we were just going for a walk, would you like to join us?" Or "First Friday art walk, have you ever gone?" Each time she would demurely tell me no or make an excuse.

After a month of attempts, I was frustrated and asked her why. "My life is given to Kali," she said, so I went away and started studying the Hindu goddess of power or "shakti," the fierce warrior goddess of time and death. Kali who was created before light itself and exists beyond time. Kali with skin as blue as Kelli's eyes.

It wasn't any one thing that won my Kelli over. It was that I never gave up. Slowly we became friends and then we became lovers and then we were married.

And my Kelli was not just a beautiful, demure veterinarian from England of Indian descent. She had the temper of Kali. She had the insecurity of a human. She could be impatient and brusque... And I loved everything about her.

***

OUR LIVES TOGETHER FLEW BY, THE DECADES PASSING IN what seemed like a blink of an eye. We loved and fought and made up. We lived in that old Victorian, most of the space going to her veterinarian practice. I began greeting patients and running the front of the house. We would sneak away to mountain trails on the weekends and soak up the calm of nature.

Not long after we became lovers, I asked her to freeze me. She told me no, of course, but I persisted. She was angry when she did it, her blue eyes like a stormy sea. "Very well," she snapped, her hands forming mudras and my world stopping.

My mouth was open in mid-sentence and she was suddenly gone, my view of our kitchen suddenly looking out of focus, the colors smearing to the left like water color done with too wet a brush. Every once in a while I would see a flash of blurry orange about a head shorter than me. Dishes stacked up in the sink, and then it was dark. And then it was light. And then that blurry orange came back and resolved into the form of my Kelli.

"There. I have misused my gift," she said, her arms crossed. "Are you happy?"

"How... how long?" I felt a bit dizzy, but otherwise perfectly normal.

"A day. I would have left you longer, but best you don't run out of oxygen." She ended with a smile and then was in my arms. It was just a few minutes to me, but a day in the world had passed. What was this creature that I had in my life?

***

My forty-eighth birthday gift was stage IV metastatic lung cancer. It had metastasized and I didn't have long. I had been feeling poorly, but had attributed that to being solidly middle-aged. We went to doctors, got second opinions, and the consensus was clear. They could extend my life with chemo, but not for long.

Kelli took it hard—her mood was a dark storm cloud for months. She locked herself in the bedroom. She drove away for most of a day and wouldn't say where she had gone. She prayed to Kali even more than usual. And then one day she woke with a smile. "We will live, my love, until we don't."

She shut the office down and we played. We went on that long talked about Caribbean vacation. I had some bad days, but some good days too. We ate decadent meals and drank expensive wine. And on really good days we hiked.

Our last hike wasn't long, just a mile out up into the foothills of the Rocky Mountains not far from our Colorado Springs home. She told me there was something she wanted me to see. She hiked me up to a deep cave that had some camping gear in it and other strange things. A couple of oxygen tanks, an LCD monitor mounted on the wall, a battery sitting below it, and wires snaking out of the cave to some solar cells.

"What is this?" I think part of me understood but I couldn't speak it yet. This was what she had been doing when she drove off. This is what she had been planning.

"I cannot be witness to..." she began, her blue eyes moist, her face hard. "I will not..." She was in my arms then and held me, her body shaking. I hugged her hard and then we talked. She was not going to watch me die, she was going to freeze me, misuse her powers again, and hope a cure came soon.

We stayed in that cave for three days, waiting until I had a "good day." She said that was important. And when the day came she rigged the oxygen tanks and froze me.

After she left, the cave was dark but for the LCD monitor which displayed the year. The numbers flicked by like random thoughts. 2015... 2016... 2017... A year passed in a minute and then the display said 2038. I had had half an hour to think about what she had done, to worry, to fret, to regret.

I didn't want to die, but I didn't want to live without her, either.

And then she was there, my Kelli who prays to Kali, dressed in orange, but so different. She was grey and stooped, her face wrinkled like a prune. And she was in my arms smelling of sandalwood but also of something sour and dank.

She shook as she held me. My heart fluttered like a butterfly. I would have asked her if a cure had been found, but I knew the answer. She had changed, so very much, but she was still my Kelli. I smiled at her and told her that we could live our last days together. The words flow out of me like poetry, like the Rumi love poems I used to read her. My love. My devotion. My desire.

She shook her head and stepped back. "I will not... I cannot..." Her arthritic hands formed mudras. "Say hello to Kali for me," she whispered.

Before I could say anything she was gone and the years on that LCD flicked by so fast I could not read them. And then the LCD failed and I was alone in the dark hurtling through time.

Kelli is dead. That was my first thought when the LCD went dark. So much time had passed, she had to be dead. What of the world outside my time bubble? What of me?

As I grieved her, a strobing, bright light filled my world as the cave eroded around me, the Earth, what I could see of it, a barren brown plane. How much time had passed? Ten thousand years? A million years? The scenery looked how I felt, wasted and barren. Everything I had loved was gone. My Kelli was gone. And then in a blinding flash, the earth was gone, and I was lost among the stars as they wheeled around me, streaks of light seen through that bubble that separated the flow of the universe's time from the flow of my time. Streaks of light that dripped to the left of me, growing farther apart as the universe expanded. And then a hulking darkness began eating up the light, pulling me and everything else into it. A black hole.

Just before I descended into its embrace, the stars, for a moment, looked blue. Azure blue. The blue of Kelli's eyes. The blue of Kali.

Some trick of the light, maybe. But I knew that the black hole that was about to eat me was Kali, the goddess of time and death. Created before light itself.

I smiled. I had found Kali. I would die now. I would be with my Kelli.

BACKSTORY—KELLI WHO PRAYS TO KALI

Genre: Fantasy
Type of Time Travel: Forward only
Nature of Time Travel: Slowing time for the protagonist so time is passing quickly relative to him

If you have read much of my writing, you know that grief is a frequent topic. For a bunch of reasons, actually.

I'm old enough now to realize that grief is absolutely unavoidable (like death and taxes) and is an absolute essential part to the human experience. It is also fascinating what we will do because of our grief or to avoid it.

Mix love into the pot with anticipated grief and power and well... you get a story like this.

The other thing I was having fun with was the imagery of time flowing so fast that the seemingly permanent is suddenly revealed as it actually is, impermanent.

PART 3
JUMP IN TIME

JUMP IN TIME

I can't make this make sense to you. I can't. It is silly to try. Stuffing a reality we perceive but a small percentage of into word boxes that fit worse than a round peg in a square hole is ridiculous. But life is ridiculous, is it not? So, I shall attempt the ridiculous and don't go blaming the result on me. Tales of magic watches and time travel bend credulity to the breaking point, but so does this "stranger fact than fiction" world we live in.

Nazis and world wars. D-Day and 150,000 troops landing in Normandy and humans dying by the hundreds of thousands. A cause for sure. Worth dying for? Of course. What strains credulity about this era I was living in is the insanity of those that would think that all others should bow to their view of life, of humans that count and humans that don't count. Power and politics and other useless things mixed in with a country given permission to hate and kill, luring the world to take sides and try to destroy each other. That is the true round peg being crammed into the square hole.

And never you mind that most say it is the square that can't go into the round. I detest square. I feel more round, so I shall say it the way I damn well want to say it. And truth be told, for one should attempt truth when cramming reality into limited word boxes, I don't identify with square at all. I am round or I am nothing at all.

My name is Margret Bellman and I was born in 1913 in San Francisco, California, as it was still rebuilding from the earthquake and fire of 1906. I believe in witches, fairies, and magic watches. This round-to-square story of mine takes place in early 1946 in London, England, not long after the war ended, the day my baby boy was born. I was a nurse working at Queen Alexandra's Military Hospital in London, attempting to put broken young men back together. I simply detest the military and went there after the war started wanting to try to do some good for those spit out by the violence. I was a fine nurse and they desperate, so they took me in despite my "wild American" to their "sedate British." Don't let that fool you. Cultural norms hide the delicious variety underneath, and I found plenty of round pegs in England. I also got shell-shocked in the Blitz and suffered a broken arm. And I got knocked up by a detestable rogue named Kenneth who...

Well, perhaps I should slow down shoving reality into the word boxes and assemble this with a bit more care and back up to 1945 when I met the aforementioned rogue.

Kenneth had swagger and charm, adored his zoot suits, and had blue eyes to die for. He loved to dance and told me my mousey brown hair was not boring but magnificent. He made me feel beautiful. He loved his cigarettes and his whiskey and he said that he loved me. He was no square peg, not even round, let's say that he was a triangular peg. He didn't fit into any of the holes, although he managed all right with me, getting me pregnant just over a month after I met him.

I remember those sparkling eyes the day I told him, my eyes

swollen with tears. We were in my little flat and I had come home to him making dinner. The man could cook, he could, but he did little if he didn't have to.

"That's wonderful news, my darling," he said, smiling and then presenting a wooden spoon with cream sauce on it to me. "Taste this. Does it need salt?"

It's like I just told him that my ingrown toenail from being on my feet all day had resolved—it hadn't. My feet were killing me, but the sauce was fabulous and made my mood a bit more reasonable. I did notice that he hadn't opened a bottle of wine, a fact that I did not dwell on at the time, thinking that perhaps we were out—we were not. "What will we do?" I asked, the tears returning.

"Well, Meg," he said with a smile, his thin blond mustache wagging above his luscious lips, "you shall get good and fat and then we shall go about raising ourselves a beautiful boy or girl. For with us as parents, how could this baby not be beautiful?"

He was the only one who ever got away with calling me "Meg." I detested that name, but with those blue eyes and luscious lips and unruly mop of blond hair, I never even told him I hated that name.

He charmed me with food. He allayed my concerns. He held me tenderly that night, not once even suggesting that we do something more.

Bastard.

Nine months flew by with morning sickness then swollen ankles and endless work as the war raged across Europe and then finally, blessedly, ended. My Kenneth was in short supply. He was always "working" as a traveling salesman, "doing the work of ten men" as he put it. He had somehow avoided conscription in 1939 when they started taking men up to forty-one years of age when he was only thirty-four. Once he told me he had flat feet and another time he told me it was because he was born in Northern Ireland. But what did I care at the time, having such a charming man in such a bleak era, and one that would happily rub my sore feet when he was around.

And after each absence he would return with his cream sauce, his dreamy blue eyes, and his being exactly who I needed.

He was there the day our son was born, relegated to the waiting room during the birth, of course, but then by my side, his eyes shining as we looked into the blue eyes of Kenneth Junior. So kind he was, attending to my every need until the day they were to release me.

I remember sitting on the bed, dressed and ready to go, my bag packed. I felt weak, but wanted to get away from the hospital. I worked in one, saw too many young men die in one, I had no desire to be there a moment longer than I had to.

"Where is my husband?" I asked the nurse, young and round, and very competent and kind. We were not married, of course, but we had registered that way "to save my dignity" as he put it.

"Oh," she said, stopping and looking at me puzzled. "He took the baby an hour ago. Said your brother would be around to fetch you before too long. Did your brother not come?"

The room spun around me and I felt as nauseous as any day with morning sickness. "I don't have a brother," I said.

We both stood there dumbly staring at each other. My mind rolling over the last ten months and everything Kenneth. At my round-peg disregard for the normal and for norms. At the lack of wine the night I told him I was pregnant. Of Kenneth's absences and behaviors. "Can you please ring the police?" I asked as calmly as I could.

THE POLICE WERE NO GOOD. NOT A ONE OF THEM. THEIR numbers were thin from the war and too busy celebrating the end of it to care much for a silly American woman who got herself knocked up and lost her baby.

"Well, 'e is the child's father, ain't he?" one slobbish Scottish detective told me, summing it up rather brilliantly.

As the saying goes, "Hell hath no fury like a woman scorned." Well, try a round-peg American in England who had her baby stolen.

I kept working at the hospital. I had to. But every ounce of energy left over I put into finding my Kenneth Junior and the bastard that sired him.

And I found signs of Kenneth, seemingly everywhere, in the innocent eyes of young women taken in by his deep blues in a time when a kind man was hard to find. And I wasn't the first woman he had done this to—impregnated and then taken the baby, that is—I was the fourth. That I found.

I did my own form of conscription and pulled his other victims into the effort. We spent eight months scouring the city and then the country, finding signs of him as far south as Brighton and as far north as Leeds. He was a traveling salesman for sure, but what he was selling was... I can't shove this particular reality into word boxes in any way that seems palatable. He was having babies and... lord save me, but he was having babies and selling them. To desperate, rich families in war-ravaged Europe.

Of the four of us, we found two of the babies—one in France and another in Scotland—but getting them back proved to be difficult. Kenneth had done everything legally. He was on all the birth certificates. He had signed legal contracts with the adopting families. The two other women did what they could, but they never got their children back, and I never found mine, or Kenneth.

He was no triangular peg at all. He wasn't human. He was a monster. My new mission was to find him and kill him.

Two years later in the spring of 1948, I was in Zürich, Switzerland, out of money and bereft of hope. I had quit my job six months earlier to chase Kenneth full time, the other victims having decided to move on with their lives. I felt no animus toward them. They were square pegs and couldn't help it no more than I could help being round.

I had tracked him to Zürich, but the trail had gone cold. I found myself feeling as low as a woman can feel on a park bench looking out on the sedate Limmat River which ran from Lake Zürich and cut through the city. My stomach was empty and my heart a void. My son had been denied me as had my revenge.

"Madam," a gentleman asked, standing above me. I slumped on a bench, all my possessions in my adorable carpet bag next to me. "Are you in need, madam?" His English was quite good and I found his Swedish accent charming, which would have made me mad at myself—I had found Kenneth's English accent charming—but he looked to be at least seventy with snow-white hair, a long goatee, that was not at all to my taste, and round glasses.

"That I am, sir. You are kind to stop, but I don't think you can help me."

He shrugged and walked away, but then turned around and walked back. "You look in need to me, madam. Perhaps you might think it forward, but if you are in need of shelter and food, I am in need of help." He handed me a white card with "Staffan Isaksson / Watchmaker" written on it in an elegant scroll. On the other side of the card was an address. He stooped down, leaning on his cane, his grey eyes catching and holding mine. "Yes, yes," he said. "I am a very good judge of character. I believe we can come to an equitable arrangement."

His three-piece suit was long out of fashion but looked clean, if a bit worn. He tipped his bowler hat at me and walked away, his cane clicking on the sidewalk as he walked among the park's greeneries, tipping his hat to the ladies that he passed.

I waited until he was nearly out of sight, my mind roiling at my need for revenge, my stomach churning from hunger, my heart weary. "Mr. Isaksson," I called, picking up my bag and running on my most tired legs to catch him. "Please, Mr. Isaksson. I'd like to take you up on your offer."

STAFFAN ISAKSSON WAS A QUIET, PRECISE MAN, AS YOU might expect given his work. He had a small shop not far from the park with an apartment above it. He apportioned me a closet of a room and gave me a small wage. For that, he expected me to cook, clean, and talk to customers at the shop. It wasn't difficult work, but there was a lot of it. And that was good. I needed time to pass with me focused on something besides my missing child and my murderous rage.

I didn't try to go get a job nursing. I didn't think about going back to England or even America. I cleaned and cooked and worked seven days a week avoiding thinking about what had happened.

One morning in the shop, which is a cacophony of ticking from the various clocks that were everywhere, I sat on the stool behind the counter, my eyes grazing over the endless watches in the display case, wondering about my sudden change. Two years of chasing a man fueled by rage and I was as still as a ship in a calm sea.

I took a deep breath, my nose filling with the smell of watch oil and a touch of solder, and sighed. I took a small piece of the dark chocolate sitting in the bowl on the display case and let its luscious, bitter-sweet flavor invade my mouth. It was for customers, but Mr. Isaksson didn't mind as long as I didn't take too many. He was at his workbench, his loupe glasses on, his body hunched over the watch he was repairing.

I didn't care much for watches and their tiny gears and mechanisms. Two months ago, when I had first started working for Mr. Isaksson, he had excitedly shown me what is inside one. The mainspring, the wheel train, the escapement, how winding it stores energy in the mainspring, its release regulated by the escapement assembly. Fascinating, yes, but my cup of tea was more flesh and blood than wheels and gears.

"I am a good listener, you must know that by now, Ms. Bellman," he quietly said, still stooped over his watch.

I let the chocolate melt, resisting the urge to bite down, trying to savor it. "You are most kind, Mr. Isaksson, but I am afraid no one can help me with this."

He chuckled softly. "I was not offering to change the world for you, madam, only to listen with a kind ear."

And he was a kind, gentle man, enjoying his watches and his solitude. He wasn't married, which made him more of a round peg than I would have originally thought. So I told him the brief outlines of what had happened and my failure to either find my son or to find Kenneth and extract my revenge.

He listened quietly as he used his small tweezers and screwdrivers on the watch. As I finished, he pulled out what I recognized as the escape wheel. It has oversized, flaring teeth and is the piece of the watch where energy from the spring escapes one second at a time and drives the rest of the mechanisms. Yes, I know I said they did not interest me, but that doesn't mean I didn't learn anything.

"It is a very sad story," he said, pushing the loupes aside, glancing at me and then searching through his drawers of tiny parts. "And what is it that you want to do now?"

I shrugged and snuck another piece of chocolate, biting down on it this time. "I want my son back. I want to see Kenneth pay for what he has done."

He turned and looked at me, his grey eyes steady and not unkind, but somehow hard. "And if that is not possible?"

"I do not know."

He shook his head and waved at me to come over to his workbench. Under the bright light, he had a clean white cloth laid out that had all the parts he had removed to get to the escape wheel. "Tiny parts, all connected. One part fails and the watch stops."

"Yes, I see that."

"I replace the defective part." He showed me the tiny grey escape wheel with two missing teeth and then the new, perfect one. "And then the watch is suddenly whole. When it does not operate, it seems the whole watch is defective when it is only one small thing."

My cheeks flushed and I backed away. Had he just told me that my missing son was one small thing, trivial to replace? "If you'll excuse me, I need to put some beans on to soak."

That night at dinner, he apologized to me. When I would finally meet his gaze, I saw that his grey eyes were so sad. What had he lost? Was there more to his unmarried status than a love of watches and solitude? "Please excuse me, Ms. Bellman. I merely meant to urge you to look for that one small thing that would get you moving forward again."

I sighed and nodded, biting my lip and stirring the soup I

had made but had hardly touched. It was made with white beans and a bit bland, but he never complained.

"I am not a conventional woman," I said. He nodded, a smile briefly appearing from beneath his goatee. "I found myself working a difficult job in a difficult time and I... I needed some fun. I did not see Kenneth for what he was, and I..." My cheeks were flushed and I felt the old anger coming back, but this time it was different. "And I blame myself for this mess. My damn round-peg self in this square hole of a world."

His bushy eyebrows lifted as he parsed through what I had said, and then he smiled and reached for his wine glass—we each got four ounces a night, no more. "To round pegs," he said, holding his glass up to me.

We talked of other things then, and I felt just a little bit lighter. I had played an important role in all of this and acknowledging it had perhaps been that one small thing that needed to change.

AFTER THAT NIGHT, WE WERE FRIENDS. HE INSISTED I CALL him Staffan and I told him to call me Margret. He had been married in his twenties but had lost his wife and child during childbirth and never remarried. More months flew by, and I was content if not happy. I still felt a hollowness where Kenneth Junior lived, and I had not really forgiven myself for being so careless, but it was a good time. I let Staffan teach me how to take a watch apart, identify the parts, and put them back together. At first, I did it only to please him, but then I found that I liked the understandability of a watch. Each part had its place and its function, each going together to make a whole greater than those parts. It was much more understandable than the human heart.

Summer had turned to fall, and I was beginning to think of Zürich as another home and learning enough Swiss German to be more useful behind the counter. One morning, the door opened, the bell ringing, and a man stumbled into the store. He wore a long trench coat and had a mop of blond hair. My heart leapt and my face flushed thinking that it was Kenneth, but it was not. This man was much younger, with hazel eyes and no mustache.

"Can I help you?" I asked in English, for some reason thinking he was local. Staffan was out on a delivery and I was alone in the shop.

He looked at me, his eyes blinking, and looked down at his wrist. There was a watch there, simple with a separate, smaller circle for the second hand. At first glance, I did not recognize its maker. He then looked back up at me, puzzled.

"I broke it," he said with an American accent. "I can't believe I broke it. What have I done?" He stumbled to the counter and I could smell the earthy scent of fall on him, but something stronger than that. He smelled of smoke.

He took the watch off, its brown leather band in tatters, and dangled it in front of me. The lettering was a clean, bold sans serif with a smaller circle for the second hand on the lower half of the watch sitting over the 6 and occluding part of the 5 and 7. Right below the 12 was a symbol, a circle, that looked like a snake eating its own tail. The watch was still. Broken.

He handed it to me. "I shouldn't have done what I did. I..." His eyes were wide in a way that I hadn't seen since the Blitz or some of those poor soldiers coming to the hospital. "I asked too much of it. She... she told me not to ask too much, but I did. It's..." His eyes stopped wandering and connected with mine. "It's yours now. The magic... it's still in there, enough so I know it's yours." His cold hands grabbed my hand and he pressed the watch into my palm. "Use it well, but don't ask too much."

He then stumbled out into the street. I looked down at the watch and felt a strange familiarity. While the band was in terrible condition, the watch itself was perfect, the face unblemished, the glass without a scratch.

Without thinking, I put the watch on. It was a man's watch and much too big for my wrist, but I liked it there and thought I felt something, a small vibration. I took it off again and walked over to the workbench, compelled to fix this watch.

I GASPED WHEN I SAW THE INSIDE OF THIS WATCH. IT HAD all the usual parts and pieces. Gears and mainspring, jewel bearings and wheels. But the metal had a golden hue that shined, the bearings seemed to be made of real jewels not synthetic ones, they looked like pale blue diamonds. The metal housing gave off an iridescent shine.

The problem quickly became apparent. A blue stone, topaz maybe, that had been embedded in the metal backing of the watch had come loose and was jammed into the escapement assembly. It was an easy repair. I used a clip to freeze the balance wheel—it is the most delicate piece of the watch and is a large wheel that rotates back and forth translating the seconds out to the toothed escape wheel. I then pulled the glowing blue gem out with a set of tweezers, and as I brought it to the back of the watch, it flew out of the tweezers and snapped into place.

This watch was magic. There was no doubt of it anymore. Before Kenneth had come along, I had spent some time with a wiccan coven in London—mostly talk of spells and smelly herbs, but they believed in magic. I had seen the pictures of the Cottingley Fairies from the twenties and wondered at them. That day I truly believed in magic. I unclipped the balance wheel and the watch came to life, a warm blue glow emanating from the entire assemblage. I put the cover back on and felt the watch vibrating, I turned it over to see the hands adjusting themselves to the current time. The room seemed warm, and I felt myself wake up. I had been hiding here with the kind Staffan Isaksson. Resting. But that time was over.

I took off the tattered leather band, pulled a new one out of the store's inventory, ringing it up and paying for it, of course, attached the new band and put the watch on.

I took a deep breath. The fearless Margret of old was back. This round peg was not afraid of any square holes. I was a bit older, and a bit wiser—I would not fall for a charlatan like Kenneth again. I took a deep breath, smelling the oil and dust of the shop, and looked around and saw it as so cramped. I had to move.

The day was beautiful, the leaves turning yellow and orange. Staffan would be back soon, and why should I spend my life in this tiny little shop? I wrote him a quick note saying I had gone out for a walk and left it on the counter. I put some money in my dress pocket—a nice green one with a few ruffles and long sleeves—and left my purse, thinking I'd be right back. I locked the door and slid the key behind the large brass clock that hung right outside the shop.

I took a deep breath and then marched away, my eyes feasting on the two-story brick buildings in this quaint area of Zürich.

In retrospect, I think the watch was trying to return the favor I had just done it. I had repaired it, now it was trying to repair me. It was the last time I would see that little shop, and I never did get a chance to say good-bye to Staffan or properly thank him for his kindness.

MY FEET CARRIED ME QUICKLY. I SMILED AT EVERYONE I passed saying "Grüezi!" wishing them good day in Swiss German. I let my brown hair out of its ponytail and shook it loose, letting the cool breeze play with my hair. I was done with Kenneth, and while I would always grieve the loss of my son, it was time to live again. Was there a festival I could visit or a place I could go dancing?

My feet took me to a market setup in Platzspitz Park which bordered the river, the ground littered with colorful fall leaves, the air cool and sharp. I bought several luxemburgerlis—a kind of macaron that is a specialty of Zürich—from a vendor and ate with gusto. My magic watch felt warm on my wrist, and I knew my life would change now. No more hiding. No more rage. Just a life, a real life.

And then I saw him. Kenneth.

Despite the cool, I began to sweat and my heart beat loudly in my head. At first, I thought, no, it must be the same man that brought in the watch, but then he turned and I saw his profile. The unruly blond hair, the slightly hooked nose. And then he turned farther and I saw those gorgeous blue eyes. The rest of the bun slipped from my hand and I gasped. The rage that I thought I had left behind came down upon me like an avalanche. He saw me, his eyes widening in fear, and he dropped his bag of groceries and ran.

I ran after him. I was in flats—never being much for heels, too damn impractical—and my skirt was easy to run in, but I was out of shape. Long months mostly indoors and not on my feet all day as a nurse had left my muscles weak and added ten pounds. But I was driven by my need and managed to keep up with him.

Gone was the zoot suit; he wore tan slacks, a blue shirt— designed to bring out his eyes, I am sure—and a grey sweater. We were in Altstadt, the historic area of Zürich, and he ran out of the park past stately old buildings along a road that bordered the

Zürich Hauptbahnhof, the largest train station in Switzerland. We ran past the Swiss National Museum with grey stone and pointed towers, over a bridge that crossed the Sihl River, where he dashed across the crowded street, horns honking, toward the tangle of railroad tracks coming out of the station.

My mouth was dry and my breath coming heavy and fast. I didn't want to run anymore, but he seemed to be in better shape than I, so I just kept moving.

I remembered the magic watch, felt it sliding on my wrist as my arms pumped. I had no idea how such a magic would be activated, knowing only the man that came in had said, "I asked too much of it." I didn't pause to think if I was asking too much, I only asked, Please let me catch Kenneth. Please.

I didn't know if it was the watch or not, but I felt a second wind. I ran out in traffic, wheels squealing, horns honking, shouts from irate drivers. I didn't care. I ran. I followed Kenneth.

This was the end of the line for the trains so the tracks leading out of the station were a dense tangle, trains slowly moving in or out. Down the street we went until the wall separating us from the tracks disappeared and he ran onto the tracks themselves.

I was past exhausted, not really even thinking anymore, something animal in me keeping me on his trail or perhaps the magic of the watch. He was my prey. I would not fail.

I danced among the tracks and gained on him, only twenty yards behind. I didn't shout. I didn't speak. I saved everything for the chase. He glanced back at me once and I saw real fear on his face. He knew what I wanted from him. He knew what I would do to him if I caught him.

He set off again. He ran right in front of an incoming train that stretched back at least a hundred yards. It was slowing for the station, but I knew if I didn't get in front of it, I would lose him. I didn't think. I ran.

The train blared its horns, my nose filled with diesel fumes. I wasn't going to make it. I had to make it. I ran up to the track the train was on, I made to leap across, but my foot caught on the railroad track and I fell. As the steel rushed up to me, I knew it was over. I closed my eyes, the train horn drilling into my head, and I came down hard and...

The world lurched and turned around me, and despite my eyes being closed I saw colors, all kinds of colors, smear across my vision and my stomach roiled. I was falling, no, I was spinning, no, I was flying up into the air. My body was not my own, and for a moment I wondered if this is what death felt like. And then...

I landed on grass, moist grass, the air suddenly warm and the sounds of birds chirping surrounding me. I gasped, struggling for breath, and cracked my eyes open, seeing only the grass. I had no idea what was going on. I rose up on my hands and knees, my stomach convulsing, and I vomited on that green grass.

I was weak, barely able to hold myself up, my mind not knowing what was going on, where I was, or how I had gotten here. The world spun and I felt something burning my wrist, but I could not pay attention to it.

"Meg?" a voice said, a male voice rough with age, but so familiar. "My God, is that you? How... how can it be? You... you..."

The voice was cut off by a deep, wet cough and my nurse's brain immediately thought consumption and that I should tell the doctor to consider a course of streptomycin.

But I hated the name Meg. Only one person had ever called me Meg and gotten away with it.

I looked up, forcing my eyes to focus, and sitting on a park bench six feet away from me was a wrinkled old man with a hooked nose and blue eyes.

He pulled the white handkerchief away from his mouth and

it was stained a bright red. His eyes met mine, and somehow, I knew this old man was Kenneth.

***

THE WATCH WAS BURNING ON MY WRIST AND I QUICKLY took it off, holding it dangling by the strap. It had a blue glow to it that was quickly fading and the time had snapped back from midafternoon to late morning. My wrist had a red welt and burned.

"You... you died," the old man Kenneth said. "You were chasing me. You tripped when you tried to run in front of that train. I... I turned away, but you must have died." He shook his head, looking like a confused old man. "That was... that was thirty-five, no, thirty-six years ago."

I didn't understand what was going on. I was still nauseous and was weak, but here was an old and helpless Kenneth. I saw a fist-size rock close to the sidewalk and crawled towards it. We were in a park, and I was vaguely aware of others in the park and heard talking, the sound of children playing, the hum of tires on the street, but I just focused on the rock. Kenneth was babbling on about how I looked exactly the same, wore the same green dress as I had at that train station. How he was so glad I was alive. How he was sorry for what he had done. I didn't care. I crawled to the rock, gripped it in my free hand, feeling like I had walked miles, and pushed myself up to my feet and swayed unsteadily and looked around.

The park was small, a neighborhood park on a hill with benches and swing sets and a jungle gym. The neighborhood dived down a steep hill and I could see the ocean in the distance and knew I was back in San Francisco. The buildings, though, looked fairly old, but the architecture wasn't anything I was familiar with. The buildings had simple, clean lines and big windows, rising four stories into the air. Apartment buildings.

I stumbled towards Kenneth. He eyed the rock and then me and he smiled. "Go ahead, Meg," he said. "Do it. You can do nothing worse to me than this damn cancer has done." Another coughing fit took him, and when it was over he looked up at me with watery eyes filled with pain. "Please. I... Just do it." He held my gaze, a small smile playing on his lips.

His eyes had always been so bright, so alive, and now they were rheumy and defeated. Time had done more to him than I could have. I collapsed onto the bench next to him, still breathing hard, my wrist on fire from the burn. I looked at the watch, which I still held by the band, and it seemed different. I mean, it looked the same, but it seemed hollow, empty, no longer magical. I must have used all the magic up getting here.

I dropped the rock and looked at Kenneth. "What is happening?"

He shrugged, a bit of mischief back in those eyes. "I don't know, darling, but it's 1982 and you look exactly the same as you did when I saw you last in 1948."

<hr>

On that bench, in San Francisco in 1982, Kenneth, a seventy-seven-year-old Kenneth, told me things. At first, he told me the things he thought I wanted to hear. That of all the women he had been with back then, that I was his favorite, that he spent more time with me, that he was there when the baby was born only for me. He apologized. He cried. He said he had been a terrible person but later in life had tried to do better. He told me that the cigarettes had done him in and it wasn't consumption he had but lung cancer. That there were no treatments left for him and he would die soon.

That last part was the only thing I believed, his stories punctuated by coughing fits and bloody handkerchiefs.

And then he told me what I really wanted to hear. "I know... I know what happened to our son."

I was still shaking but starting to feel normal. I just stared at him and blinked.

"I kept track of him, of course I did, Meg. I am not a monster."

But of course he was a monster in an era of monsters. My monster.

He promised me he would tell me everything if I would but help him get home. He was enrolled in a program called hospice that helped keep the dying comfortable, applying palliative care to the terminally ill. The hospice nurse came once a day and he didn't want to miss her. His excursions outside were frowned upon, but he said, "What is life without a bit of sun on the face?"

I helped him up, helped him to the walker parked beside the bench, guided him up the sidewalk and helped him navigate the steps to his apartment building. He was weak and thin, his once beautiful hair reduced to grey wisps, his rakish good looks an eroded wasteland.

He told me he had no family to help him. He had been married once, had a daughter, but neither of the women would answer his calls. The money he had made selling babies was soon lost to a lavish lifestyle, and he had eventually found himself in America. He told me he came to San Francisco because of how I had talked about it, that he came to feel closer to me.

His apartment was a small studio, cluttered and stinking of his illness. I was still weak, my emotions at war with each other. On one hand, I would just as soon push him down the steps as look at him, and on the other hand, he said he knew what had happened to my boy.

We didn't talk about how I got here. I knew it was the watch and put it on my unburnt wrist once it had cooled. I had traveled in time. There was no question about it. And I don't know why he accepted it so easily, but he did. Perhaps seeing me was all the proof he needed. Back in 1945 when we met, he had loved the ideas of witches and fairies. Did not blink at my assertion that there must be magic in this bleak world.

"Tell me now," I said once I had him settled in his reclining chair in front of the television—which was quite large and produced a startlingly clear color picture.

He nodded. "Can you please get me some water? I'll tell you after the nurse gets here."

When the nurse came, Kenneth introduced me as his niece Meg. The nurse, a kind, middle-aged woman named Jean, was ecstatic to have me there, rattling off all the things Kenneth needed that her hospice could not provide. I smiled and nodded, not wanting to do any of that.

"That is an... interesting dress," Jean said as she was about to leave.

"She was in a play recently," Kenneth offered from his chair, ever the charlatan, lying was still like breathing to him. "I asked her to model it for me."

Jean smiled and shook my hand. "We'll see you soon, Meg. So glad you are here."

I smiled as best I could and told her my name was Margret.

"Now," I said to Kenneth after the nurse had left.

He met me with steady blue eyes. "I need you, Meg. You help me, I'll help you. I... I don't know how you got here, but maybe there is a reason for it. I'll teach you about this world, even help you get identification so you can live here, work as a nurse. And I'll tell you about Kenneth Junior. I will." He looked away from me for the last sentence, making me think he either wouldn't tell me or I wouldn't like what he told me.

A knot formed in my stomach that didn't go away for weeks.

And so, as I had done many times before for brave soldiers, I began taking care of a dying man. This time for the man I hated most in the world because he kept dangling what I wanted most in front of me.

NINETEEN EIGHTY-TWO, AT LEAST VIEWED THROUGH THE lens of a color television, certainly strained credulity. Bars where everyone knows your name and no one ever seemed to go home; cars that talk and are smarter than people and leap into the air, defying gravity; saccharine shows of families too well adjusted with problems so trivial as to not be believed; even a former actor as president of the United States. It went on and on.

Outside, when I could escape from Kenneth, I found 1982 to be more to my liking. The world was not at war, although there was a "cold war" with Russia and the rising threat of communism. The Nazis had been truly defeated, and the world seemed relaxed, and women's clothing had gotten a whole lot more sensible, although I can't say the same for the excessively teased hairstyles. The battles fought in America were more cultural with men openly holding hands and kissing in my hometown. The AIDS epidemic was poised to crash down on us, but in that moment, it seemed to be a happy country and I seemed to fit. I was still a round peg, but the world seemed rounder now.

The burn on my wrist healed and I never took the magic watch off except to bathe. It was inert, merely a mechanical watch that kept excellent time, but I hoped that its magic would come back one day. It would be a terrible shame if I had used it all up.

Kenneth, on the other hand, was wearing me down. Hospice

would come in daily, but not for long. They had sent volunteers to sit with him, but he had scared them all off. After I had been there a week, he couldn't get up and needed help going to the toilet. After I had been there three weeks, he was confined to a hospital bed, his end coming near.

My emotions, always a chaotic jumble, were more confused than they ever had been. He was such a paradox to me. I hated him for what he had done, but still remembered the fun we had had. He was old, but my memories of him being young was only two years back. The watch had brought me here, and as the weeks passed, I came to believe it had done more than just save my life by doing this. It had brought me here for a reason, and what reason beyond Kenneth could there be?

He shed more weight and began to withdraw as his time came. The nurse, Jean, kept me supplied with morphine to ease his pain, and he slept more and more.

And still he hadn't told me about my Kenneth Junior. Every time I asked, he would grin and say, "I'm too tired now. Tomorrow."

I searched his apartment and found very little. Clothing, unpaid bills, a few paperback novels, a couple random volumes of the Encyclopedia Britannica, but no picture albums, no mementos, nothing of note. His life, whatever it had been, he seemed to have discarded. I no longer believed he knew anything about Kenneth Junior. And yet I stayed.

He had kept part of his promise. He told me about this strange world and had given me the name of some men who could, for a price, create an identity for me where I wasn't a sixty-nine-year-old woman born in 1913. But no Kenneth Junior, never anything about him.

One day, the sun filtering in through the living room window —the hospital bed was there, too cramped was the bedroom—I was feeding him ice chips, his eyes dull with pain and drugs, his face pale, his lips dry. "You don't know what happened to him, do you," I said.

His eyes widened in question.

"That's why you won't talk of our son. You don't know."

He nodded weakly. "I do know." His voice was weak and wispy. He still coughed a lot, but had trouble expelling the fluids, so his lungs were filling up.

"Why won't you tell me?" I asked. I was bone tired of being a caregiver working a shift that never ended.

He blinked, a tear escaping eyes. "Because you'll leave then."

I bit my lip and shook my head. "I won't. I swear to you I won't."

He looked away; he didn't believe me. I had seen many men die, mostly young men, and I had an idea of what Kenneth was going through. He was tired of the suffering, of the battle, but he was not yet ready to give up. If I left, he might die alone, or they might take him to a hospital where he would die among strangers. In this very odd world, I was still a fairly young woman, while he was an old man, and I his only chance of succor.

I had a thought. A glimmer. Something I could offer him. "Tell me," I whispered, "and I can see that this ends peacefully for you... and soon."

He looked at me again and I saw the desperation there. I had him. "How?"

I shrugged. "Morphine, maybe, but you are used to it and we probably don't have enough and the hospice takes great care with it."

"What then?"

"I'm sure you know where I can get some heroin. It would be a lovely way to go." I gave him the best smile I could.

His nostrils flared and his eyes flicked away from mine.

"Tell me," I whispered, trying to keep my voice even. "Or I

walk out of here right now. Today. The nurse was just here, your morphine will run out in a few hours. It will be a horrible night for you... maybe your last."

"You wouldn't?"

I laughed and I sounded a bit insane, and likely I was. "I will." I had taken oaths, it was against my nature, but he had driven me to this.

He took a breath and nodded, the smell of him dank and rotten, clinging to my nose. "Get the heroin first. I do know where you can get some."

<hr>

The money was hidden in the M volume of the Encyclopedia Britannica, a space cut out in the pages and a fat wad of 100-dollar-bills stuffed in. His emergency money. I took a bus and then a trolley to Golden Gate Park. I bought the heroin from some young scruffy men wearing headphones and listening to music on their portable "Walkman." The music, quite improbably, recorded on a strip of plastic tape.

Kenneth was asleep when I got back and I carefully prepared the heroin, mixing the white powder with water and filling the syringe.

His face was relaxed in sleep, the battle with pain briefly won, and I stared at him. It was too good a death for him. I was glad I hadn't hit him with the rock. I was glad to see him suffer. But only part of me. I hated myself for hating him so and knew I had never really forgiven myself for falling under his spell. He had his own magic of a sort. The magic of charm mixed with a horrible lack of morals or empathy. The good times with him were good, but the bad times, horrible.

"Did you get it?" he asked before a coughing fit hit him. He was almost too weak to cough, and I cranked up the back of the bed so he could try to expel the fluid, but couldn't anymore.

I held up the syringe.

"Prove it," he said, his blue eyes briefly lighting up.

He didn't trust me, despite the weeks I had spent by his side. I nodded, injected a small amount in his arm. I wasn't worried about anyone finding signs of the injection and wondering at it. When he was dead, I was gone. I would not stay any longer than that.

The drug hit him and he let out a heavy sigh. Heroin is essentially a stronger morphine, and he needed much stronger at this point. At this dose, the heroin was a kindness.

"He's dead," he whispered. "In the Vietnam war. In the jungles. In 1969. The family that adopted him was American."

I nodded and blinked, suddenly numb and heavy with fatigue, I could barely move. He nodded me to come closer and he whispered our son's name in my ear, the one his adopted family had given him, his foul breath making my eyes water.

"Now do it," he said, his blue eyes meeting with mine one last time, the spark gone from them, the Kenneth that I had loved and the Kenneth that I hated both gone.

I injected the rest of the heroin, waited for his heart to stop, and walked out.

THREE YEARS LATER, IN THE SPRING OF 1985, I FINALLY made the trip to Washington, DC. The magic watch was still on my wrist and I was starting to feel something. Not anything overt, it just felt like it was alive again. It was recovering from dragging me forward in time so that I could help Kenneth die. So I could learn how my son had died. So I could heal.

I stood on the mowed lawn and pulled my sweater tight, the

morning chill. I stared at the Vietnam Memorial, a long granite wall lowered into the ground, almost 58,000 names etched in the stone. I shook my head. What would have happened if I had caught Kenneth in 1948? Would I have hurt him? Killed him? Had any real closure?

Instead, I got to see what the life he had lived had wrought and done a kindness to a man who did not deserve kindness.

I hadn't approached the wall yet. I knew I needed to. I needed to go find my son's name. My hand went to my abdomen, as it often did these days, even though I wasn't showing yet.

I looked at the watch, at the circular symbol of the snake swallowing its own tail, a circle that could never end. New life was in me now and I had a chance for a better life in this new time. As I got to know the eighties, I found it squarer than I liked, but much more round than the forties had been, and perhaps I was a bit squarer than I used to be.

"Are you ready yet?" Michael asked, a kind look in his very normal brown eyes.

He reached for my hand and squeezed it. He was my husband. I carried his baby. I had used the rest of Kenneth's emergency funds and bought my new identity, got a job at a hospital, and slowly learned about this time and slowly healed.

Michael had been a doctor there and asked me out right away. I said no, not trusting any men. We slowly became friends and I slowly grew to trust him and that turned into more. Michael wasn't dreamy and delicious like Kenneth; he was strong and steady, trusting and loving. He didn't know I was from the past, he thought the name I was seeking today was my father's and not my son's.

Life is ridiculous, the way it twists and turns on us. This grand reality we perceive and experience only a small percentage of the totality. And even my small slice is too rich, too dripping with emotion and subtlety for the word boxes I have presented to you. And yes, my tale strains credulity, but so does World War II, the Korean War, the Vietnam War, and an unratified Equal Rights Amendment. And, in fact, most of the things this silly race does to each other every day.

Take my story or leave it. This round peg cares not. It's all true, though.

"Yes," I said to my husband, nodding slowly. "I think I am ready."

And as we walked up towards the wall, the watch seemed to wake up and it vibrated briefly like it once had in 1946. And I knew it would be time for it to move on soon. Time for it to find another life to repair.

BACKSTORY—JUMP IN TIME

Genre: Fantasy
Type of Time Travel: Forward only
Nature of Time Travel: Powered by a "magic" watch for
unknown reasons

I wrote this story back in 2017 as part of my "Short Story Marathon." I wrote 30 short stories in 33 days. And, yes, that's just about as crazy as it sounds. It was equal parts exhausting and exhilarating (you can find out more about it at *RobertJMc Carter.com/category/story-marathon/*).

This story popped out in the middle (it's story #15) and caused me some problems because of the length and complexity of the story. But, I think it worked out for the best because I might have talked myself out of following through with this one if I had had more time.

"Jump in Time" is one story in a planned series of twelve stories that interlock or "chain" via the watch featured in this story. These stories are all, in one way or another, about time.

There's just one in this collection, but be on the lookout for more. One of these years, I'll have the time to finish all twelve.

If you'd like to read another one, "Forgiveness in Time" is featured in my ebook *Bits, Bites, and Rarities: The Worlds of Robert J. McCarter*. This is a free ebook given to the subscribers of my newsletter which you can sign up for at *RobertJMcCarter.com/newsletter*.

This story received an honorable mention in the Writers of the Future contest.

PART 4
GOODBYE MRS. HOPKINS

GOODBYE MRS. HOPKINS

I'VE TRAVELED BACK IN TIME A HUNDRED TIMES JUST TO SEE her standing there, but now it's time to say goodbye.

The sun is behind her, illuminating her wheat-colored hair, long and straight, spilling down her shoulders while the breeze plays with it. She is looking off in the distance at the approaching storm, her blue-green eyes fixed on the horizon.

It's 1868 in Missouri, and she's out in front of her farmhouse dressed in a simple brown cotton dress with an apron over it, both of which she sewed herself. There's a bit of flour on her cheek, and I know the kitchen smells like baking bread.

She's only thirty but carries the burden of running the farm and raising her three children by herself. Both her husband and her father perished in the Civil War.

The horizon is dark, roiling clouds tinged with a hint of green. She suspects, but she doesn't know yet, that a tornado is coming right for her.

There is nothing I can do to save her.

"Is there somethin' I can do for you, sir?" she asks as I walk up the drive to her house. My time machine, all brass and crystals and superconductors, is hidden in a ravine not far away. I have squandered my life coming back here whenever my other missions have allowed it, wasting my jumps for this simple exchange.

But no more. Time extracts a price for our intrusion, each jump ages a body by a month or more, and mine won't take another jump.

"No, ma'am," I say, tipping my hat to her. I've got on a long brown duster, cowboy boots, and a round brimmed hat. "You are most kind to inquire."

"Well, then, what are you doing here?" She reluctantly shifts her gaze from the coming storm to me, her eyes sweeping me up and down, taking me in.

I move slowly now, my hair white as snow and not the dishwater blond it was when I first came to see her. "I just thought it'd be nice to see you one last time."

Her smooth brow furrows and she takes a step forward. I can hear the kids, Emily, Taylor, and Kyle, playing in the living room. She crosses her arms and looks at me closely and I get a whiff of her rosewater perfume and smile.

"I am sorry, sir, I don't recognize you. Perhaps if you told me your name."

"Evan Randal," I say, extending my age-spotted hand. "I was a friend of your father's. I haven't been around in quite some time. Not since you were a little girl." A lie, but one I know she will accept.

She shakes my hand, her grip strong as usual. "Janis Hopkins, but you know that, don't you, Mr. Randal?"

I smile and nod.

"Well, I don't recognize your name, sir, and for that I apologize. If you'd like to take shelter from the storm, then you can come in. The kids are rather rambunctious, but harmless." She nods back to the shouts coming from her house.

It's like a play all scripted out and we're each acting out our parts, each step a foregone conclusion.

When I was a young man, sent back here on my first mission, and saw Janis Hopkins standing there, so strong, so beautiful... well, I lost myself. Love at first sight and every other cliché you'd like to throw at it. I didn't believe in it myself, not until that day.

But I was just an observer, a historian, here to take some pictures and watch the tornado take out the farmhouse. The future was interested in Emily Hopkins and how this incident affected her young life, pushed her towards meteorology and her contributions to weather prediction.

I wasn't even supposed to talk to any of them, just record from a distance. But I could not. That hair glowing in the sun, those resolute eyes, they drew me in. She was kind despite me being a stranger and the weight of the Civil War still laying heavy on the country.

I tried to save her then, but she would not leave her children, young Taylor will twist his ankle any moment now and she will not be able to get to the storm cellar fast enough, but Emily and Kyle will.

I came earlier the next time, came in for tea, disturbed the play of the children, but this time Taylor broke his ankle when he tripped over my boot and it all turned out the same.

We travel back in time, but cannot change it. We are unwelcome guests, the fabric of time tolerating our presence, but not our interference.

"Mr. Randal, you have the oddest look on your face," she says. "Are you quite all right? I have a horse, should we get you into town so you can see the doctor?"

I tried that. The horse will have run off if we go looking for it. When I went to town to get a wagon, they were all taken. When I tried to steal horses, I was caught and barely escaped. In my youth, I tried over and over.

As I grew older, I would come back occasionally for the simple pleasure of a handshake and a brief conversation.

The past is not ours to manipulate, only ours to observe.

"You are most kind, Mrs. Hopkins, but I am just fine. I am but an old man and I have my moments."

She smiles; it is a bright thing and my old heart flips in my chest as it had every time she smiled at me. I felt young again, like the rules of this world didn't apply to me, thinking that time would yield to me if I wanted something enough. And I had wanted Janis Hopkins enough, but time doesn't yield to anyone or anything.

There's a crash from the house, a yelp, and then crying.

Janis purses her lips and shakes her head. "That would be my cue, Mr. Randal. It was a pleasure meeting you."

Her eyes linger, and for a moment I think I see recognition in them, as if she is remembering the many times I've said hello to her, or had tea with her, or tried desperately to save her. But it is only a moment, she can't recognize me. She is who she is, trapped in the web of time, replaying the narrow variations time will allow because of my presence.

She turns to go and my heart is in my throat.

I have never kissed her, never held her, only shaken her hand, and yet I feel like I was born to the wrong time, that I should have been born sooner so that I might have really known her, not just this tiny slice of her.

"One moment," I say, my voice just a croak. "If you could indulge a foolish, old man."

She turns quickly, her golden hair sliding over her shoulders. "What is it, Mr. Randal?"

I smile, trying to breathe her in one last time. "You are a fine woman. Your father would have wanted me to tell you that." Another lie. She is a fine woman, but I never knew her father. It is the only way I can think to pay her a compliment.

She looks down, a cloud of sorrow passing over her face. She takes a deep breath, puts a smile on and says, "Thank you, Mr. Randal. You are most kind."

I smile back at her, for the last time.

"Goodbye, Mrs. Hopkins."

"Goodbye, Mr. Randal."

I watch her rush into the house as the sun is swallowed by the approaching storm and the wind rushes up and I have to hold on to my hat. The air is charged with electricity and damp, and thunder shatters the silence.

"Goodbye, Janis," I say quietly, as I turn and walk back towards my time machine.

BACKSTORY—GOODBYE MRS. HOPKINS

Genre: Science Fiction
Type of Time Travel: Backward only
Nature of Time Travel: Interacting with the past without being able to change it

What if you could go back in time but you couldn't change anything? Ever. What if you fell in love and could never do anything about it? What if you were desperate to save someone you cared about but it wasn't possible?

Others have written about this "historian" style of time travel where you can only go back and be a witness, you can never change the essential facts of what was and what will be, even though you know how.

That makes this type of time travel more realistic, more reflective of our reality—there is no changing the past—and it makes this kind of story a bit wistful.

This is my attempt at that style of time travel in a short and bittersweet form.

PART 5
THE TOMBSTONE BARBER

THE TOMBSTONE BARBER

I bought the straight razor because it terrified me, that and Angela Ortega pestering me about not buying anything when she was loading up like a tourist overdue for a shopping fix.

It was one of the folding kind with a wide blade and a dinged-up mother-of-pearl handle, the words "John Barber" stamped near the hinge with the Masonic square and compass symbol below it. I pointed at it and smiled.

"What? No," Angela said, shaking her head. "Don't buy that. That's... eww."

We were inside Larry's Antiques and Things, a big corrugated metal building with a faux Western front overflowing with the old and the weird. Larry's sits on the west end of Old Town Cottonwood. It was a sweltering Arizona summer day and the place just stank of old, all moldy and mildewy. We had stopped here when with an "Oooh, oooh" and a point of a long red fingernail, Angela had spotted it on our way back from Jerome, having gone into every store there.

I love Angela. Secretly, of course. Well, she knows I love her,

I tell her all the time, it's the "in love" part that is secret. We went to high school together, after which she promptly went to California for college and never came back until now. We text. We Skype. I make it out to California once or twice a year, but it's not the same. I miss my Ang, my best friend, the only reason I survived high school.

"I like it," I said in defiance, my fingers reaching toward the straight razor. Below it was a yellowed piece of paper that said, "Tombstone, circa 1881," and a price tag of $39.99. It was part of a small shelf that had rusted pieces of railroad tracks, hunks of polished petrified wood, and a few framed stock certificates from companies long gone.

And, honestly, if Angela hadn't been asking me all day if I was going to buy something, I wouldn't have cared. I watched her buy prickly pear cactus jelly, and a red rock dirt T-shirt, and locally made habanero sauce and... well, you get the idea. You would think that she missed Cottonwood, the same small town she was so desperate to escape eight years ago.

Every time she bought something, she'd raise her eyebrow and say, "What about you?" As if my lack of purchases said something about her.

The straight razor, it terrified me, and that... I don't know how to describe it—it made me want it. I pulled my phone out and did a quick search on eBay and found a similar razor, without the mother-of-pearl handle, listed for $99. "See," I said, showing Angela my phone. "I can resell it and make a good profit."

Her black ponytail wagged as she shook her head and her brown eyes narrowed. "Ewww," she said again.

Angela was half tough Latina girl and half girly-girl, taking no shit from no one *and* liking frilly things and mani-pedis. We bonded in drama club when I student-directed *The Taming of the Shrew* and she played Katherina, the "shrew." She ended up dating the much-handsomer-than-me boy that played Petruchio and I ended up deep in the friend zone.

And I got her ewww about the straight razor. I remember my old man wanting to experience a real barber when I was, like, six, and watching the white-haired barber with shaking hands shave my father with a straight razor, the sound of the scraping making my skin crawl, my nose full of the smell of pungent after-shave. It was too many horror movies with my older brother Ben, where a straight razor would never be used for benign purposes.

I grabbed the razor, the size of my smile matching the size of Angela's frown. "See. I'm buying something."

Her eyebrows raised, she shook her head and pointed past the maze of shelves and furniture towards the register. "Well, then, Alan, I guess you best buy it."

She was disappointed, and I didn't understand why. I almost put it back, but I felt something with that razor in my hand. I felt confident, happy, like things were going to go my way. Like I wouldn't be stuck in a crappy job in small-town Arizona for the rest of my life.

JAIL TRAIL RUNS FROM WHAT USED TO BE THE OLD Cottonwood Jail down through towering cottonwoods and dense willows and wanders along the Verde River. In high school, Angela and I used to sneak out here and drink Coors beer and complain about our families.

As we walked, I felt the closed straight razor in my back pocket. It felt good there. Natural. It slid in right next to my wallet and I felt different, more confident. I felt myself walking with a bit of a swagger.

Angela was rattling on about her marketing work, giving me a data dump on SEO (Search Engine Optimization), Facebook ads, and recapture marketing. Stuff I'd usually eat up, loving just how geeky absolutely everything has gotten in the last ten years, but her words were a distant drone as I wondered at the barber that owned this blade or who it last shaved. Maybe Wyatt Earp or Doc Holliday before their fateful shootout in 1881.

Back when this was the Arizona Territory. Back when the whole state was like a good Western movie. Men riding their horses over the open range, whiskey served up at a saloon to the jangling sound of an out-of-tune piano.

"You're not listening to me," Angela said from behind.

"Ummm hmmm," I replied before my brain had parsed what she had said.

I turned and her hands were on her hips, her head cocked and lips pursed. A universal gesture. Put her in the 1880s in a dress and petticoat instead of shorts and a tank top and the man she was staring down would get the message just like I did.

"SEO. Facebook. Recapture marketing—which is, by the way, creepy. I was listening."

Her eyes narrowed further, and her head slowly shook. There was a reason Angela was cast as the shrew—she's fiery and even more beautiful when she's angry. I could almost see her in a high-collared, long dress, the amount of fabric unable to hide her excellent curves. I took a step towards her, suddenly feeling the weight of the razor in my pocket, imagining I had a gun on my hip.

"Alan," she began, "what the hell has gotten into you? You look strange, you—"

I swept her up in my arms and kissed her hard, the canopy of cottonwoods blunting the desert sun, dappled light falling all around us. Her lips were soft and she squealed and resisted, but for only a moment.

And then that fire turned from anger to something else and she kissed me back like I have never been kissed before. Need and hunger mixed into heady passion. Her warm hand went to my neck and she pulled me closer.

When our heads finally parted a bit, she whispered, "What the hell has gotten into you?"

"I..." I stammered. I felt the blade in my pocket, I still saw her in that dress, her long black hair in a bun on the top of her head. I knew it wasn't true, that I wasn't wearing cowboy boots and had a baseball cap covering my red hair, not a cowboy hat, but I felt that way.

"You just look so beautiful," I said, my heart pounding in my ears, my face flushed. "I've always wanted to do that."

She nodded, rubbed at the moisture on her lips, and then we were kissing again with such passion, like our years of not doing this had made it all the more powerful.

<hr>

MY WET RED HAIR STUCK UP IN UNRULY CLUMPS AND MY face looked tired. I smiled into the foggy bathroom mirror, the joy of Angela fighting through the fatigue. I took a deep breath of the warm, steamy air and wiped more fog off the mirror. The straight blade was in my right hand, open, my thumb pressed to the shank of the blade covering the John Barber symbol, my palm against the mother-of-pearl handle. I squirted some shaving cream into my left hand and covered my face.

"I am goddamn sick of them Earps," a graveled voice said behind me. I looked around, confused.

Out in my studio apartment, Angela was sprawled on the bed, my cheap white sheets wrapped around her olive skin. We had let our passions run wild, eaten pizza, drunk beer, and then watched the movie *Tombstone* propped up in bed holding hands.

There was no one else out there.

I shook my head and looked back down at the blade. It was

patinaed with age and wasn't sharp. I had tested that earlier. This was silly, but Ang was asleep and I just had to try.

I brought the blade to my right cheek held it at about a thirty-degree angle and gently pulled down.

I twitched, pulling the blade away when I heard the scraping sound, the one I'd heard as a kid with my father in that barber shop. I looked in the mirror and that section of my face was clean and smooth, red stubble clinging to the blade along with the shaving cream.

I smiled and rinsed the blade and did another stroke and... it worked. This dull, old blade worked! I could feel it; the blade had missed doing its job.

And somehow, I knew how to shave myself with a straight razor. First the cheeks, using my left hand above the blade to pull my skin tight. Under the jaw, the chin, under the chin. It was magnificent. My skin was so smooth.

After I was done, a few tufts of white still on my cheeks, I dabbed some more shaving cream on my sideburns. They had gotten a little longer than I liked. I went in at the perfect angle and just knew it was going to work, when the blade bit into my flesh and blood flowed down my cheek and dripped in the dirty water in the sink.

I pulled the blade away and stared at it, my blood bright against the steel.

"Them Earps gotta go," the gravel voice said again, somehow distant but close. I could smell strong aftershave mingled with tobacco smoke and, distantly, the smell of sweaty horses. A clomping noise accompanied my beating heart.

A shoop-shoop sound commenced and I found myself making long strokes with the blade in the air from my waist down. The word "strop" popped into my head and I felt leather in my left hand as I moved the blade back and forth, the blade always pointed in the direction opposite my motion. I was stropping the blade, smoothing out the hone so it would be perfect when I laid it to Billy Clanton's face.

Billy Clanton. He was one of the Cochise County Cowboys, the outlaws that went up against the Earps and Doc Holliday.

"You listenin', Billy?" the graveled voice said again. "Them Earps don't care for hard-workin' men like you and me. The Northern carpetbaggers have found us. They're not here for the ranchers, or the law, they're here for themselves. You get your boys together. You do something, ya hear me?"

I shook my head. We had just watched *Tombstone* last night, that must be it, but why did the razor work even when dull?

***

I COULDN'T LEAVE IT, THE RAZOR, EVEN AFTER IT HAD BIT me. It fit so nicely in my back pocket, the metal tang sticking up.

Angela was sweet when I kissed her goodbye, and then she noticed the cut. The bleeding had stopped, but it was a straight red slice an inch wide right at the base of my sideburn.

"What the..." Her hand went to my face, the sheets falling from her body as she sat up, making me wish I didn't have to go to work.

"Shaving," I said with a shrug.

"You used it." Her voice was hard. She pulled the sheet up as if cold.

I nodded. "Feel." I guided her hand to my chin. "Smoothest shave of my life. Don't worry about the cut. I'm still figuring it out."

What I said was the truth, kind of. I didn't tell her the blade was dull or about the voice I heard.

She nodded, seeming to accept my explanation. Yawning, she said, "I wish you didn't have to go. It's Sunday."

"All hands meeting," I said with the best smile I could

manage. "I'm the assistant manager now. Besides, Sunday is a big grocery day."

She kissed me, and I slipped out, not wanting to let her ask more questions.

———

THE MEETING WAS FULL OF PEOPLE WHO LOOKED AS TIRED as I felt, huddled in the break room of the Safeway, sipping coffee, sitting on the cheap furniture, trying not to inhale the strange scent of too many meals put through the microwave. No one was listening to Herb, the manager, as he droned on about the upcoming Labor Day holiday.

I wasn't listening either, the break room looking more like a saloon, a long bar with a mirror behind it where the sink and refrigerator were. Round wooden tables with cards and whiskey bottles on them, miners and ranchers in wide-brimmed hats slumped in the wooden chairs smoking instead of bored employees staring into empty space.

I could almost see Frank Stilwell, one of the Cochise County Cowboys, with short brown hair parted to one side and a smooth face. His gaze was intense, he was watching someone, and I knew it was Virgil Earp, the City Marshal of Tombstone. The famous gunfight was over, the McLaury brothers and Billy Clanton dead.

And then the meeting was over and the illusion shattered, but I was still staring at where I had seen Frank Stilwell. In Stil-well's place was William Smith, a beefy boy I went to high school with. A football-playing prom king to my soccer-playing, theater-loving geek. We weren't friends, especially not when I got the assistant manager job over him.

"You got any questions, Will?" I asked.

"Yeah. How'd a loser like you get this job?" He stood, his

arms crossed over his barrel chest. He was acquiring a spare tire, but he was still a lot bigger than me.

Part of me wanted to laugh that he was bent out of shape about my crappy job, but his insolence, that made me furious. Without thinking, I slammed him up against a vending machine, packages of cheap chips swinging on the other side of the glass. I didn't remember doing it but the razor pressed to his cheek.

"Now hear this, Frank," I said, my voice sounding gravelly. "I'm only going to say it once." Will's eyes were wide and his sour breath came in gasps.

Except it wasn't William Smith, it was Frank Stilwell up against the wall of the saloon late at night when everyone else had gone home and the barkeep was in back cleaning up.

"You and Curly Bill better wise up," I continued, my razor scraping down his dry cheek to his chin, making that eerie sound as it scraped off his stubble. "Don't confront the Earps in the open again. You fools. Find a dark spot, use your rifle, take them out." I slid the blade over his chin down to his neck and rested it against a mole. "Get rid of them Earps."

Frank/Will didn't speak, his eyes wide, his carotid artery pulsing against the blade. I didn't like Frank Stilwell, I thought him stupid, but I didn't want the Earps to drive the Cowboys away. I liked all the money they threw around town, how loose their tongues were in my barber's chair, what I could do with that information. I had my girls to take care of, three dowries to save up for. I couldn't have them Earps interfering with my business... my...

I shook my head, trying to clear it. I'm Alan Lester. I'm not a barber in 1881 in Tombstone, Arizona. I found this stupid razor at an antique store.

"You're so dead," Frank/Will said. "Herb will fire you in two seconds once the cops drag you out of here in cuffs."

I felt a wave of shame, but anger rose up and took it over.

"You breathe a word of this, Frank... and..." I flicked the blade, neatly slicing the mole off his neck and I stepped back. Frank/Will cried out, his hand flying to his bleeding neck.

"You tell them lawmen about our little talks and..." I slashed the blade across the air at the level of his neck. My voice was still gravel and I could feel the heat of my anger reddening my face. "Besides, you'll look better without that mole. I usually charge for such procedures."

I turned on my heel and strode out of the saloon, my boots pounding against the wooden floor.

⁂

"Do you believe in past lives?" I asked Angela. It was late and we were sprawled on my bed, the flat-screen playing some inane comedy, the white sheets against Angela's olive skin making me wish I had more energy for what we had been doing most of the night.

"What?" she asked, sitting up, brushing her long black hair away from her eyes. "Is that what's been on your mind since that meeting? You've been awfully quiet when we've... not been..." Her grin faded into concern. "Are you having second thoughts?"

"No! God no." I hadn't told her about the meeting, about Will, and no cops had come knocking on the door, so I guess the crazed barber had scared him enough to stay quiet. "No second thoughts." I grabbed her hand and squeezed it. "But... do you believe in reincarnation?"

Her brown eyes searched mine, her forehead wrinkling in concentration. The straight razor was on my bed stand, not far away. I could feel it and I longed to touch it almost as much as I longed to touch Angela again.

"Maybe you better tell me what's on your mind," she finally said, her arms crossed over her chest.

I glanced over at the closed razor, its mother-of-pearl handle looking so beautiful. I licked my lips and looked back at Angela's hard eyes. I knew that look. She would not relent until I spilled. "I... I think I was a barber in Tombstone in 1881."

Her eyes widened and a smile played on her lips like she thought I was joking and then she got deadly serious. "You're not kidding."

I shook my head.

"Give it," she said, her hand extended.

I froze. It was *my* blade. I had bought it from that English chap that came through Tombstone a few years back. I honed it and stropped it. I did shave after shave with it, day after day. It was part of me.

"I'll get it myself then," she said, crawling over me, her hand slapping down on the closed blade, her nude form lost on my seething mind.

My blade. Mine. "No!" I growled, the gravel back in my voice as my hands went for the blade. But she was on top of me, her hands quick.

Before I knew it, the blade was open and pressed to my throat, Angela's eyes suddenly beady, her voice an octave lower and full of gravel. "Listen here, Frank Stilwell. I know you're scared. Good for you shooting Virgil Earp, he'll never use his arm again, but that's not enough. Get back out there, take out Wyatt and Morgan and the rest of them Earps."

Those eyes, they scared the hell out of me.

"You're right," I said slowly. "Them Earps got to go."

"Now you're talking sense, boy," the possessed Angela said. And she was possessed, just as I had been.

"I best get to it then," I said, trying not to move at all.

Angela nodded, her jaw muscles bunching as she sat up and closed the blade. She was still sitting on me, her eyes vacant, and then she blinked and threw the blade across the room. "What the hell was that?"

WE DROVE THE REST OF THE NIGHT, FUELED BY COFFEE AND terror, as if the Tombstone barber was chasing us, seething about the Earps and how the Northerners were changing his town.

We took turns driving Angela's Mazda 3 out of the Verde Valley, down to Phoenix, through Tucson, and finally to Tombstone in the southeastern corner of Arizona.

Whoever wasn't driving was madly tapping on their phone, reading about Tombstone, the Claytons, the McLaurys, Frank Stilwell, and the Earps. How the gunfight didn't occur at the O.K. Corral—that myth set by the 1957 movie *Gunfight at the O.K. Corral*—but on Fremont Street next to a photographic studio. How the conflict between the Cochise County Cowboys and the Earps and Doc Holliday was in many ways a conflict between North and South, Republican and Democrat, an echo of the Civil War, and ultimately, about how the West was changing.

But we couldn't find anything about our barber. Nothing.

The razor was in the trunk. I had transported it out with barbecue tongs held at arm's length as if it were radioactive.

"I still want it," I said quietly, the rising sun a diluted yellow as we rolled into Tombstone. I could feel the blade and the barber calling to me. He had failed to stop the Earps, but somehow part of him was still there in that straight razor.

"I do too," Angela said quietly. She was behind the wheel and only glanced at me briefly, her eyes wide in the dim light.

She parked in front of a saloon on Allen Street and we got out and wandered around. It's a strange place. Old buildings restored with wooden sidewalks. Faux-fronted modern buildings. A stagecoach parked on the side of a paved road not far from a pickup truck. And then if you wander out of the boundaries of the tourist area, it's just a small desert town with old motels, houses, and RV parks.

We left the razor in the car and I felt the separation. I wanted to feel the power that I felt when I had it, that sense of confidence that had let me grab Angela and kiss her.

It was early, not quite seven a.m., and the town was quiet, just the occasional car humming by on Fremont Street. Angela was quiet, her eyes flitting from building to building like she was seeing something.

I could see it too. The streets were dirt with horses and wagons, not cars, men in wide-brimmed hats and women in full-length dresses. I heard the creak of leather saddles and harnesses and the clomping of hooves.

"You see it," I whispered.

She nodded, her hand grabbing mine, her grip painful.

And then I saw him. Our barber. He was short and barrel-chested with a white shirt, tie, and apron, the straight razor open in his hand. He looked up and down the street, a fearful expression on his face, as if he were looking for someone.

He scurried down the street, his head swinging from side to side.

The gunfight was over, Frank Stilwell had killed Morgan Earp, and Wyatt Earp had gone on his vendetta ride. The Earps had won and our barber was afraid his part in it had become known, that Wyatt Earp was after him.

The barber's path took us right by the car and, without talking about it, Angela unlocked the back and I grabbed the razor and...

We weren't in the tourist trap of Tombstone anymore, we were in the real Old West Tombstone in 1882, the smell of dust and horses filling my nose.

We followed as the barber left the main street, passed down an alley, and came out at the back of a small house and paused behind a rickety wooden outhouse placed under the shade of a scraggly tree. But I wasn't following the barber anymore—I *was* the barber.

One of the local town kids, who I paid in candy and pennies, had run into my shop as I was shaving my first customer, told me Wyatt Earp was back in town, that Curly Bill was dead, the Cowboys in disarray.

My heart beat loud in my ears and my breath came fast and heavy, sweat trickling down my back. Images of women flitted through my mind, one older, three younger. My wife and daughters, the eldest busy planning her wedding to the undertaker's son.

I looked down and the straight razor was in my hand, the blade open. You couldn't carry guns in Tombstone, or bowie knives, but no one would think twice about a barber with his razor. Maybe I could surprise Earp.

I stepped out from behind the outhouse and he was there. Wyatt Earp. He towered over me, his blue eyes piercing, a blond handlebar mustache dominating his face.

"You and me, George Pacher," Earp said. "We have to have ourselves a talk."

His long coat was covered in trail dust. He had on a wide-brimmed hat and a pistol on his hip.

I blinked and shook my head. "You kill me, an unarmed man, it won't go well for you."

He smiled, his eyes narrowing, an evil look on his face. "I'm not going to shoot you, George. I'm going to watch you tried and hung. I'm going to confiscate every last dollar you got from your association with the Cowboys. I'm going to see your pretty daughters penniless and forced to make a living on their backs."

I licked my lips and rubbed the sweat from my forehead. "You have nothing on me," I said, but I didn't believe it.

He laughed, and I felt as if the devil himself were in front of me. "I got plenty. Billy Clanton spoke your name with his dying breath. Frank Stilwell told me everything before I killed him."

I backed up a step, slamming into the hard wood of the outhouse, but Earp just stood there, relaxed.

"There is one way out of this for you, George." He said it gently as if we were friends, but no friend ever looked at me like that. He glanced at the razor in my shaking hand. "You end this here. You end this now. And I'll leave your family alone."

He just stood there staring at me, smiling. I lifted the razor and looked at it. It'd be quick. One clean cut to the neck and my life would flow out of me and soak into the ground.

I looked back into the devil's blue eyes and... I thought I could hear shouting, a woman's voice, she was desperate, but it was a distant echo, barely louder than my beating heart.

I licked my lips and nodded, agreeing to the lawman's terms. My wife, my girls, would have a hard time without me, but at least they would have money and status.

I brought the razor to my neck and—

"No!" Angela screamed at me, her eyes wide, her hands on my wrist wrenching the razor away from my neck. The past faded, the outhouse gone, replaced by a gazebo, the tree that had been producing scant shade now large. We were in a small park.

I fought her, the barber still with me, the need to protect my girls strong. "Please, Alan," Angela cried. "Don't do it!"

It's my name that reached me. I dropped the razor and fell to the ground, exhausted. Angela was by my side, hugging me, her tears wet on my cheek. Or maybe it was my own tears.

"I hate straight razors," I said after my heart had stopped hammering so hard.

She laughed. It was strained and too high pitched. "Well, why'd you buy it in the first place then?"

I shrugged. "You bugged me all damn day about buying something."

We laughed and then, seeing a loose stone at the base of the gazebo, I pulled it out, slipped the barber's razor in and put the stone back. I knew that being here, where the barber died, would quiet the razor and end its master's eternal quest to stop the Earps.

WE LEFT TOMBSTONE IMMEDIATELY, STOPPING ONLY LONG enough for fast food and gas, and drove until we got back to my apartment. We slept for sixteen hours and then it was time for Angela to go.

I stood there next to her Mazda 3 like a dummy, my hands shoved deep into the pockets of my shorts. I didn't have that razor in my back pocket next to my wallet, making me feel like I was someone, like I knew what I wanted and could have it.

Angela had her arms crossed and wasn't meeting my gaze. Our passion had been under the influence of that razor, and what was left? She turned and opened the door, the car dinging its warning that the keys were in the ignition. She was leaving, maybe for good.

"I..." I began, swallowing hard, my mouth dry.

She turned back, her brow furrowed, her eyes soft.

"I... Ang... I..."

"It's okay, Alan," she whispered. "If you think this was a

mistake, that the razor did this, then..." She trailed off, her eyes looking down.

"No!" I said, my voice way too loud. "No," I said again, quieter. "I've loved you since high school, this... this wasn't a mistake."

And there it was out in the open and my breath caught, and my heart pounded as she stared at me blinking.

Didn't she feel it too?

And then she was in my arms and I knew the razor had made me bold, but the passion had been real. Maybe it was finally time to leave small-town Arizona and find a different life... with her.

BACKSTORY—THE TOMBSTONE BARBER

Genre: Fantasy
Type of Time Travel: Backward only
Nature of Time Travel: Experiencing the past

This story has a history. I don't think I'll go into details, but for a while it seemed like this story about a cursed object was, itself, cursed. It got the attention of several editors, an honorable mention from the Writers of the Future contest, but no sale. Then I sent it to Dean Wesely Smith and it found its home at *Pulphouse Fiction Magazine.*

This is another one of my very Arizona stories. It takes place in modern day Arizona in Cottonwood and in Tombstone back in 1881.

This one took a bunch of research and takes a different view of the conflict between the Cochise County Cowboys and the Earps and Doc Holliday. It turns out the gunfight didn't occur at the O.K. Corral. I also rewatched the movie *Tombstone* as part of my research (the life of a writer can be so tough).

The story imagines another party involved and behind the

scenes pulling strings; a barber, the Tombstone barber. The story revolves around his straight razor which is cursed.

This was a fun one to write and I'm glad the story itself has a happy ending. It was originally published in *Pulphouse Fiction Magazine, Issue #19*.

PART 6
THE PEARCE SHOOTOUT

THE PEARCE SHOOTOUT

The following was assembled from the logs and mission briefings of Evan Price, Timeline versions 6.02–8.21

Mission Briefing

Prepared by: Intelligence version 6.01.153 for Agent Evan Price

Mission Narrative:

A lone cowboy riding into Pearce, Arizona Territories, in the early fall of 1893 was not an unusual sight. This one hit the small mining town an hour before sunset in early September, the cowboy's tawny horse kicking up puffs of dirt with each step on the dusty road.

At forty-two hundred feet in elevation, Pearce is considered high desert, with thorny bushes and scraggly mesquite trees. It is a rocky, gently rolling landscape with low mountains sitting on the horizon in all directions. Hot in the summer, cool in the winter, and a bit of snow now and then.

Miners were the most common sight in Pearce, with tons of gold and silver ore being pulled from Commonwealth Mine every day, and the many miles of tunnel ever expanding. The town was built for the miners and for them to spend their money. Saloons. A newly built general store, post office, and a stamp mill for the mine. A brothel. Boarding houses. A smithy. Several stables.

It was typical of a boom town, buildings hastily erected and freshly painted with an optimistic view towards a bright future, but many of the buildings would not survive long when the boom went bust. Some Tombstone residents even going so far as to dismantle their homes, haul them over the Dragoon Mountains, and reassemble them here.

There was a lot of money coming out of the ground and that always brought people, and not always at their best.

Not much notice was made of this cowboy because someone with chaps on, a worn duster, a gun holstered to each hip, and a Stetson "Boss of the Plains" hat on their head wasn't anything to take note of.

But the undertaker did. He was on his way back from the brand new general store, his arms full of the provisions his wife had tasked him to get. He stopped and watched the cowboy, his morbid sense of humor forcing him to calculate the odds of his services being needed. He wrote a few paragraphs in his journal about this.

He was an odd one. Short, to be sure, but it was the lack of spurs that first stood out and caused my eyes to linger. Did he think he had such mastery of his beast that a spur would never be needed? He rode well, his hips moving contrawise to the horse, keeping him straight and tall, a proud air to him though his hat was pulled low and his head was swiveling to and fro as if expecting danger. The horse's reins were held loosely, but his gloved grip on them was tight. I didn't see much of his face, the strong sunlight of a cloudless afternoon shining in my eyes, but I did notice a splash of freckles and a lack of whiskers.

I couldn't pin it down that moment, but I would have wagered I'd be seeing this cowboy on my table.

The cowboy rode straight to the saloon, again, not unusual, but stopped, still astride their horse, and stared at the door for a full minute, the sounds of men laughing and the smell of cigars and alcohol filtering out. The cowboy got down slowly, the leather of the saddle creaking loudly in the relative quiet of the late afternoon. The cowboy didn't tie the horse to the hitching post, but wrapped the reins around the saddle horn and spoke in low tones to the horse, kissing its brown hair before standing in front of the doors, taking a deep breath, and striding in.

MISSION: ENSURE THE COWBOY LEAVES THE SALOON ALIVE.

Mission Parameters: Minimize associated changes to the timeline but use any means necessary. Study attached biographies and sketches and photographs of individuals you might encounter in Pearce.

ONE

THURSDAY, SEPTEMBER 7, 1893

**Bisbee, Arizona Territories
Timeline version 6.02**

MY STOMACH IN KNOTS, I SAT ON MY COT AND READ THE mission briefing again, the cool, damp air of the abandoned mine suddenly feeling stifling. The silence of it, which was usually comforting, made me nervous.

The narrative portion was simple and straightforward and sounded like I had written it. And given how all of this works, I could have. The mission was assembled in version 6.01 of the timeline and we were on version 6.02.

I stood and paced over the fairly flat dirt floor across my room, holding the reading tablet and flipping through the biographies, the faces looking like so many I had seen before on other mission briefings. Three strides and I came to the end of the abandoned mine shaft that were my quarters, and four more to the larger tunnel. I didn't have a door, the concept of personal privacy fairly new. In any case, we were safe down here and I could easily hear someone coming.

My room wasn't much. A cot, a chair and table, and a trunk for my belongings in an abandoned mine shaft several thousand feet under Bisbee in the Arizona Territories. It was cool, a constant fifty-three degrees Fahrenheit, but still, it was a marvel to me.

My own room. My own space. Not packed into the crowded confines of the future. I had plenty to eat and far too much to read. I had the infinite silence of the mine or, if I wanted, music to listen to and videos to watch. And not far away through the tunnels, I had my fellow time travelers to have meals with and talk to.

I was born in 2365, engineered really, for a single purpose. My genome was assembled. I have no parents, not in the normal sense. I was raised and trained to be sent, at the age of fifteen, back in time to change the future. To help save humanity from itself. From the radical climate change and following population shift, wars (nuclear and otherwise), famine, and pandemics. In the twenty-fourth century, humanity is barely holding on. Living underground, growing crops and raising animals under large transparent domes, never going out into the maelstrom that is the earth's surface.

We are time travelers, but not how the literature of the twentieth and twenty-first centuries thought it would be. Our trip back in time is one-way and so hard on the body that we are genetically modified to survive—and we barely do at that. We call ourselves Butterflies, because we come back and make the smallest of changes that cascade into larger change, like the proverbial butterfly flapping its wings on one side of the planet and causing a hurricane on the others.

Given a few centuries, a small change here can be that dramatic. At least that is our hope.

But this mission the Intelligence had tasked me with is more than that. It is—

"You comin' to dinner, Evan?" Bella asked from the open tunnelway. I hadn't heard her coming. Isabella Reynolds, at twenty-one, is a few years older than me and...

In reviewing the histories and the logs I have written, I have waxed poetic—well, as poetic as I am capable—about Bella. Her round face and prominent cheekbones. The mole resting to the right of her nose. Her lustrous, long black hair. Even in the gray jumpsuits we all wear down here and her hair pulled back into a ponytail, she looked... well, like everything I wanted but could never have. Relationships are forbidden among the Butterflies.

"It's this mission," I said with a sigh, looking at the tablet in my hand so I didn't think about her. I shook the reading tablet and tossed it on the cot and sank down next to it. "There's almost nothing here. A cowboy riding into Pearce, the observations of the undertaker." I shrugged weakly. "It doesn't seem right."

"The Intelligence knows us and knows what we need to do," she said, which she had said to me many times before. "It gives us just the information we need to complete our mission."

"You know," I said, "the next century will call them *artificial intelligences*."

She pursed her full lips and crossed her arms; we'd had this "discussion" before. The Intelligence, while non-biological, was the only thing capable of determining the correct moves for us Butterflies to make. The small changes that will snowball into a better future.

"There is nothing here," I said, picking up the tablet and offering it to her.

She walked in and her rosewater scent overtook the damp dirty smell of the mine, and I could barely keep myself from smiling. Bella was engineered to be beautiful, of course, for the role she was to play here in the nineteenth century, for the effect she would have on men. And knowing that did not do one thing to diminish the effect she had on me.

Her eyes scanned the tablet as she flicked between the scant pages of the briefing. "Ahh," she said after reading.

"What?"

She nodded and handed the tablet back, her face darkening. "The Intelligence knows more, to be sure, but this is all you need to know. But..."

"Just spit it out, okay?"

She sighed. "This is a new mission, Evan. A version zero mission. You've never done it before."

"What about the briefing? That sounds like my writing."

She shrugged. "Maybe the last version of you was sent just to observe. The Intelligence suspects that this is a nexus here, that this is important. It's version zero for sure."

I bit my lip and nodded. I had heard of them before, but never been assigned one. The Intelligence had good reason to change things, but couldn't guide me much, couldn't tell me what the small action here that would cause the butterfly effect was.

I slumped back onto the cot.

"And..." she added, her green eyes refusing to meet mine.

"Please, Bella. Just tell me."

She nodded, our eyes connecting and the compassion there more frightening than the scant mission briefing. "Things have gotten worse in the future the last few versions. Something is fighting the changes we are making. This feels like a..." She sat next to me and her presence and her scent nearly overwhelmed my dread. "This one is important, Evan. I can't tell you why, but if this works, the next version will be better. I can feel it."

We sat there in companionable silence for a minute, my mind spinning with nowhere to go.

"Now, come on," Bella said, grabbing my hand and standing up. "You've got to leave in the morning and you must eat. You've got the future to save." She tugged on me and I couldn't resist her, even though I was a time traveler stepping into a history I knew almost nothing about.

PEARCE IS IN THE SOUTHERN PART OF THE ARIZONA Territory, forty miles from the Mexican border in the Sulphur Springs Valley. What brought men of European descent here is what brought these men to the rest of the West. Resources and the money they could bring. In this case, silver and gold. Pearce was destined for disaster, a series of collapses in the coming years causing the Commonwealth Mine to shut down and let go of the 200 men employed there. With the mine gone, Pearce would be quickly abandoned. In 1893, Pearce was a mining town and only a mining town.

Before arriving in Pearce, I had to read every diary entry, every newspaper article, every scrap of information the future had about its past. And there wasn't as much as I would have liked, Pearce being easily overshadowed by its famous neighbor, just southwest over the Dragoon Mountains, Tombstone.

The characters that inhabited Pearce and when exactly John Pearce discovered gold and staked his claim, and when the mining accidents happened, varied a few years from version to version, but the story was always the same. Rapid mining. A few getting wealthy. Many miners dying underground.

My stomach fluttery and nervous, I reined in my horse as soon as Six Mile Hill resolved on the horizon. I had made my way from Bisbee and spent the night in Tombstone. This morning, I had ridden over the Dragoon Mountains, and could just see a corner of the tin roof of the new stamp mill glinting in the sunlight. It was a new addition to the Commonwealth Mine where ore was crushed before the precious metals were extracted. Pearce was just on the other side of the oblong hill.

I pulled out my pocket watch, which was biometrically secured and was the sole piece of future-tech I was allowed to carry on this mission. The silver cover popped open as I pressed the fob, revealing a high-density screen with a countdown timer that had just passed 3:00:00, giving me only a few hours to accomplish my decidedly vague mission.

I indulged myself for a moment and remembered the feel of Bella's warm hand in mine. Her kind reassurances that even if I failed this version zero mission, the Intelligence would learn and the next version of me would know more, could do better.

And then the mission wouldn't be version zero but would be a butterfly mission. A tiny change, strategically placed, perfectly timed, that would eventually lead to a positive shift in the timeline.

Our one-way trip back in time is a strange one, the changes of those sent back further than us always changing things, always changing reality and changing us. It is these logs that keep us oriented to what the different versions of ourselves have done.

My youth in the twenty-fourth century, the memories that I have, are part of the sixth version of the timeline. The sixth major version of myself that has been sent back, and as bad as it seemed to me, it was much worse for the original version of myself.

Keeping these histories straight is difficult, to say the least. The future sends us small pieces of tech back, just digital memory etched into synthetic diamonds, that have the latest compilation of all the versions of history.

Through version four we were making progress, good progress, the future I came from in that version had a sliver of hope, the storms not so terrible, more of humanity had survived. But things had changed and the Intelligence that guides our actions suspects that there is a force resisting us.

Whether it is time itself resisting change or intelligent actors, we do not know.

I tilted my head up so the sun could get under my cowboy hat and shine on my face. I took a deep breath of the dry air filling my nose with the smells of horse sweat and warm leather. I was a cowboy in 1893. I was riding across the Arizona Territories. This, given my first fifteen years, was a miracle.

My dread didn't quite diminish, my mission was a mystery, I might not even survive it, but this moment was worth enjoying.

THE SALOON WAS NOISY, FILLED WITH THE SOUND OF laughing men, cards being shuffled, boots on the wooden floor, the jangle of spurs, scraping chairs, and the occasional higher octave sound of a woman's voice.

Angelina Cortez smiled brightly at me, her strongly floral scent barely competing against the bouquet of cigar smoke, sour beer, and body odor that is a saloon. "You are so different, señor," she whispered to me, her red lips near my ear, her warmth palpable. "I like that."

My heart beat hard because of her presence, because of how it made me think of Bella, and because I knew the mysterious cowboy would be walking in at any moment. I had slipped her a few coins to talk with me—not her usual request, I'm sure.

We stood in a corner of the small, rectangular saloon. A faro table set up towards the front of the building, the bar at the back of the building, rough round tables filled mostly with miners, their faces dirty from the job, and a set of stairs leading to the rooms on the second floor.

When the mysterious cowboy walked in, the saloon doors flapping behind them, the room didn't quiet, no one noticing the lack of the clatter of spurs or looking up from their cards or their drinks for more than the briefest of glances.

Well. That's not true. The two women in the saloon noticed. Angelina glanced away from me, and Rosie glanced over the railing of the second floor, having left her client snoring in his room.

They saw what I did. Something was off. The cowboy's clothes were too big, the gun belt cinched tight, a few stray blond hairs leaking out from under the Stetson that were rather long. They noticed and they watched.

The cowboy's gaze raked over the saloon quickly, stopping at the faro table where Bartholomew Jenkins was playing, laughing loudly, his pinstripe suit clean and barely wrinkled, his jacket off and white shirt sleeves rolled up. His black hair, with a few strands of gray, was slicked back, his mustache waxed up into a curl.

It wasn't quite a stare, but almost, the cowboy's lips pursing before moving on to the bar.

"Whiskey," the cowboy said with a voice that was a bit rough but sounded young. The bartender, a thin man with balding gray hair and a nervous look to him, nodded and pulled a bottle and a jigger from underneath the bar.

Angelina stared at the cowboy and I stared at her. She could see it, but I couldn't. "Excusa, señor. Un momento," she said to me, lapsing back into Spanish. She didn't apologize, but rushed upstairs, her whispers with Rosie floating down through the noise. It was fine by me; now that the cowboy was here I needed to focus and wouldn't have to worry about her.

I went over to the faro table as if to get a better view of the cards and stacked chips laid out on the green felt, my back against the wall.

The bartender filled the glass and the cowboy at the bar shot it back, giving the bartender a good look at the cowboy's face. He suddenly found a reason to go into the back room, mumbling something I couldn't hear.

While I knew something was different about this cowboy, I couldn't have told you what it was. And the rest of the saloon didn't notice either.

Time travel will just give you a headache, and whatever version of me that is reading this, I am guessing you have one right now. Just in case things have changed, let me pause and summarize how all this works.

The future, barely holding on to survival after radical climate change, population shift, war, famine, and pandemic, figured out how to send things into the past. It's a one-way trip and if a person is to be sent, they must be young, fifteen at the oldest, and the cost in terms of energy is astronomical. It doesn't happen very often.

But small inert things can be sent more frequently and at a reasonable cost. About once a week, the future will send a synthetic diamond wafer with the histories encoded on it. We will add all the data we have to it, bury it in a prearranged location, and thus send it back to the future the old-fashioned way.

The "versions" I mentioned are changes, large changes in the timeline that the future is able to detect and catalog. Version 3 being one of those. We catch some smaller changes and those get cataloged after the major version, like version 3.50. We miss some versions, for sure. It's all a matter of timing.

Think of space-time as a pond and a change we make is a pebble being tossed into that pond. Changes take time to ripple through, a change in the timeline is not instantaneous. The future will send back a history to us that isn't the same as the one we are living in. This is how we know the timeline has "versioned."

It is not perfect, but it is the only tool we have to gauge our efforts here.

IN THIS "VERSION" OF AMERICA, THE WOMEN'S SUFFRAGE movement is about five years ahead. At one point it was ten years ahead, but things have degraded.

There are many factors the Intelligence considers in how to make the future better, but human rights are at the forefront. If man can take care of each other, then man (and woman) can take better care of the planet.

In that saloon in 1893 in Pearce, a small part of that movement was playing out.

The women and the bartender, knowing what was coming, have left. The cowboy turned around and leaned against the bar, taking off her Stetson and shaking her long curls out.

At first nothing changed except for my small intake of breath and then the smile on my face as I realized what was going on and what this meant. Her hair was long and curly, the color of winter wheat in the light of an orange-red sunset. Her duster was swept back, exposing the guns on her now noticeably wider hips.

The cowboy was a girl. A woman. Gayle Smythe. I recognized her from the biographies I'd read, and it was now clear what was about to happen. If she survived long enough, it could cause the timeline to version.

The faro dealer was the first to notice, he sucked in a breath, inhaling some spit, and then started coughing. Eyes turned to him and saw his stare and then turned to her.

The talking subsided, slowly at first, and then suddenly the only sound was the intake of surprised breaths, coughs, and the scraping of a few chairs.

She was dressed like a man, wore guns like a man, and wanted revenge like a man. I was briefly distracted wondering why the Intelligence didn't want me to know her identity, but the unfolding drama left no room for that.

"Bartholomew Jenkins," she said, her voice raspy like she hadn't spoken in a long time. "I am calling you out."

Jenkins turned slowly, a smile lifting his curled mustache. "Well, whatever for, my darling?" he said, his Southern origin clear in the lilt of his voice.

"The murder of my husband," she said, her voice stronger, but the emotion there now clear. "Either you step outside right now or I will gun you down in here."

He sighed and smoothed his vest. "Mrs. Smythe, now really. That was nothing but a tragic accident, and besides, I am a gentleman, I won't shoot a woman even if she has the poor taste to dress up like a man." His smile twitched briefly into a sneer.

I slowly stepped back from the faro table spotting the two men I knew to be associated with Jenkins. It didn't look like Gayle Smythe had much of a chance of leaving this saloon alive, but that was why I was here.

In this version of the timeline, Bartholomew Jenkins is the owner of the Commonwealth Mine, having bought it from John Pearce. The mine has the same problem the mine always has. The timbers used to shore up the tunnels are substandard and the tunnels collapse, killing and trapping miners.

Jerome Smythe was one such miner, a learned man originally from Boston who had been telling Jenkins of the danger for months. Jerome was ignored and was in the mine for the first big collapse, and perished with four other men.

The Smythes had a small plot of land outside of town in the rolling foothills of the Dragoon Mountains, where they were raising cattle among the rocky hills. Jerome worked at the mine to pay down their debt while Gayle ran the ranch.

They had met in Boston, Gayle finding Jerome's shyness appealing and his encyclopedia-like mind fascinating. Jerome was a kind and thoughtful man who longed for the open countryside of the West. He kept a diary, but he wrote in it infrequently. He did write this about his longing for the West and for her:

They say it's quiet out there in the vast desert among the prickly cactus. That all one can hear is the breeze during the day and the yip of a coyote at night. Land is plentiful as well as are opportunity and danger.

If not for meeting Gayle, I would have left already. Her brown eyes and red-tinged golden locks mesmerize me, but it is her fierce heart that I long for the most. She, the only child of an adventurous man, is better with a gun than I, a better shot I have never seen except for maybe her idol, Annie Oakley. She is built for this adventure, more than I am, but yet she hesitates to take my hand and go with me.

I have the dreamer's heart, she has the gumption. We shall make a team such as the West has never seen if I can but convince her.

***

Jenkins set his cigar in a metal ashtray and leaned over and spoke to another man at the faro table, a willowy older gentleman by the name of Mayer. Jenkins stood slowly as I backed myself into the corner of the saloon so I could see everyone. About half the contents of the room rushed out, including Mayer, the remaining were either with Jenkins or too curious for their own good.

The older man didn't draw his gun or act afraid, he just stood slowly and tugged his vest down, pulled out his pocket watch and said, "Well, it's past high noon, my darling, and I believe you just might have read too many dime novels. But, let's say we all meet back here tomorrow?" He ended in a smile that I am sure was meant to be charming but was nothing less than menacing.

Gayle Smythe remained relaxed, leaning up against the bar. "I thought I made myself clear. I shoot you down in here or we go outside. And if you call me 'my darling' again, I won't be able to stop myself from drawing."

Jenkins slowly nodded. He was likely buying time, waiting for one of his men to sneak around and come in the back. "What happened in the mine was most regrettable," he said with a sigh, his voice getting thick. "Truly regrettable."

"Jerome warned you," she said, blinking rapidly, the emotion back in her voice.

Jenkins looked puzzled, his brow furrowing so deeply it was almost comical. "I do not recollect any such warning, my darl— Missus Smythe. Perhaps your husband did not have the courage to voice his concerns."

Smythe pushed away from the bar, her freckled face reddening as Jenkins backed up against the faro table, his hands out to the side.

"You are a liar!" she yelled, her hand straying and stopping inches from her gun.

My heart thudded in my chest. From my studies, I figured I was the third best with a gun in the room after Smythe and Jenkins. I had never killed anyone, nor had I been in a gunfight, but I could shoot.

The stories the future told of this past, of how men were always lining up at "high noon" to see who was the fastest draw, are apocryphal. In truth no one in their right mind wanted to stand still on a dusty street in front of someone else that was even a decent shot.

For me, death, if it came, would be real... to this version of me. The past could be tweaked so that a future version of me would get past this point in the timeline, but death was still death and my body responded in kind and I wanted to do nothing more than run from here.

While Smythe fumed at Jenkins and I worried about my mortality, one of Jenkin's men, a thin man with graying hair of the name Walters, flanked her and pulled his gun.

Smythe caught it out of the corner of her eye, drawing and firing with her right hand at Jenkins and swinging around her left hand to fire on Walters.

And then guns were drawn and bullets fired, I fired, and the room filled with the acrid smell of smoke and then the iron smell of blood.

It was a blur to me. I remember firing on several of Jenkin's men. A searing pain erupting in my shoulder and my gut. And then I was down on the hard wooden floor, my nose filled with the scent of sour beer before all I could smell was my own blood and my own waste as my bowels let loose.

After it had quieted and all I could hear was the sound of groaning men and distant shouts from outside, I looked through the legs of the chairs and tables and saw Gayle Smythe dead on the floor, her brown eyes open and empty.

TWO
THURSDAY, SEPTEMBER 7, 1893

Bisbee, Arizona Territories
Timeline version 6.03

"You comin' to dinner, Evan?" Bella asked from the open tunnelway. I hadn't heard her coming. Isabella Reynolds is a few years older than me, engineered to be beautiful, and not currently my biggest problem. This mission was.

"I died," I said with a sigh, slumped on my cot, the reading tablet in my hand.

She put her hands on her hips, her curves quite clear in the utilitarian gray jumpsuit we all wear down here. "What are we talking about, Evan?"

"This mission. I died. Multiple times. Enough times until I got lucky and had wounds my nanites could contend with, and survived long enough to make the report." I was standing with no memory of getting up, my face feeling flushed. "The Intelligence knew more, didn't give me enough information, and... I died!"

I handed the tablet to Bella, her green eyes serious, and she paced while she read the briefing which included my version 6.02 log. This reality, the different timeline versions, was something I had been taught about from a young age, something I intellectually understood. Versions of me would die for the future. My one-way trip back in time guaranteed it. But I had never confronted the reality of it before.

"This was a version zero mission," Bella said as I paced. "You know things haven't gone that well these last few major versions. Maybe the Intelligence didn't know about Gayle Smythe and her intention but had enough data to suspect this could be an inflection point."

I ended up in front of her and sighed. "I died, Bella. How many times did I die on the floor of that saloon after the bullets flew? Each of those Evan Prices were as real as I am. And now I have to go back?"

Her green eyes were unwavering but compassionate as they met mine. "We've all died, Evan. We've all faced this in our briefings."

I slowly nodded, my heart beating harder as her nearness moved my mind to yet another reality I couldn't affect. Butterflies were not to fall in love with each other. Fraternization was forbidden. We had to stay focused.

She gently took my hand. "Come on now, let's go eat. Let's talk this through with the rest of the team."

I nodded slowly. I couldn't refuse her.

MY FEAR COST GAYLE SMYTHE HER LIFE. HOW MANY times that happened in the hot, smoky saloon in Pearce, I couldn't say. One time at least, so that a former version of me wrote it down and sent it to the future, and that the future sent it back to us so I would know.

I rode hard into Pearce this time and thought about riding to the Smythe ranch in the foothills of the Dragoon Mountains to intercept Gayle Smythe on her way into town. But that was not my mission. It was still the same. Make sure she got out of the saloon alive.

I rode through town a couple of times, obsessively checking my future-tech pocket watch and the countdown timer there, hoping, wondering if I was creating enough of a sight for the undertaker to note it in his diary. It didn't take long, the main street of Pearce being maybe two hundred yards from end to end. I eyed the saloon with more distrust than the cowboy had in my initial briefing, than Gayle Smythe would soon be doing. We all go in the saloon and many of us don't survive. With a grieving and angry woman and a room full of guns, how was I supposed to stop that?

But I eventually went in. I was a well-trained Butterfly and knew I had to play my part.

I found Angelina, using her attentions as cover since I was a stranger. She was beautiful in her silk red dress, her dark hair twisted and piled up onto the top of her head. And she was charming, making my silver disappear in the most intriguing way, but I was distracted by more than how she made me think of Bella.

I was skilled with a gun, having practiced endlessly before the time jump and after. In simulations in the future and deep in the Bisbee mine that is our base here in the past. But that didn't really matter much. What really helped you survive in a gunfight was not speed or accuracy (although those certainly helped) but keeping your cool.

The tales of Wild Bill Hickok are greatly exaggerated, even in his time, but the one thing that helped him survive so many encounters was that he kept his cool. The only gunman that survived a fight with him was the one that shot him in the back.

When the cowboy that was Gayle Smythe walked in the saloon, I stiffened and Angelina could see what this version of me could see. The cowboy was not a "boy." Gayle Smythe's skill with a gun was well known in the area and Angelina must have recognized her.

"Oh Dios mío. Discúlpame, por favor," she mumbled, and swept off to go upstairs to tell Rosie, leaving me with the quickly disappearing floral scent of her perfume and my own rapidly increasing dread.

Soon the bartender was gone and Gayle Smythe took off her Stetson and revealed her identity, and Jenkins and she sparred verbally. The time was slipping past so fast, my stomach tight, sweat trickling down my back as I positioned myself in the front corner of the room.

After Jenkins denied that Jerome Smythe ever warned him about the conditions in the mine, Smythe surged forward. "You are a liar!" she yelled, her hand straying and stopping inches from her gun.

This was it. Right here. The bullets will fly. She will die. I will probably die. My heart was pounding so hard I could hear little else, the smell of my own sweat overwhelming the smoky scent of the saloon.

One of Jenkins' men, a man with the last name Walters, with graying hair and suspenders tight against his lean belly, was using Smythe's distraction to flank her. If she noticed and drew, it would all be over, the small space filling with bullets.

I took a small step forward and caught Walter's eye and nodded my head, resting my hand on my Colt 45. My hand was shaking, but I was hoping he didn't notice. He stopped, blinking, his chest heaving. The rumors of the woman's talent with guns must be well known, that was why no one had drawn yet.

"Women are not welcome in the saloon, you know," Jenkins was casually saying, his Southern lilt dangerous, his fingers lazily stroking his mustache. "At least not dressed like you are, they're not."

There were some snickers, but when her hand got closer to her guns, they stopped.

Smythe was midway between the bar and the faro table with Jenkins right in front of her and Walters and a man named Teige almost in a position to flank her on either side. If she drew and fired, I had little doubt that Jenkins would end up with a bullet in him, but it was a sure thing she would die.

I had to do something.

"You know," I said, my voice sounding much weaker than I wanted it to. Suddenly all eyes were on me and sweat sprang to my neck, sharp and prickly. "I met Jerome Smythe once. Right here."

The air was thick, the scent of sweating bodies overcoming the smell of sour beer and tobacco smoke.

Jenkins, with his eyes on Gayle Smythe, said, "And why the hell would anyone care about that?" His tone was no longer relaxed.

"Oh. Well... he told me about the problems with the mine," I continued. "This was on... let me see... in July, the first Sunday, I believe. He wasn't a man much for saloons but had just come from talking to you, Mr. Jenkins, and needed a drink. I bought him one. He told me of the problems with the mine."

"You are a liar," he said between gritted teeth.

And I was. I had never met Jerome Smythe, but I had read every scrap of information we had from this incident from all the versions, so what I was saying was true enough.

"What was it that you told him...?" I went on. "'You breathe a word of this to anyone, Smythe, and I'll make sure you never come out of this mine alive.'"

Gayle Smythe's warm brown eyes briefly strayed to mine and I gave her a small nod, wanting to let her know she wasn't alone. She recognized those words, because her husband had said them and she had written them in a letter to her sister in Boston in version 4.0 of this timeline, a version of her not quite bold enough to do what she was doing today.

"Liar!" Jenkins hissed.

I inched my hands closer to my guns, my heart pounding, but the specter of death was no longer close now that actual death was. "He said those words. I swear it."

There were tears in Smythe's eyes, her rage edging back towards grief for her lost husband. I wished my mission had been earlier in time, to prevent Jerome Smythe from going to the mine that day, or even earlier, intercepting John Pearce and preventing him from stumbling across the gold ore on Six Mile Hill.

"Hands up," a young man with russet-colored hair said, his Colt Peacemaker shoved into my side. He had been cowering under a table last time I had seen him. I had lost my focus, lost my "cool," and hadn't noticed him.

"Let him go!" Smythe said between gritted teeth, her guns drawn, one pointed at the young man next to me, the other at Jenkins.

Jenkins' men drew their guns, pointing them at Smythe and me.

The seconds ticked by as sweat trickled down my forehead, the saloon preternaturally quiet.

My mind raced. I was about to die. Again. I likely had died in this situation multiple times but hadn't survived to write about it so that a future version of me could learn from my mistakes. My thoughts were no longer on the mission, well at least not in the short term. In the short term, I needed to survive, write about this fourth person, so a different version of me could complete the mission.

"Bartholomew Jenkins," I began, my voice loud and droning.

"Born July sixteen, eighteen fifty-nine, in Atlanta, Georgia, to Bartholomew Jenkins Senior and Mary Jenkins. You were a colicky baby and nearly died of pneumonia at the age of five. You will meet your end in nineteen-oh-two when you are underground for a rare inspection of the Commonwealth Mine and the collapsing tunnel kills you and most of the miners."

There were cries and curses as I droned on, breaking all the rules that had been drilled into me, revealing details of the past and future I should not know. After Jenkins, I did it for Walters and the rest of Jenkins' men. One at a time, revealing their birth and their death and some key event in their history.

When I got to Malcom Thomas, the young man with his gun in my ribs who I had finally recognized, the routine spooked him enough that he relaxed his gun, and I shoved him away and dove to the ground as those with drawn guns started firing.

I took a bullet to the chest, my right lung collapsing, and I hit the floor hard. After the thunder of gunfire ended and the saloon became eerily quiet, as I lay on the sour-smelling wood, I saw that both Jenkins and Smythe were dead.

My breath labored, I hoped that the nanites flowing through my bloodstream would do their job, would keep me alive, and I would survive enough to write this tale.

I smiled, just briefly, as consciousness faded. The next version of me, if I survived, would be better informed, and hopefully a bit smarter and a bit luckier than I.

THREE
THURSDAY, SEPTEMBER 7, 1893

Bisbee, Arizona Territories
Timeline version 6.04

"This is impossible, Bella," I said in the dimly lit, abandoned mining shaft outside my quarters deep under Bisbee in the Arizona Territories. She was coming to tell me about dinner, her long black hair caught in a ponytail and her rose-water scent a welcome relief from the dusty, damp scent of the mine.

"What?" she asked, her cheeks flushing briefly as she looked me up and down. I wasn't the scrawny kid that had been sent back in time at the age of fifteen. I was nineteen years old now, my body having filled out. I too was genetically designed to be pleasing to the opposite sex, with hair as dark as hers and light blue eyes.

My mouth moved, all the words I had meant to say getting logjammed by what I thought I just saw in the dim light of the tunnel. But how could I be sure?

"Umm..." I stammered, waving the tablet absently, trying to get my mind back on track.

"Let me see that," she said, relief on her face as she took the tablet from me and read my mission briefing.

"Oh..." she mumbled as she read. "Oh my." She took me by the arm and led me back into my quarters, just a cot and a trunk and a small desk, lit with oil lanterns.

"I'm tired of dying," I said weakly when we were both seated on my cot. I knew Bella, I knew her well, and while I was thinking of my mission, I was lost in her reaction, her faint blush. She had never given me one hint that she might feel about me the way I felt about her. Not one.

"I get it," she said. "I've faced missions like this, missions where..." She trailed off.

"Where things worse than death happened to you...?" I offered. This time was not a gentle time for men and even worse for women.

She nodded, and unthinking, I took her hand. Much to my surprise, she didn't pull away, but squeezed it.

"How did you deal with it?" I asked quietly.

She shrugged. "I did what I was trained to do. I did my job. We don't matter, all that matters is the future and making it better."

The silence was thick as we sat there, my heart pounding hard just because I held her hand. Just because she had blushed for a moment earlier. Just because she was Bella and I was Evan and we were two Butterflies stuck in the past trying to make a better future we would never see.

"Come on," she said with a sigh. "You have to eat. Let's talk this through with the rest of the team." She stood and pulled on my hand.

I didn't want to be with the rest of the team. I wanted to be with her.

"Come on," she said again, this time with urgency.

I nodded and stood up and she held my hand until we got close to the common area. I wasn't thinking so much about my mission to save the future, but about Bella who made my present worth being in.

I HAD FOUR MEN TO KEEP AN EYE ON WHILE I FLIRTED WITH Angelina in that saloon in Pearce.

Bartholomew Jenkins, loud and chomping on a cigar at the faro table. Jake Walters and Orville Teige, both older and clearly his men, and Malcom Thomas, the young man who got the drop on the last version of me.

Angelina was beautiful with her deep brown eyes, her body encased in red silk, her floral scent the only pleasant-smelling thing in the small room. I couldn't help but wonder if the former versions of me enjoyed this more, versions of me who hadn't held Bella's hand back in Bisbee.

I think I was less afraid of death than some of my former versions, but that was counterbalanced by having something to truly live for. Someone to live for. My heart beat hard and I was sweating in the warm fall afternoon.

Jenkins played faro, the other men drank. Angelina smiled and hung on my every word while I nursed a beer and waited for the future I needed to change to walk in the door.

This time when Gayle Smythe walked in, her eyes raking across the room, lingering briefly on Jenkins, Angelina was laughing and looking away. She hadn't noticed.

I leaned in close and whispered, "I reckon that was the widow Smythe that just walked in. You best get you and Rosie to safety."

Her brown eyes widened, and she covered her mouth when she saw Smythe at the bar. "Gracias," she said with a small curtsy and moved off.

I rather wished my mission had been to prevent Smythe from entering the bar. That I could have done. How was I going to get her out of here alive was a mystery. My past versions' logs were helpful, but the situation was too dynamic, always changing, like Angelina not noticing Smythe's entrance this time.

I moved to the corner of the saloon, but the back corner near the bar this time, where I could see Thomas if he made a move.

I watched as Jenkins and Smythe sparred verbally. As he denied that Jerome Smythe had warned him of the dangers in the mine. As Smythe prepared to draw and Walters and Teige moved in to flank her.

What I needed was a way to deescalate the conflict, get it out the door, without adding fuel to the fire, without presenting myself as a threat. Or... not as a threat that could be taken care of with a revolver.

I'd watched a lot of Westerns in the future. They were full of historical inaccuracies, like the two fastest guns meeting on the street at high noon. The hot, sweaty climate and lack of quality personal grooming, though, was pretty much on point, the rest overly romanticized.

Even in this era it was romanticized, like the dime novels that Gayle Smythe had clearly read and Jenkins teased her about.

Jenkins knew she was likely a better shot than he. What in the world could make him go out onto that street with her and fight fairly?

In my mind, I could see it. Like Clint Eastwood's Blondie facing off against Angel Eyes in the climactic scene in *The Good, the Bad and the Ugly*. Except in this case, one of them was a woman. One who dressed like a man and got revenge like a man in one of those dime novels. If she won... well, the word would spread, the legend would grow, and this world, it would change.

Smythe was standing in the center of the bar, an easy target from all directions.

"Women are not welcome in the saloon, you know," Jenkins said casually, his fingers lazily stroking his mustache. "At least not dressed like you are, they're not." His eyes raked up and down her body encased in baggy clothing that must have belonged to her husband.

Smythe's mouth opened to speak when I cut her off. "Then, perhaps you two should take this outside."

The four men looked at me, and Smythe briefly glanced over.

"I mean, I personally would like to see that. The mighty Bartholomew Jenkins, owner of the Commonwealth Mine, master of Pearce, brave enough to face a scrawny woman on the street on his own."

"Who the hell are you?" he growled.

I shrugged. "I'm the man who knows, without a whisper of a doubt, that as soon as anyone in this room draws, nearly everyone in this room dies." I caught young Thomas's eye as he was preparing to get up and was pleased to see him stay under the table.

I stood straight, my hand well away from the gun on my hip, but close enough.

"You best mind your own business," Jenkins growled.

I did my best to chuckle, but it came out strangled. "Getting out of this saloon alive is all of our businesses. Especially those of us that have wives at home, and daughters, and sons."

Walters and Teige were both married with daughters, that was aimed directly at them, but I wanted to get back to Bella, live long enough to see if there was something, anything, there.

Walters and Teige had stopped their movements and were eyeing each other. No one wants to die.

My heart was a roaring rush in my ears, my hands sweating and I could barely keep them from shaking.

"Missus Smythe," I said. "I suggest you back up slowly towards the bar and make yourself less of a target."

"Again," Jenkins began, stepping towards Smythe as she took a step backwards. "I ask, who the hell are you? And do you realize what a bad idea it is to interfere with my business?"

"Me?" I asked. "The name's Price. I'm just a historian on my way to Tombstone. Like I said, I'm just trying to get out of this saloon alive. Get back to the woman I love." The words snuck out of me, driven by the adrenaline of the moment, but the words rang true. I did love Bella. I think I always had.

Smythe took another step back and I stepped in front of her. My mission was that she got out of this saloon alive. She now had a bit of a chance.

Jenkins took another step forward, but the other three men stood their ground—maybe my words had gotten through.

I was about to whisper to Smythe to get behind the bar when she stepped to my side and drew both of her guns. Protecting her like that had been my mistake. She was not a woman that hid behind men.

And then the rest of us drew and far too many guns were cocked and ready to fire.

"See," I said, trying to keep my voice calm. "Now we all die."

"Fine by me," Smythe said. "As long as he's the first to go." She nodded towards Jenkins. And he would be the first to die, an easy shot for her.

What was I going to say, that the future needed her alive? That while she might not have anything to live for, the rest of us did?

I was beginning to see why a lot of scores were settled in this era with one man shooting another in the back. My pocket watch, my piece of future-tech, buzzed in my pocket, but I had no time to think about it and quickly forgot it.

"So," I continued, nodding towards Jenkins' men, "since your boss is not brave enough to face a woman alone, you all get to die with him in this saloon, never to see those you love again."

Thomas was the first to break, putting his hands up high as he scooted out the door. He didn't have a daughter, but maybe he hadn't had enough years to build up his nerve yet.

The saloon seemed to get hotter as the five of us stood there, everyone eyeing each other. I was grateful that Smythe hadn't started firing yet, perhaps I had gotten through to her too, that her need for revenge didn't extend to others losing their lives.

A bead of sweat rolled down Jenkins' forehead and I could hear the murmuring sound of voices outside. Word must have spread as to what was going on in here.

The minutes dragged out and I didn't say anything else. I had made my case and it was as clear as I could make it. If the firing started, no one would leave without a bullet or two in them.

Walters' attention wavered as he rubbed the sweat off his forehead, and then he swore under his breath and ran out the saloon, quickly followed by Teige.

Smythe took a deep breath, both of her revolvers pointed at Jenkins' chest. "Which will it be?" she asked. "I gun you down right here, right now, or we step outside."

Jenkins swallowed hard and nodded, lowering his Colt, his shoulders slumping. "Outside," he mumbled.

As soon as he got through the saloon's swinging doors, he started to run.

"Who are you?" Smythe hissed as the saloon doors flapped from Jenkins' passage.

I took my hat off and tilted my head toward her. "The name is Evan Price. Like I said, I'm a historian and just trying to get out of this saloon alive."

Her brown eyes were fierce as she stared at me, her round face decorated with freckles, the constellations of them made dense by a lot of time in the sun. Her face didn't look like that of a killer, at least it didn't look that way to me, but circumstances drive us to be what we never imagined we would.

She blinked twice and slowly shook her head, her shoulders slumping and her head falling with a sigh. She didn't believe me, but the relief of the moment survived and the dread of the moments to come seemed to sweep her doubts aside.

"I guess you best go, then," she said, her voice low, almost mumbling. She holstered her guns and walked back to the bar, donned her Stetson, this time leaving her reddish-gold curls spilling out.

She slowly walked out of the saloon, the murmur of the waiting crowd intensifying when she got out those doors. I heard snatches of conversation. "Did you see that Jenkins run, just like his tail was on fire," "That there woman is dressed like a man," "... Gayle Smythe, she's just a miner's wife."

I holstered my gun, backed up and slumped against the bar, my own heart pounding and my knees feeling weak now that the moment was passed. Now that my mission was done.

And then I heard the tone of the voices outside change. It went from curiosity to fear. I heard a few curses and then the voices suddenly got quiet.

Something was wrong.

I walked out and blinked against the late afternoon sunlight and saw it. Gayle Smythe was standing in the center of the dirt road, her duster swept back, her hands out to her sides, but close to her guns.

On the other end of town, just coming into sight was Bartholomew Jenkins flanked by two other men. Rough-looking men with dusty clothes and hard eyes, men I didn't recognize. Jenkins hadn't run away. He had run to get more guns.

Smythe didn't stand a chance.

FOUR
SATURDAY, SEPTEMBER 9, 1893

Pearce, Arizona Territories
Timeline version 6.05

THE THREE MEN WERE WALKING OUT OF THE WEST, THE sinking sun and orange sky silhouetted behind them in a scene straight out of a dime novel or an overly romanticized Western movie. Except in this case it was the bad guys beautifully haloed in golden light, while the good woman stood alone in the street and people scattered into buildings and behind walls, getting to where they felt safe, but to where they could still see.

My legs felt like rubber as I stood on the boardwalk in front of the saloon and watched. Three against one. She didn't stand a chance. Everyone knew it.

"Thank you for being so kind as to wait for me, my darling," Jenkins yelled from about a hundred yards away, the two men flanking him letting out brief chuckles. "I would hate for our little disagreement to go on too long."

"The mine isn't safe," Smythe yelled back, "and you know it. More men will die. Good men."

"Have you ever been in the Commonwealth Mine, my darling?" he asked. They were now about eighty yards apart and had slowed their walk while Smythe stood still right in front of the saloon. "Have you any experience with mines and how they are best run?"

"My husband—"

"Was a learned man," Jenkins said, cutting her off, the tone of his voice sharpening. "I will give him that. He was well educated back there in Boston, but he knew as much about mines as you do. I was kind enough to give him a job, and what did he do? Spread rumors that attacked my very integrity."

Smythe looked around, looking for support, someone to back her up. Her brown eyes met mine briefly and I saw something there I hadn't seen before. Doubt. Fear. She doubted she was in the right and that made her afraid.

I opened my mouth to speak, because I knew Jenkins was lying, but I had no way to prove it. I heard some noise in the saloon behind me but didn't turn to look, figuring it was someone moving to one of the windows to watch from there.

The three men stopped when they were about fifty yards away, Jenkins heaving a big sigh. "I will give you this one last chance, Missus Smythe. Go home. Pack up. Leave the Arizona Territories and I will let this whole unfortunate incident pass."

Smythe's jaw moved, but she didn't speak.

"You all hear that, don't you?" Jenkins yelled. "The woman knows not of what she speaks. She came here armed and threatened my life, there are many witnesses. I am giving her the chance to leave."

Pearce was growing and Cochise County marshals made their way through from time to time, but it was still too small for a lawman to be posted here. Jenkins was making his case clear before he gunned her down.

"My... my husband saw the danger," Smythe said, her voice

breaking but gaining strength. "He warned you and you ignored him. How many other miners did he talk to this about, how many have noticed the same issues that he did?

"You can pretend nothing is wrong in the Commonwealth Mine, but everyone knows there will be more accidents like that one that took Jerome."

Jenkins shook his head and sighed. "So, I take it you are turning down my most generous offer."

Smythe snorted and nodded her head.

"And I also take it that you intend to gun me down right here and right now."

Smythe paused, licking her lips, and I took a half step forward, my hands going to my guns. I had to help her.

"No you don't," a feminine voice said as I felt the cold steel of a pistol pressed into the small of my back. "Stay right there, cowboy."

I sucked in a deep breath, my heart pounding hard and then I smelled it. The distinct scent of roses over the barnyard scent of the street.

Out on the street Smythe said, "I intend to defend myself against three armed men, is what I intend to do."

"Bella?" I whispered, not turning. "What are you doing?"

"Keeping you from doing something stupid," she said, stepping closer. "Didn't you check your watch? Things have changed."

I remembered the buzzing a few minutes back and shook my head. "I've been a bit busy. I've got to help her. She doesn't stand a chance."

"Think about it, Evan. If she lives or dies today, what will this mean to the future?"

The talking had ended as the three men and one woman faced off in the street, their hands close to their guns.

And what would it mean if three men gunned down an

armed woman in a little Western mining town? Word would spread and the tale will grow. It would soon be six armed men and an unarmed woman. People would cry out for justice. Things would change.

But what if she survived unaided against such odds? Would Annie Oakley's offer of lady sharpshooters to serve in the Spanish-American War be accepted? How many other women would start standing up for themselves? How much sooner would women get the right to vote?

And how would it look if I stepped out there and helped her, if a man came to her aid? Would it change the timeline at all?

It was a dizzying thought even trying to speculate what would come of it, making me glad the Intelligence was not human and could weigh all these factors.

"I don't want her to die," I whispered to Bella.

"Me neither," she said.

And then it hit me. Bella's mission had come in after I left Bisbee, which means a former version of myself had stepped out onto that street and tried to aid her, and considering my briefing, that former version of myself must have died.

I stepped back, Bella by my side, as we watched three men draw and fire while one woman returned fire.

***

I'M QUITE SURE SMYTHE COULD HAVE DRAWN A FRACTION of a second sooner than she did. I've played it over in my mind a thousand times.

Jenkins and his two men with the sun low on the horizon golden orange behind them drawing, their knees bending slightly, their arms bent at the elbow, smoke belching from the barrels of their three guns while sharp retorts rang out.

Smythe did not draw when they did, but instead dove to the ground and rolled.

Bella by my side, sucking in a breath and gripping my bicep painfully.

There were faces peeking out of windows and around corners watching the drama unfold, better than any dime novel, looks of shock or surprise or just plain lust on their faces.

The air was still hot but carrying the promise of a cool evening on the breeze as it licked at the sweat covering my body.

The three men fired, as fast as they could, puffs of dirt flying up all around Smythe as she moved. She came up out of her roll into a kneeling position with both guns drawn and fired each gun twice. The two men flanking Jenkins dropped to the ground, and in his surprise, Jenkins stopped firing, his gun lowering a bit, his hand unsteady.

Smythe slowly got to her feet, both her guns pointing at Jenkins. "I will give you this one last chance, Bartholomew Jenkins. Close your mine down. Pack up. Leave the Arizona Territories and I will let this whole unfortunate incident pass."

Bella's grip became vicelike on my arm and my heart clanged in my head as the seconds ticked by.

Jenkins' face, which was backlit and I couldn't see it clearly, tensed and then he brought his gun level and fired.

And she fired.

And they both dropped to the ground.

I DON'T LIKE THE SMELL OF BLOOD. METALLIC AND cloying, smelling of rusting iron, smelling of death.

I escaped Bella's grip and ran to Smythe, not thinking about Jenkins, not thinking that he might get up and start firing, not thinking at all.

My breath was sour in my mouth and my heart clanged even harder, the breeze's promise of a cool evening drowned by my nervous sweat.

"I've got you," I said, taking her hand. Her hat lay on the ground behind her, her red-tinged blond hair splayed inelegantly on the dusty road, her brown eyes finding mine.

Jenkins had gotten her good, a single shot to the chest, her wheezing breath speaking to a collapsed lung. She had the same kind of injury a former version of myself had suffered in the saloon. The kind of injury that wasn't survivable under these conditions.

"Mister Price," she said with great effort, squeezing my hand, "how did I do?"

I nodded, glancing down the street at the three unmoving men. "You did good, Missus Smythe, you did good."

She nodded weakly. "For Jerome," she wheezed and then closed her eyes, her hand going slack in mine.

And then I smelled roses rising above the animal smell of the street and the iron scent of blood and Bella was there, her hand going to Smythe's neck. I saw a flash of something small and round and matte black in her palm as she pressed and held it to Smythe's neck.

"You're not..." I began.

She smiled and shrugged. "Part of the mission, I—" She stopped speaking because others were gathering around, but I knew what she was doing. She was injecting drugs and nanites into Smythe so that she would have a chance of surviving, and I was glad.

Glad that this brave woman would survive. Glad that the future would have a new legend. A different kind of legend.

Bella's blue eyes were shining and she smiled widely at me and I finally noticed what she was wearing. A tan jacket over a white blouse and gray trousers. They were not quite what

Smythe was wearing, they fit her well and were more feminine, but they weren't what women wore in 1893.

"Hey," she whispered, glancing down at Smythe. "She started it. Any excuse not to wear a bustle."

Thirty minutes later, Smythe was sitting up and Jenkins and his men most definitely were not. You could see the look of the ladies of Pearce as they eyed Gayle Smythe and the dead men fifty yards away, as the wheels turned in their minds as to what it meant to be a woman. I could see them staring at Bella, still beautiful in her unconventional clothing. You could practically hear the future changing.

Those women swarmed around us, took over Smythe's care, speaking to her in hushed, excited tones. Angelina was among them and gave me a warm smile and a bright, "Gracias."

They helped her off the street and towards the saloon where they could get her in a bed and better tend to her.

The sun had set, and I looked over at Bella as she watched the woman go. There was something in her beautiful face that I hadn't seen before. It wasn't just hope that this mission of ours to better the future might actually work, it was more than that. It was as if she were eager to see the future.

It was a beautiful night, a sliver of a moon surrounded by glittering stars, the air finally cool. Bella and I rode together, clear of Pearce and heading towards Tombstone.

If I felt a lightness now that the mission was over, I also felt a giddiness that made me think of holding Bella's hand in the mine deep under Bisbee.

"Thanks for coming," I said, the sound of coyotes yipping in the distance and the clop-clop of the horses the only other sounds in the quiet.

"It was a mission, Evan."

"Thank you, all the same." I tipped my hat and stared at her. The scant light only let me see the outline of her lovely face, but I was sure she was smiling.

"You are welcome."

"I'm guessing that the former version of myself went out onto the street with her and..."

"And history wrote that a stranger by the name of Price lost a gunfight with three other men, an innocent bystander, a woman named Smythe, dying too."

I sighed. Knowing what the right thing to do was beyond me, at least where it concerned the future. My instinct to protect Smythe, as men protect women in this time, was the exact kind of thing the Intelligence was trying to change. We all need saving at one time or another—Bella saved me from dying on the street today—but a woman like Gayle Smythe or Bella most definitely did not need me to step in as the clichéd big strong man of the era.

We rode for a time in companionable silence, the Dragoon Mountains rising on the horizon, blocking out some of the stars.

"When I was in that saloon, when everyone had their guns drawn," I finally said, my heart clanging in my head once again, "I thought of you. Of seeing you again."

"Evan, please—"

"No, Bella, hear me out. This world, this version of us will soon be gone, replaced by the next version, our missions refined, our duty always for the future. What if we...?" I trailed off, I couldn't say it.

I could feel Bella's stare, but she didn't say anything.

"If the Intelligence doesn't like it..." I said, my mouth dry, my words faltering. "It... it can tweak the next versions of us so... so we never have this moment. But, Bella, we are here. Now. We are having this moment. And we had a moment in the mine two days ago."

In the darkness she sniffed and nodded. I extended my hand to her and it hung out there in the void between us.

"I know we are in service to the future," I added. "I know we must follow our missions. But I... Bella, I think I—"

"Just shut up, Evan," Bella said, but her tone was gentle and I heard her sniff again. She maneuvered her horse close and took my hand and squeezed it.

I shut my mouth and let that gesture do all the talking. We rode off into the transient future hand in hand.

EPILOGUE

TUESDAY, NOVEMBER 1, 1904

**Pearce, Arizona Territories
Timeline version 8.21**

I DIDN'T NEED TO RIDE THROUGH PEARCE, IN FACT I shouldn't have. The mission eleven years earlier was long done, the Pearce shootout having become a legend near that of what happened in Tombstone just outside the O.K. Corral in 1881.

But I knew that Gayle Smythe was still here, and it was almost election day and I just wanted to see her.

As I rode into town, the quiet was unnerving, the once-bustling mining town that inhabited over a thousand souls was now nearly abandoned. One too many collapses and the Commonwealth Mine had finally been closed down and would stay that way for a while.

Gayle Smythe stayed in Pearce for the last eleven years, fighting with the next two owners of the Commonwealth Mine, trying to get them to take the safety of their miners seriously.

I stopped in front of the saloon, one of the swinging doors hung tiredly by a single hinge, dirt and debris on the floor inside.

The once brightly painted buildings were now tired, their paint peeling, windows broken, the breeze whistling through the streets was the only sound I heard.

Pearce was a ghost town, or nearly so. A chill ran down my back.

I hitched my horse in front of the saloon and walked out onto the street where Gayle Smythe had stood and fought. I looked to the west where Jenkins and his hired hands had fallen.

The timeline had versioned many times since that battle. I had been back each time with Bella as over and over each version of us acted out this conflict. Each time Bella had to come save me from walking out into the street. This was odd. The Intelligence could have given me enough information to prevent it without sending Bella, without us holding hands as we rode away. But I think the Intelligence played it out that way every time because I had something to learn.

That shootout had helped the future or the Intelligence wouldn't have us doing it version after version.

"Who the hell are you?" a rough voice asked, accompanied by the sound of a revolver being cocked.

I turned and slowly raised my hands. It was Gayle Smythe, the years having wrinkled her face some, but little else had changed. Her brown eyes were soulful and warm, her reddish-blond hair had a few stands of gray, but otherwise she seemed the same. She still wore pants, although these were much more fashionable and much better fitting.

I smiled at her and bobbed my head. "Ma'am. Just passing through and I felt the need to stop. I've got some memories here."

Her gaze intensified. The years had changed me too. I was thirty years old, not nineteen. I had been on many more missions, but none quite like this one. "Mister Price?"

I nodded. "At your service, Missus Smythe."

She holstered her gun and looked around, as if afraid something terrible was about to happen. "What are you doing here?"

I shrugged. "Just missing my youth, I guess. If that makes any sense."

She nodded as if it made all the sense in the world, her eyes skating around the slowly dilapidating buildings. The boom town was bust, but it had taken far more lives than it should have for that to happen.

She had stayed here after the celebrity of the gunfight had faded, after her biography had netted her enough cash to buy the general store. She had fought for the miners against two more owners of the Commonwealth Mine, but those fights had been without guns.

"Come on," she said, nodding towards the general store. "I've got some coffee on."

Inside the shelves were half bare, but the high-ceilinged room was clean and warm and smelled of smoke and baking bread.

"I failed them," she said, sinking into a chair by an iron potbellied stove. She pulled an enameled pot off the top and poured a dark brew into two cups, handing me one. The coffee was very strong and very bitter. I loved it.

Maybe she was telling me this because of the intensity of the few minutes we had shared. Maybe just because the words needed to be said.

I shook my head. "No you didn't. If Jenkins had continued on his course, it would have been much worse."

Her freckled brow furrowed and her eyes narrowed. "How can you possibly know that?"

I smiled. Bella tells me I have a good smile. "I am a historian and I have studied the last century extensively. Let's just say it's an educated guess. People are who they are. Jenkins wouldn't have changed anything until utter disaster had struck."

It's not like I could tell her I was a time traveler and many more died in previous versions of the histories.

She sighed and nodded, sipping her coffee.

The silence between us felt awkward. I knew so much about her, having followed her in the histories since that day eleven years ago, but I didn't really know her. She changed the world, I helped her do that. But that didn't make us friends.

We chatted, mostly about small things. How the West was changing now that the boom period of the mines in the area was waning. How she had seen a few automobiles rumble through town. How Pearce had changed when the railroad came and then left.

After I finished my coffee, I stood up. "Well, I best be on my way, Missus Smythe."

She smiled and nodded. The smile was genuine, but wistful. I'm sure I reminded her of difficult times.

She stayed by the warm stove as I walked to the door. When I was almost to it, she said, "Thank you, Mister Price."

"What for, ma'am?"

She smiled, this time widely, her smile pushing up her round, freckled cheeks. "For letting me fight my own fight."

I smiled back and nodded, not telling her it was Bella that had stopped me from fighting it with her. "It was truly a pleasure, ma'am."

She got up and rushed over and hugged me fiercely. Maybe I didn't really know her, but there was a strange bond between us.

After we parted, I said, "I trust you'll be voting in the upcoming election."

She snorted and nodded. "God and his archangels couldn't stop me."

I smiled and nodded. Women had gained the right to vote in the United States in 1902 instead of 1920. This was the first election that Gayle Smythe or any other women in this country could vote.

"That makes me very happy, ma'am," I said, bowing my head to her.

I left her and Pearce behind. While we had made a difference, it wasn't enough yet. Not nearly enough. Bella was waiting for me back in Bisbee and there was a lot more work to do.

BACKSTORY—THE PEARCE SHOOTOUT

Genre: Science Fiction
Type of Time Travel: Backward only
Nature of Time Travel: The Future can be changed

I love this story. In fact, this collection only exists because of this story. Wanting to get it out there again motivated me to do the work to create this collection.

In some ways this is one of the most serious time travel stories in this collection, but in another it's lightened a bit by the "Groundhog Day" nature of the time travel. The stakes are high, very high, the timeline is not fixed, but you get more than one shot to get it right, leaving room for the protagonist to be quite human.

See the backstory for "Butterfly in Training" for a little more on this world.

This story was originally published in *Pulphouse Fiction Magazine, Issue #13* and in the introduction to the story, Dean Wesely Smith said, "In this issue, Robert J. McCarter gives us a stunningly original and wonderful science fiction story set in the West, sort of."

That about covers it.

This story was also reprinted in *There'll Be Blue Popcorn Without You: Stories from Pulphouse* and received an honorable mention in the Writers of the Future contest.

PART 7

THE TRAVELERS

THE TRAVELERS

Even with all the trouble that ensued, the endless scrambling, and the breathless getaways, I would not give up my time as a time traveler.

I, you see, am not the sort that longs for the endless scramble or the breathless anything. I am no longer fond of exercise—at least not the kind that has no purpose beyond exercise itself—and I prefer time to come at me at the normal speed and in the normal sequence.

That said, we did some things when we were time travelers, didn't we?

Although, we didn't call it that, "time traveler," that is the common vernacular and a bit too long. We called it "traveling" and we were "The Travelers."

It began in 1946 on an oppressively hot summer's day in Lincoln, Nebraska. I was fifteen on my way home from school, my hands shoved into my jeans pockets and my mind obsessed with Alison Rodgers and not giving one thought to my father just back from the war with one less leg than he left with or my mother out of work at the factory and having trouble coming to grips with being back at the house all the time with a man that drank as much gin as he did water.

Those thoughts were too heavy, too empathetic for my hormone driven, teenage, heterosexual male body.

All I could think of was Alison. Curly hair the color of wheat that glistened in the sun and fell to her delicate shoulders. Eyes green as jade framed by a heart-shaped face. A light spray of freckles on cheeks. And that day she had smiled at me.

Smiled. At me!

It was a random walk-by in the halls of Lincoln High School and those green eyes connected with my blue eyes, a feeling like electricity coursing through my skinny body, her beautiful lips pulling up into a small smile.

It was just a moment, but what a moment. Suddenly I couldn't hear the chatter of my classmates or the clanging of the metal lockers. I couldn't smell the sour scent of too many bodies mingling with the smell of floor cleaner. All I could hear was my beating heart and all I could smell was a sweet whiff of her rose perfume.

She was perfection itself, her wheat hair pulled back into a ponytail, a pink sweater encasing her lovely curves, a black skirt swishing around her knees.

My addled brain didn't stop to wonder if she even knew my name, didn't consider that maybe that small upturn of her lovely lips was the beginnings of a smirk. That smile was kind of like a big bang, it created a whole new universe for me and that universe was her.

As I walked past the picket fences and nice houses on Randolph Street, barely seeing my surroundings, my mind and body focused on Alison Rodgers, I didn't see the strangely dressed man until I ran smack into him.

"Hey!" I shouted from the sidewalk, my right hand scraped

and my Alison illusion in tatters. I was back in the real world and mad as hell about it. I didn't want to deal with reality, which was pimples and the football players throwing me in the girl's bathroom and snide derision from all the kids who ranked higher on the keen-o-meter than I—which was most of the school.

The man was tall and lanky with pockmarked cheeks, short brown hair, and some kind of awful silver jumpsuit on. His blue eyes widened as he looked me over and I swear that look was full of snide derision. Adults seem to have terrible memories and quickly forget their hormone-addled teen years.

He seemed to recover, took a deep breath and said, "There you are, Gene. We need to talk." He extended his hand.

I didn't know why then, but I trusted him. He felt familiar even though I couldn't place him. I took his hand and let him pull me up.

I WON'T HOLD OUT ON YOU, DRAW THIS OUT IN SOME laborious way and then like a cheap street magician reveal my secret and expect you to be aghast. That would be tiresome.

I am a Traveler, so there are things I can experience that you cannot.

Like that day on Randolph Street in Lincoln where I, as a thirty-nine-year-old Traveler, met my fifteen-year-old self.

See. Best we just get that right out there as I try to tell my story. I will tell you, remembering the encounter from one side while experiencing it from the other is more than a little bit disorienting... and on top of the physical jar of traveling, quite nauseating.

When I first saw the younger me on the sidewalk I couldn't think. There was this feedback loop as I looked at my younger-self and remembered looking up at my older-self not yet knowing who I was. It was like standing between two mirrors, the reflections going on into infinity.

I had experienced this from one side and now it was time to experience it from the other. I couldn't remember exactly what I had said to myself, but I remembered the broad outline. The boy and me had important work to do, a life was at risk, one that we both valued. But it wouldn't be simple, and it wouldn't be without its cost, but it had to happen, had already happened, and in the facing mirror effect of time travel, perhaps, it was always happening.

While my younger brain recovered from the Alison illusion, I stood there trying to orient and had the briefest, oddest thought. If I killed my younger-self would that be considered murder or suicide? Or, maybe, both. Would this endless loop between me and myself be like a photon escaping the endless bouncing between two facing mirrors when one of the mirrors is broken?

I shook my head to clear it of such morbid thoughts. It was the jump, my body was still recovering from it. The sounds from the quiet street overloud, colors bright and oversaturated, and I could feel the small breeze as it flowed over my skin, evaporating the sweat there.

Jumps are... I can't describe it, the passing between one time and another. It's like a dream, a vague sensation of rushing, a noise that is so loud and sounds like it should have meaning, but it just slips away from your mind. And then you are in a new place hot, sweaty, and wanting to puke.

And then I really saw myself. Brown hair, a bit too long, hanging into my eyes. Levi's and a button-down blue shirt. Lots of pimples decorated a young face, one without lines or character.

I didn't envy myself the youth and was, frankly, aghast that I had ever survived being that self-conscious and awkward. I was skinny and lanky, but not devoid of hand-someness.

Like being between those two mirrors, a shadow of the teenage self-consciousness descended on me and I couldn't stand it. I wanted to look away but didn't, knowing my younger-self would think even less of himself if I did.

I took a deep breath and said, "There you are, Gene. We need to talk."

———

The odd man in the awful silver jumpsuit had a clean handkerchief that he pressed to my hand after he pulled me up. My hand was bleeding and I thought my pounding heart might make it bleed more.

I was still of an age where minor wounds like that felt personal, as if the world had set out to harm me for reasons I couldn't fathom. But then again, at fifteen, the whole world seemed to be one big experiment to see how terrible I could feel.

Shreds of my Alison fantasy/memory were still in my brain and I wanted to get back to them, but this man with the pock-marked cheeks was so earnest, so confident, his blue eyes so intense.

"Listen, Gene," he began, a bit breathlessly, "we need to move fast. It's—"

"How do you know my name?" I asked. It seemed a proper question of some random man you happened to bump into who knows you by name.

He tilted his head, his hand rubbing at the stubble at his chin and I felt the usual jealously that I felt of any boy or man with what looked like a proper beard. I was entirely in the peach fuzz camp and entirely too old for it.

"I know all about you, Gene," he said. "You were born in

1929 in Chicago, Illinois, to Gene and Mary Baxter. Your father moved your family here in 1941 after Pearl Harbor to be closer to your mother's parents. I know he was a prisoner of war and has just recently returned home with only one leg and is over fond of gin and yelling..."

He went on, but I couldn't really hear him anymore. He knew everything about me, even little things like I hated Cheerios (although thought the name better than CheeriOats) and wished we could afford a TV. It was all too much, and then he hit me with it.

"...and I know you were just thinking about Alison Rodgers and I can tell you that she is a colossal waste of your time."

All that other stuff about me was weird, I mean, my buddy Trent might have put him up to it, but Alison? No way he could know that. No way *anyone* could know that.

I did what any reasonable American teenager with respect and dignity would do. I ran.

GENE RAN FROM ME. I REMEMBER MY YOUNGER-SELF running from me and still it was a surprise. He was quick, in shape from running track, and while I still jogged to keep in shape, as much as I hated it, I was no teenager.

I ran after him down the street, through a well-manicured lawn and through the backyard of a house that clearly had several children who never picked up a single toy in their lives.

A metal Tonka toy tripped me and I went down on the soft grass and cursed, taking a deep breath and trying to remember what happened next.

The memories of this encounter are twenty-four years old. They've faded over the years and have the warm patina of age.

Given what my life has been like, I hadn't come back to them very often until recently.

Actually, if I am being honest, I didn't come back to them because once I found out who that older man was... well, it just wasn't comfortable. I wanted to come back to it no more than I wanted to come back to my Alison Rodgers fantasies once her disdain for me became clear enough for my hormone addled brain to comprehend.

I got up and kept running, just trying to keep my younger, fleet-footed self in view. Youth brings speed, age brings endurance, and I knew I could outlast him.

But his speed was too much and soon I was left sweating and panting in front of a two-story, picket-fenced home, wiping sweat from my brow.

The facing mirrors of my echoing memories was making this much harder than I had imagined it would be. I could remember much more clearly what I felt at fifteen than exactly what I did. That crushing sense of doubt, the eternal sense of uncertainty, the unquenchable desires. These are the things I knew my younger-self was experiencing, as all teenagers do. But what exactly I was doing, which houses I ran between and which streets I tore up, I could not recall.

But then I did remember where I ended up.

I smiled and walked at a leisurely pace knowing where my younger-self would soon be.

I freaked out. I'll admit it. Old men that know everything about you will do that to you.

Well, he wasn't "old" like my grandfather, but he was old like my father. And how could he know I had been thinking about

Alison Rodgers? I hadn't told a soul about her. No one. Not my best friend, not even my dog.

I ran until my spit was thick as molasses and I had a stitch in my side and then I ran some more. I ran until the little neighborhood park came into view, the squeaking of the swings a comfort. Life was much simpler when I was younger and frequented such parks, when all girls had cooties and I had no interest in them.

I slunk over to the metal water fountain and drank deeply, the green-leaved trees swaying above me, the chatter of children all around me.

When I stood up, the *old* man was there.

"Gene," he began with a smile. "We really do need to talk." I would have run, but the smile stopped me. It wasn't the condescending smile of an adult, but the empathetic smile of someone who knew exactly what I was going through. The kind of smile another teenager would give me when I recounted the latest embarrassment suffered at the hands of my mother or the latest terror executed by my drunken one-legged father.

"Who are you?" I asked, his face so familiar, but I could not place him. Likely some friend of the family who I had been introduced to once long ago and was expected to remember everything about.

"We'll get to that," he said, his smile still warm and empathetic. "Right now we need to go. Your mother is in danger."

It was a risk. Telling my younger-self that his mother was in danger was as complicated as a teenage boy's relationship with his mother is.

I knew my younger-self loved my mother... I still did, but I was aware that my current love of my mother was warmed by age and distance. A boy trying to find his way in the world still needing his mother, but not wanting her, that is complicated. Not as difficult as a daughter breaking away from her mother, but still quite difficult.

But no, there was no risk. I was a Traveler, so I knew that ploy had been used on me and I knew it would work.

"What?" my younger-self asked, his hand going to the water dribbling down his chin from the fountain, some particularly shrill sounds of children at play emanating from behind us on the jungle gym.

"That's why I'm here," I said, gesturing down to my silver jumpsuit, which was collecting stares and frowns from watchful mothers. We don't dress this ridiculously in the future, but it is either come through naked or come through looking ridiculous, and I will tell you, ridiculous is the far better of the two.

"Mom?" he said.

His brain was clearly having trouble getting traction. And in the memory hall of mirrors this encounter was becoming for me, I was having trouble thinking straight too.

"Yes. She needs us," I said flatly while my heart thumped hard in my chest. The thought of seeing Mom young again, with her full faculties, was...

I don't have the words, but let me say that my mother, in my present time, has a mind that never has traction on anything anymore. She often doesn't know who I am.

The thought of seeing her young again was the sheer definition of terror. Her slide had been gradual at first, but was gaining momentum now and she wasn't who she was anymore. She wasn't my mother. Senility had taken her away—could I bear seeing her whole again? Would I be able to do this here, see my mother young and all there, and go back and visit an old woman who doesn't know my name and is terrified of every little thing?

We walked, the two of us, down the sidewalks of Lincoln at a fast clip. The old guy could keep up with my long strides, which surprised me. I looked at him and noticed we were the same height and again wondered at his familiarity. A distant cousin of my mother's? A friend of my father's from before the war?

It also surprised me that he seemed to be the more nervous of the two of us and I was hoping that would loosen his tongue, that he would spill a few details about who he was and how he knew my mother was in danger, and what that danger might be.

The third time he caught me looking at him, his cheeks flushed briefly red and he asked, "Why do you think Alison is so special?"

The look on his face when he asked it was strange. Desperate and wistful at the same time. I wanted to ask about that, but hearing her name brought back together the tattered shards of my Alison Rodgers memory. I didn't want to talk, but I couldn't help it.

"She's... I don't know," I began, my cheeks hot. "She's beautiful and smart. Her laughter is like music. Her smile is like sunshine on a cold day after a big snowstorm. She smells like flowers and everyone loves her."

"Not everyone," he said, his voice low.

"What?" My heart leapt at the thought of it. Of course everyone loved Alison. She was perfect.

"Miles Kenner rather hates her, you know," he said.

I stopped and stared at him. Miles and Alison had broken up, the rumor was, because she refused to go all the way. And so she should—Miles was a Neanderthal and she was right to refuse him. But how did he know about Miles? And a dim part of my mind was aware that he was distracting me, not that the rest of my brain could do anything about it.

"Well... he's... that's not a fair example," I sputtered.

"She's just a girl, Gene," he said, his tone dry like he was reading from the phonebook. "Your hormones tell you she's the most important thing in the world right now, but your hormones lie."

I chewed on my lip and stared at him. He seemed serious and sad. My hormones lie? Who says things like that?

"She's just a girl," he said again, and started walking down the sidewalk just like he knew exactly where he was going.

I wanted to rescue myself from the horrors of being a teenager, from the endless, crippling self-doubt. From the pathological need to fit in and be accepted. From the heartbreak that was coming and the deep pain it would cause.

We can do a lot of things by going back in time, but that is not one of them and I knew it.

My younger-self would throw himself against the impenetrable defenses of Alison Rodgers until he broke himself. Until he learned. And sometimes breaking yourself is the only way to truly learn.

I sighed as I walked just ahead of him down the sidewalk to the home I still remember so well, toward my young and healthy mother. It would be silly to try to spare my younger-self the pain. Imagine if Alison had returned his affection and he ended up thinking that the world was that simple, that easy, really did work that way.

"Who are you?!" my younger-self asked, catching up to me.

"Who do you think I am?" I shot back. A wave of dizziness tumbled down on me, because this exchange I remembered well. The facing mirrors effect of memory was making me want to puke.

"I don't know," he said. "Some long lost uncle or someone

who has been talking to my friends, snooping around my life, who likes to dress like a dope."

That last comment hurt. I didn't like dressing this way at all. Just like my teenage self, I didn't like to be stared at or suffer ridicule, I just wasn't pathological about it. I wore the silly silver jumpsuit because it was a necessary sacrifice. After all, it wasn't as if I was going to hit someone over the head and steal their clothes.

Between the memories of the moment and the sting of his insult I got mad. "Alison doesn't even know you exist, Gene. Can you please grow up, just a little, just for today? She will never know you exist. She will never love you back. We've got to help your mother. We don't have time for this."

I watched his face fall as I said this. Like a balloon deflating, the defiance and energy just melted off his face, his cheeks flushing red, his hands shoved deep in the pockets of his jeans.

And I felt my own cheeks flushing in embarrassment for what I had said, and for having said it, how real it felt again to be on the receiving end of it.

I had just delivered and received the insult and the facing mirrors effect was too much. My stomach rose and I doubled over and puked in a nice bed of colorful pansies.

I SHOULD HAVE LEFT THE FAMILIAR OLD—BUT NOT SO OLD—man. He was puking his guts out on Mrs. Layton's flowerbed, doubled over in his stupid silver suit. He couldn't follow me. He was crazy. He said Alison will never love me. I should have run away again.

But I couldn't. I told myself it was because he'll somehow know where I'll be next, but that wasn't the real reason. Well, it was *part* of the reason, not *all* of the reason. It was Mom that kept me there. If there was a chance that he was right and she was in danger, well... I couldn't just walk away from that.

As he continued to puke, I felt this knot of guilt in my stomach. About my mom. I loved her, but it was weird to be with her anymore. She wanted to help me like I was still a boy, and I wasn't. She wanted to still hug me and kiss me on the cheek and that just felt weird and she didn't seem to fathom how that could even be.

So I had been avoiding my mother, spending time with the chess club or Junior Achievement. Going away on every Boy Scout trip I could. Leaving her alone with Dad and his gin and his missing leg.

As he continued to heave, it hit me. Dad was going to hurt her. That's what the man was on about.

I grabbed him by his arm, the fabric so slick it was hard to hold on to him, and pulled him towards home while he was still spitting and gagging.

Dad only had one leg, but he was strong. Not a gangly chess playing kid like me, but a former wrestler and football player.

And then I wanted to puke too, imagining my mother dead on the kitchen floor, blood pooling around her head, my father standing over her with a cigar in his mouth, his beard unshaved, and a bottle of gin in his hand.

TIME TRAVEL MESSES WITH YOUR BODY. SEEING YOURSELF, young and pimple-faced, messes with your mind. Arguing with your past self can make you sick.

But as Gene, the younger me, pulled me down the sidewalk, my head began to clear, the facing mirror disorientation still there but more background noise. I remembered dragging the weird guy in the silver jumpsuit towards my house, just like

Gene was doing, but my mind was able to separate it better now. I was adjusting.

It didn't take long until he was tugging me up the sidewalk to his home... my old home.

It was older than the rest of the houses, a white rectangle box with a screened-in porch, no picket fence, and a small grass yard that was overdue for mowing. I stood there as he tugged, his hand slipping from the silver fabric and felt a different, more natural rush of memories.

We had moved here when I was six and I lived here until I was sixteen. I was an only child with a mother that doted and a father that was mostly absent, and then too present. I slipped off the roof, trying to be the man of the house and patch the roof while my father was away at war. I landed poorly and broke my arm.

I painted the house. By myself. Twice.

I mowed the yard and helped weed the small flower beds below the living room windows.

I kissed Jenny Oster, my first kiss, under the oak tree when I was thirteen.

"Come on!" Gene said. He was shouting, he had my hand now and was tugging me towards the door. "She's... come on!"

I shook my head and jerked my hand out of his. The heat and the running had made them sweaty so it wasn't hard. It's not that I didn't want to go into the house, even though the thought of seeing my father slumped on his tattered recliner, his stub of a leg sticking out his shorts, out for everyone to see, was a bitter knot in my stomach.

I turned away and kept walking because this wasn't the right place to be.

"Where are you going?" Gene shouted, his voice high with stress. It was good. He was believing me. And he had changed in my mind since I puked. He was "Gene." Not my younger-self, but Gene. I was Gene, too. I had the same name, but I was not him.

As an observer, safely looking on, you might quibble with the definition. While I did share many of Gene's memories and we had the same DNA, twenty-four years separated us and that made us very different people.

I ignored Gene's protestations and walked as fast as I could down the sidewalk to where I knew my mother would be in just a few minutes.

HE'S NOT RIGHT, THIS OLD-ISH GUY, HE'S JUST NOT RIGHT. He was walking away from the house. It was Thursday after school, and I knew Mom would be in there making meatloaf for dinner, that dad would be slumped in the living room pretending to read the paper and sneaking swigs out of his hip flask, which he thought we didn't know he did, but of course we could tell. You can smell it, for God's sake.

There were good odds she was making lima beans and would make me eat them although they are so disgusting.

If this pockmarked-faced man was right, my father must have gotten some bad news, like his VA benefits getting reduced and maybe he'll actually have to go do something with his life despite having only one leg. So he got the letter and he got drunk, and my mom tried to cheer him up and, maybe, accidentally spilled her afternoon tea on him, burning him, and he just lost it, grabbing the poker from the fire and hopping around one-legged after her, swinging it and...

My mind was out of control. How had this guy gotten in my head so fast? The house was quiet, and he was walking away from me fast, he was almost to the end of the block, the honking from Twenty-Seventh Street filtering up the hill.

I looked back at the house, plain and white and in need of painting again soon. I was born in Delaware, but we came to Lincoln when I was young, and I don't remember much about it. Just vague images, mostly of my grandparents, and a cherry tree blossoming. This was the only home I really had ever known.

I knew it wasn't as nice as the other houses on the block, but it was my house. My mom was in there, and apparently in danger. Wasn't she?

The man rounded the corner and went to the west. I hesitated for a few more breaths and then ran after him.

THERE ARE TWO WAYS TO LOOK AT WHAT WAS ABOUT TO happen. Since I had already experienced it twenty-four years earlier, it was predestined, fate, and there were no choices to make, they had already been made.

Or you can think that these experiences were brand new for the current me, that I was making each choice fresh, that I was exerting my free will with every action I took, despite it being the same actions I remembered.

They teach classes on this at the Traveler's Academy. Everyone gets a headache.

The conclusion, after the head-pounding semester, is that both viewpoints are perfectly and totally correct. It looks like fate. It functions like free will. Both are true. Choice and destiny are not separate, kind of like space and time are not separate. They are part of the same thing.

And that's where it gets tricky. Does the memory of my past actions as observed by my fifteen-year-old self twenty-four years ago determine what I do now?

Well, that imagines memory as something perfect and inviolate. It imagines a container like a tough stainless-steel bowl that holds all memories perfectly, when it's much more like a colander with plenty of holes for memories to leak out.

But that doesn't quite do it, either. Each memory remembered is a memory rewritten by the brain, it's this constant rewriting and perversion of the memory.

Up ahead I could see the Mobil station with the old-fashioned gas pumps out front, a long, sleek Cadillac pulling away, and I paused. Perched above the blocky letters spelling out MOBIL was a red Pegasus horse rearing, one hoof extended slightly, the other curled back a bit.

Unlike some other of my young memories of this day, this place, this gas station, these moments, I had remembered many times, my brain pulling it back out and rewriting it as it stored it again. In the last year or so, as I knew I was the right age to return for this, I had been thinking about it a lot and always I would remember the red Pegasus perched above the MOBIL sign.

Except its wings weren't as high as I remembered and the red was dingy, closer to the color of blood than the bright cherry red I remembered.

What else was wrong with my memory? What other details had been perverted by the process of remembering? I thought I knew what was about to happen, but in what way were my memories dulled and twisted? How had the lens of a fifteen-year-old colored what was about to happen?

I swallowed hard and shook my head.

I saw the brown 1936 Ford Deluxe pull up in front of the red gas pumps. It seemed like such an old car, the models they were making now after the shutdown for the war were much sleeker, the Deluxe with its rounded fenders and narrow hood looked ancient, even then.

My mother got out and my heart flapped in my chest like a scared bird. She wore high-waisted, long, flaring pants, navy blue, and a white blouse, her long brown hair pinned on top of her head. She paused and looked across the busy street and I swear she looked right at me, a wistful smile forming on her round face.

I couldn't breathe.

She was beautiful, even from this distance, but not in a way that felt strange... or *too* strange. She was slim, but it was clear there was strength in her frame. She had worked in a factory for the entire war and had refused to wear dresses ever since unless we were going to church.

This, almost as much as my father losing his leg, had driven him to drink. My mother, strong and independent, happily driving the family car, dealing with running the household and earning a living.

The factory shutting down had been hard on her. She didn't want to go back to being just a wife, a mother. My father's injury, delivered by a German land mine, had let her retain part of that responsibility, but not at a price anyone would have wanted to pay.

My mother hugged her chest, just briefly, took a deep breath, and turned away from me and walked resolutely into the garage.

I turned around and saw Gene running towards me, but he had been out of her sight. She wasn't looking at me, but looking back towards her home, something on her mind.

"What are you doing?" Gene yelled, but I didn't listen.

I saw a break in the traffic and ran out into the street. There wasn't much time.

The traffic was heavy on Twenty-Seventh Street and I stood there on the curb looking for a break, wishing I could see in the Mobil station where the man disappeared. I glanced to my left, there was a streetlight and a crosswalk there, but that would take too long.

I looked back at the gas station and really noticed the brown Deluxe parked in front of the red pumps. It had a ding over the front right wheel. Just like our car.

I glanced back up the street, although our house was out of sight. The car had not been parked there. That was our car. That meant that Mom was in there, but how? How did the man know she would be there? Who was he?

He said she was in danger, that we had to help her. He had known where I would be. He knew where she would be. He had to be right.

There was a brief break in the eastbound traffic, so I sprinted into the middle of the street, horns blaring. I stood there while heavy cars passed way too close to me and then ran the rest of the way.

My nose was filled with the smell of exhaust fumes and my heart pounded in my ears when I pulled open the door to the Mobil office and saw...

Nothing unusual.

The man was sitting in a seat, his leg crossed, flipping through the *Saturday Evening Post*, like being dressed in a silver jumpsuit was the most normal thing in the world.

My mother was at the counter talking to Mr. Peters, the man who ran the station. He had on dark grey coveralls and was wiping his greasy hands with a rag and nodding slowly.

The radio was playing Frank Sinatra, singing "Five Minutes More" which was drowning out the sound of the traffic. The smell of oil and gas was potent. Time seems to stretch out.

"...oil change today should do it," Mom was saying as Sinatra was singing how he just wants five more minutes on his Saturday date. "I'll just walk home and pick it up in the morning."

The strange man slowly turned, his blue eyes catching mine, a small smile on his face as the crooning continued.

My mother's fine. She's not in danger. She didn't turn when the door's bell rang when I entered and didn't know I was there. I wanted to leave. I didn't want to explain to her what I was doing or how I got there.

My cheeks flushed red and my ears grew hot. What kind of cruel joke had the old—but not that old—man played on me?

I opened my mouth to confront him, my anger taking over my good sense, when a screeching noise erupted outside, followed by the crunch of metal and the bright sound of shattering glass.

And then the man was up. He grabbed me by my shirt and yanked me away from the door and I went stumbling across the room where I ran into my mother.

Outside the noise was getting louder, all mixing into a cacophony where I couldn't make out the shearing of metal from the breaking of wood or the honking of horns. It was a wave of noise that assaulted my ears.

Time seemed to slow further. I could smell my mother's floral perfume and see the surprise in her blue eyes as I ran into her and then the wall of the office imploded, the sound deafening.

In that moment, my mother's eyes caught me. They were slowly widening in surprise. Her eyes were blue like the ocean on a sunny summer's day. The exact same blue as my eyes. The exact same blue as the man's eyes.

And then the noise was so loud, I couldn't hear anything. I grabbed my mother and held her close, pivoted her away from the imploding wall, wood and plaster flying all around us, slapping into my back, and...

It all went black.

Time is an ouroboros, a snake eating itself, at least for some of us Travelers. The intermingling of free will and fate is the fabric of our existence.

I wasn't thinking anymore in that little service station office. I wasn't remembering my past and I knew Gene would do his part. I was just reacting.

I threw him into our mother as soon as I heard the accident starting outside. It was exactly what I had done before, except I was doing it for the first time, finally free of the facing mirror effect of past, present, and future.

I got a single look at my mother as I threw Gene, her blue eyes meeting mine. I swear there was a flicker of recognition there, but I can't be sure. She never talked to my teenage-self about me afterwards.

And in that moment, my dread at seeing her alive and vibrant and whole melted away. Here she was, thirty-six-years-old and so strong. In a year, she would leave my father and take me to Los Angeles and start a new life. She would work two jobs so I could go to college and study physics. Once I was recruited as a Traveler, she would endure all the oddities of my life, strange absences, sudden changes in appearance, with her usual warm grace.

It was just a moment there, a second maybe two, and I felt such love and admiration for the woman that birthed me and raised me. She had a difficult life and was far from perfect, but she was so courageous forging the life she did in this male-dominated era.

Relief filled me and love. I knew it would be exquisitely hard to see her again, old and afraid, her demented mind turning everything into something terrible, something fearful, but it was worth it to see her whole one last time.

And then Gene was shielding her body with his and I couldn't see her anymore. The violent roar of the accident filled my ears right before the imploding wall smashed into my body and I knew nothing.

***

Smoke, acrid and oily, assaulted my nose as I coughed my way to consciousness. I heard distant shouts and the crackle of a hungry fire, but it was blessedly quiet compared to what it had been.

I was on the floor, my mother next to me coughing and groaning. I shrugged debris off and helped her to her feet. She had a cut on her forehead and was bleeding, but otherwise looked unharmed.

"Hurry," Mr. Peters yelled from behind the counter, frantically gesturing for us to climb over.

I glanced back, looking for the not-so-old man with the blue eyes like my mother and the pockmarked cheeks. My hand strayed to my own pimpled cheeks. I was in the midst of a bad outbreak and we didn't have the money for a doctor to look at it.

I couldn't see the man, the front and side of the service station was slumped in, a fire slowly growing. He had to be buried there.

"Gene," my mother said softly, "help me."

I turned my back on him, helped my mother up and over the counter, and back into the garage with Mr. Peters. I could just hear the sound of a distant siren approaching.

Mr. Peters led us into the garage, the front of the bay caved in, the roof collapsed on a tan Chevrolet, the fire burning there, but there was a back door out into an alley.

I blinked at the harsh sunlight, my mind still not working

right, and watched as Mr. Peters led my mother away. I just couldn't leave the man in there.

I turned and walked back in when a strong hand grabbed me by the shoulder.

"I got this, Gene," a deep voice said. "Your mother still needs you."

I looked and it was the old, but not so old, man in his silver jumpsuit, whole and well, except the right of his face was this massive scar, his right eye half-closed by it, and his hair was much shorter, buzzed all the way off.

I was so confused, my mouth opened to ask him who he was, but he was already running past me to the debris. "You know who I am," he called back as he disappeared into the service station office.

I leaned against the door suddenly dizzy, my hand going to my pimpled cheeks, where the first man's pockmarks were and the second man's scars. Those blue eyes. How he knew everything. I thought about the book, *The Time Machine,* and H.G. Wells who had just died a couple of months ago. It couldn't be, could it?

The sirens grew loud and my world spun, maybe from the trauma I had just been through, but certainly from the truth I had just uncovered. He was me. They both were me.

The Travelers have an academy, of course they do, populated by experienced Travelers who have had enough of the madness of jumping. I suspect I'll be teaching one of these days.

One of the things they try to teach us is to ignore the coming pain that our profession often lets us know is coming in no uncertain terms.

Like going back to do my part in saving my mother's life

when the car plowed into the Mobil service station. I knew from my fifteen-year-old perspective that I would be buried under the rubble, that I would survive, but would end up with a badly scarred face.

They teach us that pain is coming for all humans, the only difference with a Traveler is that sometimes it's clear exactly what and when instead of not having a clue. Travelers get that kind of pain too, the sudden and the unexpected, but it's the known trauma that they teach us not to tense up for.

If I hadn't been trained, I probably would have missed that moment, that flicker of recognition in my mother's eyes as part of her knew who I was. What the fifteen-year-old me had trouble putting together, my mother saw in a glance.

Of course she did. I'm her son.

"I got you," a deep voice said, strong hands pulling me as consciousness sparked to life with pain, such pain. I had a broken arm and second and third-degree burns over much of my right side, my silver suit providing some protection from the flames and saving my life, my face taking the worst of it. Besides the broken arm, I had bruises all over my body. The constellation of pain mixed into something that is hard to describe, it's like I *was* pain, there was little else to my world.

But I had a question, a question unbecoming of a Traveler and I asked it as I cracked my left eye open and saw the burning debris I had just been pulled out of. "Is Mom all right?" I asked. "Did we save her?"

"Of course we did, Gene. Of course we did."

It was odd hearing my own voice, but not the fifteen-year-old version I had been hearing, but the older, rougher version of my voice.

I wasn't conscious long, the pain pulling me back down, and as the darkness slipped around me, I remembered that look of recognition in my mother's blue eyes.

I BECAME OBSESSED WITH TIME TRAVEL AFTER THAT OLD—
but not so old—man dressed in the silly silver jumpsuit helped
me save my mother's life. Of course I did. I read *The Time
Machine* over and over again hoping there was some glimmer of
truth there, not just the inventiveness of a clever mind. I started
reading every book on science I could get my hands on for clues
to how it could happen, but this was 1946 and Albert Einstein
said it wasn't possible, but I knew he was wrong.

My brain was obsessed with time travel with nearly the
fervor it had been obsessed with Alison Rodgers before I ran into
myself.

And my older self was right, Alison rejected me summarily
the next week. The incident with my mother had given me
enough courage to actually ask her out. Enough courage to do it
enough times until it became embarrassing, the kind of thing my
schoolmates would snicker behind their hands about.

In some ways I was just being stubborn. I did it that many
times because my older-self had told me it wouldn't work. That's
the insanity of being a teenager—you can't even believe yourself.

It hurt, of course. But eventually I learned. There were
much bigger mysteries in this world than Alison, and a lot more
girls.

I kept looking for him, for me, or for anyone in one of those
silver jumpsuits. Thinking they would be back to get me, it was
inevitable after all, wasn't it?

In 1951 when *The Day the Earth Stood Still* came out, I
nearly had a heart attack seeing the silly silver jumpsuit the alien
wore. It wasn't the same as my future-self had worn, but it made
me wonder if the people who made the movie knew something.

About a year after the accident at the gas station, my mother
left my father and we left Lincoln for Los Angeles, and then I

finished high school, and then I went to the University of California to study physics, which is as close as I could get to studying time travel.

And then I forgot about all of it. Well, "forgot" is the wrong word, it was more like that day got buried under the rest of my life. I finished college, fell in love, got a job, got married and lived. I didn't really forget, I was just too busy living to think about it much.

And then one day I saw him... or me, rather. My wife was pregnant and off with her mother in San Diego and I had come down to the beach, which was my favorite part of living in LA.

It was early on a Sunday morning, the air cool as the seagulls wheeled and cried. I walked barefoot not paying much attention to anything, watching the birds, hearing the gentle roar of the surf when I almost ran into me.

Silver jumpsuit again, but this time I was older, maybe ten years older than the last time I had seen myself back in Lincoln. One moment I was alone at the beach and the next moment I smelled ozone and I almost ran into myself again.

"Gene," he said. "Good to see you." His hair was shorter, shot with grey, and his face, while still scarred, was not nearly as bad as the version I'd seen running into the garage.

My heart raced and I was sweating despite the cool morning. "Now you come?" I asked.

He nodded, his face solemn, but then again, he remembered what I was going through. I had a wife and a life and a child on the way. I was past fantasies of time travel and youthful romantic notions like that.

I did wonder what it was like to be him, having the other side of a conversation that he remembered.

"And that's why it's time," he said, pursing his lips.
"But..."
"Your wife won't even know you're gone," he said.

He handed me a silver jumpsuit and said, "Put this on. There's not much time."

I stood there for a moment staring at him. "Not much time." How can a time traveler say that? I opened my mouth to speak but he cut me off.

"Don't argue with yourself, Gene, it's not becoming. Now get that on, we've got work to do."

And we did, and in some ways I guess we still do as the different versions of me loop through time.

BACKSTORY—THE TRAVELERS

Genre: Science Fiction
Type of Time Travel: Bi-directional
Nature of Time Travel: Causal loop

It's obvious that we all change over time, that the people we once were are not the people that we will one day be, that the very nature of our lives, if we are lucky to live long enough, is very similar to having multiple lives.

I can see this in my own life. I have empathy for my past-self, but perhaps I don't understand him as well as I once did, because that is no longer the person I am. And I imagine that my future self will not think kindly of all the choices I am making right now, especially with the clarity of hindsight that I lack.

This story uses time travel to explore this phenomenon up close.

This was my first attempt at a causal loop story, something that I explored later in "My Love's Past" and "Which Came First: The Chicken or the Time Traveling Egg?"

There is one other thing that fed into this story. My mother had passed away several years before I wrote this one and from time to time I find myself writing stories with characters that wistfully remember their mother.

This story received an honorable mention in the Writers of the Future contest.

PART 8
BUTTERFLY IN TRAINING

BUTTERFLY IN TRAINING

Evan Price woke with a sneeze, the straw of his bedding tickling his nose. A rooster crowing far too close turned his thoughts murderous, and he threw his arm over his eyes to protect himself from the dim light filtering in through the wide cracks in the barn's walls. It was well past 2:00 a.m. when he had arrived. Sleep, he needed sleep, but the air was cold and the rooster was proud of its call and kept up the reveille until he sat up on the straw-covered pallet softly cursing under his breath.

Even though it was a violation of mission protocol, he would happily kill that rooster, he would, but Mrs. Reynolds would be mad, and that is not a woman you want to get mad. It's not her sharp tongue or her withering looks, but the disappointment in her green eyes that always got to him. Actually, her eyes got to him no matter her mood. When she was happy, everything in the world just seemed right, and when she was sad, there was nothing that made any sense.

He rolled his shoulders, stretched his aching back and yawned. He was nothing to Mrs. Reynolds, just another cowboy that would sleep in her barn on the way to and from Bisbee in the Arizona Territory. He got up, tucked in his shirt, pulled his hat from the hook on the wall and put it on. He pulled what looked like a watch out of his pocket, popped the lid, and glanced at it. It was round with the date, September 23, 1885, and the time written in clear letters with the seconds spinning by. It wasn't a pocket watch, it wasn't from the 1800s, but then again, neither was Evan. Once he saw there were no new orders, he closed the device and it looked just like any other pocket watch. Because of the growth hormone treatments, his young body felt old, but he got himself moving. Time to get to those chores that were the price of a place to sleep.

"OH, YOU'RE HERE," MRS. ISABELLA REYNOLDS SAID TO Evan as the entire household sat down to breakfast at a long table just outside the main house. There was Mrs. Reynolds, her younger sister Camila, her brother Trent, and two ranch hands. Mr. Reynolds had died three weeks ago of cholera, and it was all his fault.

"Yes, ma'am," Evan said tipping his hat to her, trying not to get lost in those green eyes. She was a few years older than Evan, around nineteen. "Your hospitality is much appreciated. The horse stalls are mucked out and I thought I might work on the fence east of here a bit. I noticed some damage when I rode in last night."

She gave him a tight smile and a small nod, which was as much as he could hope for. He sat and breathed in the scent of bacon, coffee, and eggs, and caught a whiff of her rosewater perfume. While she said the Lord's Prayer, everyone else closed their eyes, but he didn't. He stared at her round face, studied it. She had a mole to the right of her nose, sharp cheekbones, and long black hair piled up on the top of her head. She was beautiful, yes, but there was something else about her, and he hoped if he studied that face long enough he would figure out what it was. Or maybe he just liked looking at her, and when those sharp eyes were closed, he really *could* look at her.

Her brow was furrowed even while she prayed. This was a tense time for the Reynolds family. Mr. Reynolds' death had set off a series of small incidents that had compromised their financial standing. He knew that her bankers would ride out tomorrow and attempt to foreclose on the ranch. He couldn't let that happen. Mr. Reynolds shouldn't have died and they shouldn't be in this position.

His original mission was to save Mr. Reynolds' life, but he had failed. Now he had to try to save the ranch if he could.

THE REYNOLDS RANCH SAT ON THE SAN PEDRO RIVER, between Fort Huachuca and Bisbee in the Arizona Territory. Deciduous trees lined the small river—a creek really, but this was a desert and nearly anything with water in it was a river. The surrounding land was flat and full of tall brown grass and sagebrush, with the Huachuca Mountains to the west and the Mule Mountains to the east. Land not good for much more than raising cattle and riding horses. But compared to the future he was born to, it was an oasis. He loved it.

As he worked on the wood rail fence that he himself had knocked over on the way in, he set his trap. He installed two small pieces of electronics they had just built at their base in Bisbee. One piece he buried right next to the road, the other one he put under one of the fence rails. It would be triggered by motion in a given timeframe, and if he was lucky, buy the Reynolds the time they needed. As he did this, Evan wondered why this little ranch was so important, why he had been ordered to keep it in the hands of the Reynolds family. He was new to this time, had just completed his training, and didn't feel fully acclimated. It was his first mission, and he didn't want to fail.

Time travel was an expensive and dangerous endeavor and there were a lot of rules. Big changes were never done directly, like detaining Lee Harvey Oswald before he shot Kennedy or stopping the assassination of Archduke Franz Ferdinand to prevent World War I. Instead, small butterfly-effect-like changes were made, generations back, calculated by the AIs to be reasonably safe in areas where it seemed nothing ever happened. Like the high desert of the southern Arizona Territory in 1885.

The operatives of his organization called themselves Butterflies to embody their way of working: avoid conflict, light touch, in and out.

He didn't know what change he was here for and he never would.

THE SUN WAS HOT, BEATING DOWN ON EVAN AS HE gathered his tools to head back to the Reynolds's ranch. He was tired. The fence repair had taken longer than he'd expected; he had been a bit enthusiastic when he kicked it down.

Butterflies were gene-modded to enhance strength, endurance and speed, but mostly so they could survive the trauma of being sent back. In time travel, mass mattered, so Butterflies were sent back at their minimum viable weight and when they were about sixteen. Sixteen was an adult in the 19th century as well as the 24th. He had only been back in the west for four months, he was still very thin, and although his body was stronger than when he came, it was not up to par.

He sat down under the thin shade of a mesquite tree—he

was not close to the river—and closed his eyes. Just for a moment, he told himself, until his tired muscles had recovered.

Moments later—or at least it seemed that way—he woke to the distinctive clicking sound of a revolver being cocked.

"Now, why don't you explain yourself, Mr. Price."

He sucked in a breath, smelling roses, and opened his eyes to Mrs. Reynolds squatting in front of him and pointing a gun at his head.

"I beg your pardon, ma'am," he said, his heart thudding in his chest.

She nodded to the fence and the work he had done. "There was no cause to dig that hole. You covered it fairly well, but it was plain enough to me."

He looked around, the sun was leaning towards the horizon, several hours must have passed and she must have come looking for him. The thought of her concern made his heart race faster. His eyes strayed to the hole, which was no longer cleanly covered.

"What is this?" She tossed a small black device on the ground between them. It was star shaped, about three inches in diameter, with a small green light in the center. "I've never seen anything like that."

He licked his lips, he was very thirsty, and looked deep into her green eyes. There was nothing he could say that would help this situation. "I mean you no harm, Mrs. Reynolds. I—"

"Like when you came storming into my house saying you had the cure for my husband while he was lying on his deathbed?" Her nostrils flared and her cheeks flushed red.

That was when they had met. His mission had been to get antibiotics to Mr. Reynolds, but she had stopped him. She wouldn't listen to him then, and he didn't think she would now.

"You showed up with that potion out of the blue," she continued, "and now you are planting this..." She looked down at the device between them, her brow furrowed. "This... this thing."

He couldn't tell her it was a neural disruptor, that it would leave the men coming to foreclose on her property catatonic for an hour, just long enough for him to turn them around, separate them, and leave them in the desert. They would awaken with nothing more than a horrible headache, but disoriented enough to head right back to Bisbee. It might have made more sense for him to do this farther away from the Reynolds ranch, but this had been his orders. You always followed your orders.

Her lips were pursed, and her hand trembled slightly as she stared at him. He had no doubt she knew how to use that revolver, but he didn't think she was a killer. "I wish I could convince you that I am only here to help."

She stood up and stepped back, the gun leveled at his chest. "You'll be emptying your pockets and tossing everything between us. Let's see what other kinds of things you got."

He nodded and slowly emptied his pockets. There wasn't much. A few matches, a shoelace, two silver dollars, a quarter, and his pocket watch. He had left his gun back in the barn.

"Now step back." He did as he was told and she stepped forward, squatted down, her hand going right to the pocket watch. She popped it open and saw the digital display in there, her eyes going wide and her mouth forming an "O." Evan was confused; the watch shouldn't have opened. Her brow furrowed and she shook her head. "Why does it say, 'Kill Isabella Reynolds'?"

ISABELLA REYNOLDS KEPT HIS HORSE AND GUN, LEFT HIM with his "strange things," and forced him to leave her ranch at gunpoint. She promised to shoot him if she ever saw him again.

He believed her. He headed east, towards Bisbee, off the stage-coach road and into the open desert.

After he was out of sight of the ranch, he popped open his pocket watch. Instead of the date and time, it said "Kill Isabella Reynolds," with a countdown timer below that was ticking down from three minutes.

He stood there for the longest time unable to move, staring at the display. There was nothing he could do in three minutes, and he wouldn't kill her anyway. It wasn't in him, and it was a violation of protocol. Large changes, like murders, wreaked havoc with the timeline. With a sigh, he closed the lid on the watch, shoved it in his pocket and kept walking east.

It was a long walk from the Reynolds ranch back to Bisbee, and as he walked, the look she had given him haunted him. As he was walking away, he turned back for one last look. She raised the gun, her hand no longer shaking, a hard look on her face, but fear in her eyes. She thought him a monster.

The gibbous moon provided enough illumination and the evening was cold, so he didn't stop, except to drink when he could find water, and cut across land when it would speed him up. He walked until noon the next day, his body tired and sore, his stomach empty, his heart aching.

Before town, just over Mule Pass, he headed up Morales Creek to a hidden entrance into an abandoned section of a copper mine that had played out quickly. He lit a lantern waiting inside the entrance, made his way down a series of tunnels and ladders and through locked gates that opened because of his pocket watch. The twisting path took him deep into the earth.

This is where he had come into the 19th century, and although he knew there was no going back to the future—even if he wanted to—there would be no more missions for him. He would be relegated to an isolated part of this world to live out his life in a way that didn't affect the timestream.

And what damage might he have done by not saving Mr. Reynolds, and then not succeeding in saving the ranch? He couldn't even imagine why he had been ordered to murder. It didn't make sense.

A steady light up ahead told him that he had arrived at their base. He heard the sound of voices and a melodic laugh that made him stop in his tracks. There was something so familiar about it.

"Well, about time you got here," Isabella Reynolds said when he walked in the large cave. Her black hair was not in its normal bun and flowed down around her shoulders. She wasn't wearing a dress, but a simple, grey, utilitarian jumpsuit all the Butterflies wore when they weren't in the field.

There were several other people in the cavern, not to mention equipment and monitors, but he didn't see any of it. His jaw moved, but he couldn't get any words out. He took a step towards her and she smiled widely, her laughter echoing around the cavern.

"We wouldn't just send you on a real mission before testing you," she said. "You didn't think that, did you?"

He blinked and kept staring. This had all been a test. She could open his pocket watch because she was a Butterfly too. He should have seen that.

"But... But... I was ordered to kill you?" he finally got out.

She shrugged. "That part of the test you passed. We aren't assassins and don't betray our mission parameter under any circumstances."

He was still struggling with it all and was now close enough to Mrs. Reynolds to smell her rose scent, and that just confused him more. "But if I had tried?"

She laughed again, looking him up and down. "Don't flatter yourself, Price. I can handle you."

His cheeks flushed and he looked around the room and saw

Mr. Reynolds at one of the monitors. He smiled at Evan, tapped on the keyboard and then pointed at Evan's pocket. His watch buzzed and he pulled it out and opened it. It said, "No one was hurt in this training exercise."

As Evan stared at Mr. Reynolds, Trent, the man he thought was Isabella's brother, walked in. "Alastair here was in one of the first waves," he said, pointing at Mr. Reynolds. "Back before they got the gene mods right and stopped sending adults. He sustained some neural damage getting here. Can't talk. Can't smell. But boy, can he hold his liquor."

Alastair nodded and held up his hands as if to say, "What are you going to do?"

"Got the time capsule, Bell?" Trent asked Isabella. Trent was a couple of years older than Evan, dark haired and strong. Evan felt a stab of jealousy.

She nodded and pointed at Alastair. Time travel was one way, but they sent information forward to the future the old-fashioned way. They regularly buried time capsules with dense information stores about the current state of the timeline, so the AIs in the future could track how things had changed.

A different team of Butterflies had greeted him when he arrived in 1885, helped him recover from time travel sickness, and trained him. They must still be in Tombstone on mission. He had known there were more Butterflies in the area, but had never suspected that the Reynolds family were Butterflies. "What... what now?" Evan asked Isabella, his head still spinning.

She smiled and turned to Alastair. "How's the historical records look for Bisbee today? Any reason not to go up?"

Alastair shook his head and gave them a thumbs-up.

She turned back to Evan. "I'm going to change into my dress, put on a bustle, for God's sake, and then we are going to a saloon."

Evan stood there, a puzzled look on his face.

She walked to him and put her hands on his shoulders, her green eyes locking onto his. "We Butterflies do drink, you know. The future couldn't spare calories for such indulgences, but the past can. Besides, you look like you could use a drink."

He nodded.

"Your real training starts tomorrow." She laughed again; he liked that sound. "Everyone goes through something like this so they get a feel for how hard this is. We are foreigners here. We've got to blend in, get our job done, and change as little as possible."

"Yes, ma'am," Evan said. "I'll do my best."

She sighed. "'Ma'am' just makes me feel old. And I'm not old. Call me Bell."

Evan nodded, getting lost in those green eyes. This wasn't the end, this was just the beginning.

BACKSTORY—BUTTERFLY IN TRAINING

Genre: Science Fiction
Type of Time Travel: Backward only
Nature of Time Travel: The future can be changed

I wish I could remember exactly what was going through my crazy writer's brain when I came up with this story. I can only remember a few things:

First was the thought that if time travel into the past was real and the timeline could be changed, then the application of this awesome power would be as precise as possible, surgical even. Thus the "Butterflies" concept was born.

The second thing was that I enjoy writing things set in the Old West. It was an absolutely fascinating time when the world was changing so very, very fast.

The third thing was I wanted to try my hand at difficult, high-stakes time travel. These time travelers can never go home and that implies quite the commitment and speaks to the high stakes of this world.

This story is the prequel to "The Pearce Shootout." While it establishes the world, "The Pearce Shootout" really takes advantage of the concept.

I hope to write more Butterfly stories in the future.

PART 9
FOLD. SHIFT. GOODBYE.

FOLD. SHIFT. GOODBYE

She is a creature not of this world, not of this time, not human at all. She looks like a woman, curves in all the right places and a smile playing on her full lips, her curly black hair like a halo around her head.

She moves like one of us, sheathed in loose fabric that shimmers like sapphires that make her dancer movements seem like she is flowing water, not flesh and blood.

"Tim," she whispers to me that night we met. There is no question in her voice, no doubt in her eyes, like she knew me, had always known me.

I am standing on the grass in front of the cool mountain lake, the stars glittering in the night sky, my heart broken into pieces, the sticky remnants of salty tears fresh on my cheeks.

I look around. The cabin is secluded, a vacation rental that I had retreated to after the accident that took my wife and my daughter from me. After the funeral and all the people looking at me with such pity in their eyes. After I returned to a home filled with enough memories to crush me. After the need to crawl back into the bottle and never come back became too much for me to deal with.

The woman dressed in the folds of sapphire cloth is eight feet from me when she whispers my name, her feet hidden behind the shimmering fabric, and still I can hear her clearly. She glides to me, but her path is not straight, more like a water droplet finding its way down a wet window after a long storm, her path is erratic, unpredictable, but graceful.

"Who are you?" I ask.

She smiles as if such a question is too trivial to even reply to.

"What do you want?" I meant to pull my phone out of my jean's pocket just in case she was dangerous, but my hand only went halfway there when it seemed to forget what I asked it to do and fell to my side. She is almost to me and she smells of the ozone of lightning, a fresh smell like a summer monsoon.

She lays a hand on my cheek, soft flesh against my unshaved stubble, and I feel a tingle of energy as if she had been struck by lightning, the electricity still escaping her. "You grieve," she said.

I nod, but slowly, I don't want her smooth warm hand to leave my cheek.

"As you must," she adds, her eyes narrowing slightly. Her face is smooth, not one wrinkle, yet she did not look young, nor did she look old. It is as if she is perfectly balanced at the brief moment when a human can look ageless. It doesn't last. Nothing lasts. But I get the sense with her that it will last. That she always looks like this.

That face is beautiful. Not in the way of Hollywood or the kinds of faces you see in advertisements trying to sell you things. Her face is not perfectly symmetrical, no single feature perfect at all really, but together she is not just beautiful, she is beauty itself.

The slight crook in her nose, the splash of freckles on her cheeks, her flat brow and thick eyebrows, her blue eyes showing the barest hint of an epicanthic fold. Her skin tone is not one single thing either, a light brown as if she were a mixture of all the races.

I nod because I have much to grieve. It is why I came up here, so that I could be alone while the grief made my eyes red? So I could cry without thinking of what people might think of me, without worrying about how much noise I make, or what someone might think if I have to break something... or many things?

And I am up here to stop myself from drinking. I had climbed out of that pit once and I did not want to fall into it again.

Life is the gift we are all given, but it can be capricious and cruel. We love. We lose. We grieve. It is the way of it.

A smile plays on the woman's lips. "Capricious and cruel," she says. "I like that."

She can hear my thoughts and somehow, I am not surprised. Her hand leaves my face and I miss it, but then she takes both of my hands and pulls me into what I can only call a dance.

It is not like people dance at bars when they are drinking and looking for companionship. It is like she has to keep flowing, like water, and she guides me along with her.

Not that my movements are graceful. We take a step in the grass and then she pulls me low, my middle-aged knees creaking and then another step with our centers of gravity so low and then a half turn and up again.

I don't resist. Her will, carried on the wings of her beauty, is undeniable. She laughs and at first I think it is at my awkwardness but then I realize it is in celebration.

Of what? Merely moving. Only being. For her that is enough to bring joy that required expression.

For me being is loss, being is grief. I am not ready to die, but without my wife, without my daughter I do not know how I can possibly live or what I would live for.

The woman pulls me across the grass in her dance. Small steps then large. Squatting low and then standing tall. Always twisting and moving in unique ways. She spins me around and I see the dark, placid lake under the glittering stars. Another turn and then I see the dimly glowing peaks of the snow-covered mountains illumined by starlight. The fir and spruce tree forest. The small log cabin.

"Should we go?" she whispers.

My body is warm from the effort, and while I can't claim I am graceful, my middle-aged version of her dance has gotten easier. My breath comes quick and I am sweating, unused to such exercise or such movements.

"Yes," I whisper back because escape is what I long for even though part of me knows what she is offering is not simple escape. She is not a bottle of vodka or too many sleeping pills.

She smiles, just barely, as if she is glad for my choice but worried at how naively I made it.

She pulls me close. She is tall, so her face is right next to mine and our feet continue to move across the grass.

A tingling sensation, like when she touched my cheek, fills my entire body and I see the lake fold in front of my eyes like it is a piece of paper until it becomes one dimensional and is gone. But behind the folding lake is another scene, another place, another time.

The present has folded away and we have shifted into the past.

Fold. Shift.

A boy with short black hair, a long nose, and a wide forehead runs laughing down a narrow, paved road, trees leaning in close and thick as if they want to reclaim the land that the road has stolen from them.

He has on dirty shorts and his knees are scabbed. From behind him comes a high-pitched call "Timmy... Mr. Frog wants to *kiss* you."

The sapphire woman and I are up the hill a bit, our view somewhat occluded by the thick trees, but we can see enough.

The boy runs faster and a girl comes into view. She is taller than the boy, lanky even, dressed like the boy in dirty shorts and an old T-shirt, her long brown hair pulled into pigtails, a plump frog clutched in one hand. The flip-flops they wear slap on the old pavement and echo through the forest.

"I remember this," I gasp, my heart lurching in my chest and tears springing to my eyes.

That is the nine-year-old me being chased by the eleven-year-old Stella Young. My future wife chasing the boy me.

"Of course you do," she whispers. "But be quiet, we don't want them to know we are here."

I stare at the beautiful woman with the unconventional features and she gives me the kind of look my mother did when she wanted me to shut up and listen. Her head cocks to the side a bit and her eyes narrow.

Timmy lets out a gasp, stops running, and clutches his side. "A stitch. I've got a stitch."

And then the older girl is on him and pressing the frog to his face and they go down in the soft leaves on the side of the road, Timmy trying to shield his face quite unsuccessfully, both of them laughing the whole time.

I forget about the mysterious woman, a smile on my face as I watch. I am caught in the slight dissonance between the memory and what I am seeing. They are so similar, but not the same.

And then the two kids are staring at each other, the forgotten frog hopping away into the forest. The girl pecks the boy on his dirt smeared cheek, her cheeks blossoming red. "I like you," she whispers.

The boy's jaw drops open and his cheeks turn scarlet too. "I like you, too."

Up until that moment, I thought of Stella Young as my cousin. She is the daughter of my mother's best friend. My mother considers her a sister and so I think of Stella as my cousin and my friend.

But she isn't really and that peck on the cheek changes that. It changes everything.

Looking on, it is so sweet and innocent. Just the first glimmers of something more, a moment of hormone-free affection, two kids being just a little less like kids.

But it is just a moment and is quickly over.

Timmy gets up suddenly, lurches into the forest and retrieves the frog. "Your turn," he said with boyish enthusiasm. Stella turns and runs back the way they had come from and Timmy chases, their flip-flops slapping against the old pavement.

"More?" the woman askes, mischief in her blue eyes.

My heart pounds in my chest as if I had just run as hard as those children. I feel a bit dizzy but I nod my head. I am a starving man and Stella Young is my food.

She grasps me, guides me in a watery dance and the forest folds away.

***

Fold. Shift.

The scene unfolds into a backyard barbecue, the sapphire woman and I behind a sprawling maple tree. Smoke is flowing out of the large stainless-steel gas grill as people mill about with drinks in their hands and kids squirt each other with cheap plastic squirt guns and run and laugh.

This is my backyard. The one I lived in while I went to high school. That is my mother, her dark wavy hair cascading down her back yelling at my father about the smoke.

My mother ruled the roost when it came to cooking except with the barbecue, and then it was my dad.

But we aren't here to watch them. I remember this day, my eyes quickly finding my sixteen-year-old self standing stiffly in front of the eighteen-year-old Stella Young.

In my memory she was so mature and so beautiful and I felt like I was still a kid.

The younger me—I'll keep referring to him as Timmy—is wearing shorts and flip-flops but put on a nice blue shirt with a collar and buttons knowing I was going to see her for the first time in three years.

Stella is wearing a pale green sun dress with a yellow flower pattern that accentuates how she wasn't as lanky as she had been the last time I saw her. The dress intensifies the green in her eyes. Her brown hair is still long but pulled into a graceful pony-tail instead of pigtails. A riot of freckles still rest on her cheeks and she has the scar on her chin from that fall she took the summer after the frog incident.

From behind the tree, I just stare. Timmy has his hands shoved in his pockets and he isn't saying a thing. It's been three years since they were together, Stella's mother having gotten remarried and moved away. Now Stella is back in town for college and I have finally gotten a moment with her alone and I can't find any words.

The strange dissonance is back, the difference between what I remember and what I am seeing. But more than that, it is the difference in perspective, remembering being Timmy so nervous to see Stella and watching my younger self from a distance of twenty-five years.

I open my mouth to urge my younger self to say something. To not be so pimply and awkward. To rely on our long friendship and forget what a beautiful woman she's turned into for just a moment.

But the sapphire woman squeezes my bicep with surprising strength. We are only a dozen feet away and it is the chaos of the yard that lets us stand here unnoticed.

Timmy licks his lips and swallows hard. Stella smiles shyly. While she may look like a mature woman from Timmy's point of view, from my middle-aged perspective they are both still children on the cusp of adulthood, but not there yet.

I watch Timmy take a deep breath and puff his chest out, folding his arms so his biceps look a bit bigger. I choke down a laugh.

"How have you been?" Stella asks.

Timmy shrugs. "You know... okay, I guess. Played a lot of soccer this summer. I..."

Just say it. Tell her that you miss her.

"And you?" he asks.

I remember being worried that she had found someone when she had been away. She was eighteen, she was officially an adult, surely she had fallen in love. Surely she didn't want a kid like me.

"Pretty good," she says with a shrug that moved her body in ways that distracted Timmy. "Glad to be... you know, glad to be back."

Come on, Timmy. You can do it. Just give her something. Anything.

The banalities continue and I just want to tear out my hair, until my mother is calling everyone over to the brightly festooned picnic table to eat.

"I guess we better..." Stella says with another distracting shrug.

Timmy purses his lips and nods, but after she has taken a few steps he says, "Wait."

He runs to her, digging something out of his pocket and shoves it in her hand. "I still like you," he says and then is gone.

Stella looks in her hand and there is a tiny little frog sitting there and her cheeks flush and her freckles darken. She stares at the retreating Timmy and whispers, "I still like you too."

From behind the tree, my heart skips a beat. I had never witnessed that part, my nervous energy having carried me away too quickly.

"More?" the sapphire woman asks.

I swallow hard and nod.

She embraces me, we move in a brief liquid dance, I feel the electrical tingle, and then the backyard is gone.

FOLD. SHIFT. WE ARE IN THE RESTAURANT FOR TIMMY AND Stella's first date. He looks so awkward in a tie desperate to look older than he is.

Fold. Shift. The first kiss under the maple tree in my parents' backyard.

Fold. Shift. On the college campus, a jealous Timmy making a fool of himself about an older boy, a senior he's seen her with. Stella storms off.

Fold. Shift. At her dorm room where Timmy has a dozen roses in his hand pleading for forgiveness.

The scenes spin past, marking the hesitant steps of a young romance between two young people. I was so intimidated by her age, by her being in college while I was still in high school.

It's painful to watch my younger self. It's wonderful to see my Stella again so young, so healthy, so beautiful.

In a strange way, it palliates the loss while at the same time making me even more aware of it. This dance through time with the sapphire woman is wonderful and I think it just might kill me too.

Watching it all spin forth so quickly makes me start to worry about what is to come. The challenges. The fights. And the last goodbye.

I want to keep saying hello to Stella. I want to be that boy on that narrow road in the thick forest that is admitting that he likes a girl even before he knows what that means.

Fold. Shift. It is Timmy's seventeenth birthday and the sapphire woman and I are back in that yard hiding behind the maple tree watching Timmy and Stella.

I have to think of it that way. I am Tim, he is Timmy. He is my past but not my present. He is who I was but not who I am now. We are different people. It is the only way my brain can handle this.

The sapphire woman is folding time and space in on itself to shift us from event to event. I don't want my mind to fold in on itself. He is me, but he is not me. What I was, not what I am.

"I saw you," Timmy hisses, his face red. He had pulled Stella aside, the older girl having arrived to the party late.

"What are you talking about?" she asks.

"I came to surprise you. I saw you with that senior—what's his name?—Geoff with a 'G'?" He lowers his voice again. "I saw you. Coming out of the library. Laughing. Holding his arm. Happy."

She shrugs, not a sundress this time but a dark green sweater against the chill of fall, the maple we are hiding behind fiery in their fall colors. "Not this again. He's just a friend, he's tutoring me."

"Is that what they call it in college?" Timmy spits out.

I want to step out from behind the tree and stop this. It's petty. It's ugly. It's about to cost Timmy what he wants the most, but the sapphire woman holds my bicep in her iron grip.

Stella's mouth drops open. Our relationship had been growing slowly, the friendship turning physical in gentle turns, but we hadn't "gone all the way" yet and my teenage hormones wouldn't stop telling me that she was going all the way with someone else. With "Geoff with a 'G'."

There is a moment, a stillness, like the air stilling before a hellacious storm, Stella's smattering of freckles reddening with her cheeks. My parents and friends and the rest of the people in the yard seemed to notice it too, all eyes turning on us.

But Timmy doesn't notice. His eyes too wide, his breath coming too fast, his cheeks burning too red.

Stella doesn't notice, she takes a half step back and slaps Timmy. Hard. The sound seemingly obscenely loud in the silence.

That slap seems to reverberate through time and I feel my much older cheeks redden and sting.

The sapphire woman pulls me once again into our liquid dance and I am so glad to leave.

JEALOUSY IS MAKING YOURSELF AND YOUR NEEDS MORE important than the one you love. Jealousy is you feeling separated from what you want the most, what you think will make you whole.

I thought Stella Young was the only thing in the world that could make me whole. What I didn't understand is that I had to be whole to be worthy of Stella Young.

That would be a hard lesson to learn. The harder lesson was

that I needed to be whole to be worthy of myself. Of this precious and fleeting gift of life.

Fold. Shift. Timmy coming out of a two-story upper=middle-class home, much nicer than mine, sloppy drunk with a petite, curvy blond on his arm. Loud music is playing and teenagers are spilling out in small groups. He stops her, kisses her hard and sloppy, grabs her short-skirted behind and laughs some more.

Angela Ratner. Timmy just realized that she has had a crush on him all through high school. He will get her pregnant in a fumbling, awkward losing of his virginity in the back of his parents' minivan.

Timmy will... no, I will... no, I did... it's getting all confused in my head.

FOLD. SHIFT. TIMMY AND ANGELA ARGUING OVER HER pregnancy, the seventeen-year-old boy's face red with shame, stricken with fear.

Fold. Shift. A hasty marriage in my parents' backyard, Angela Ratner's round form extra round at the waist in her lacy white dress.

Fold. Shift. Eighteen-year-old Timmy walking a squalling baby in front of his parents' house, his exhausted wife sleeping inside. Timmy should be in school, but after the baby came, he got himself a GED and a night job stocking shelves at Wal-Mart.

Fold. Shift. Timmy walking out of a country and western bar, three days of stubble on his cheeks, dark circles under his eyes, and a cowboy hat on his head. He's twenty, still married, and has lost his job at Wal-Mart but hasn't told his family. The brunette on his arm is twice his age and he kisses her on the mouth when he opens the passenger's side door of the minivan for her.

After they drive off, the sapphire woman looks at me. "Shall we dance some more?" she asks.

"Am I dying?" I ask. "Or dead?"

She smiles, it's a playful expression of her full lips, a deepening of her dimples, a sparkle in her blue, blue eyes. "Living is dying and to me you are both alive and dead. But no, not like you think of it."

The music from the bar is loud, a converted grocery store in an otherwise moribund strip mall.

"Then why show me all this?" I ask. "It is Stella that I want. Stella that I need."

She lets go of my hand and steps away from me, her bare feet sliding across the cracked pavement with such grace you would think it was freshly cut grass. She dances her liquid dance, her blue clothing flowing around her like clouds, her curly black hair sweeping behind her, her lips quirked into her usual smile.

This is the night I stepped out on Angela and ruined my marriage. I would lose my daughter, Elizabeth. I would lose the support of my parents. I would crawl to the bottom of a bottle and hope to never leave.

All because I was jealous and ruined my relationship with Stella Young. It was all so clear now. All so simple.

"Take me back," I say. "Let me change it."

She sweeps me into her arms and I do my best to flow with her over the cracked parking lot in a bad part of town, the sodium glow of the city reflecting off the clouds.

She smells like a thunderstorm, her flesh tingles with electricity. "Are you sure?" she asks.

"Yes. God, yes."

Her smile quirks even more when I say "God" and she nods her head sharply and...

Fold. Shift.

My cheek burns and the sound of Stella Young slapping my seventeen-year-old face seems as loud as a thunderclap.

Stella marches away and I gasp at the pain. I gasp at the feeling. I am young. I am strong. My back doesn't ache. I feel like I could run for miles. And my emotions... they are so turbulent, like an unstoppable tsunami.

Stella is so beautiful she must be more than just "friends" with that college senior with his perfect hair and his mouth so full of too-white teeth. He must be touching her in the ways I want to touch her.

It's awful. I love the feeling of youth in my body, but my mind is like a wild horse, uncontrollable.

But I fight it back as my family and friends stare at me, as the smoke rises from the stainless-steel grill, as the fiery fall leaves of the maple rattle in the breeze, as Stella marches into the house, her back straight.

How did I ever function this way with all of my feelings so strong, so raw? I shake my head and take a deep breath trying to throw it off. That is Stella, the love of my life, leaving.

I trot after her and marvel at how easy it is for this young body to move. So smooth. Such power.

I catch up to her in the front yard with more maple trees and more fall colors, the sweet smell of it filling my nose. "Wait!" I call.

Stella turns, lips pursed, her jaw set, her arms folded over her green sweater.

She doesn't speak and I have a hard time finding my words, the words that I want to say knowing the future.

"I'm sorry. I'm an idiot." I want to be eloquent. I want to truly speak my feelings but it is like my younger self doesn't have the words, doesn't know how to speak his mind or his heart. It's everything I can do to keep more jealous words from escaping.

"You *are* an idiot," Stella says dryly.

"And you are my everything," I say, finally getting some feeling out.

Stella blinks, her green eyes going wide and tears forming in her eyes.

"I can't imagine my life without you," I say, finally getting some control over the hormone-fueled emotions. "I don't want to live my life without you."

And then Stella is in my arms crying and kissing me. She's so young, her lips sweet. She is all my world and I want to lose myself in her and never come back. I want to touch her until time ends. I want to love her every second of every day. I want to—-

Suddenly I am old again, standing across the street with the sapphire woman watching Timmy and Stella kissing. It is passionate but it is not subtle, not artful.

The sapphire woman smiles up at me, her dimples deep and her smile more quirky than usual. "Want to see what happens next?"

FOLD. SHIFT. TIMMY AND STELLA ON THE COLLEGE CAMPUS with its smooth rolling grass covered by bits of snow, the old brick buildings with white splashes clinging to the red bricks. The air is cool and crisp. Stella keeps holding her belly, almost cradling it. I hear the word "pregnant" float over the quad and I suck in a breath.

I had gotten Stella pregnant.

Fold. Shift. A hasty marriage in my parents' back yard, Stella Young's lanky form extra round at the waist in her lacy white dress.

Fold. Shift. Eighteen-year-old Timmy walking a squalling

baby in front of his parents' house, his exhausted wife sleeping inside. Timmy should be in school, but after the baby came, Stella quit college and he got himself a GED and a night job stocking shelves at Wal-Mart.

Fold. Shift. Timmy walking out of a country and western bar, three days of stubble on his cheeks, dark circles under his eyes, and a cowboy hat on his head. He's twenty, still married, and has lost his job at Wal-Mart but hasn't told his family. The brunette on his arm is twice his age and he kisses her on the mouth when he opens the passenger's side door of the minivan for her.

"No!" I cry, sinking to my knees on the worn pavement. It's happening again with Stella Young instead of Angela Ratner. I wanted to fix my life. I wanted more time with Stella, but here I have less.

And I can feel it, this version of me. After the divorce and a few hard years, I won't eventually run into Stella and find a reason to crawl out of a bottle, a reason to be a better man. I won't fall in love with her again and I won't start a second family.

And I won't lose her and our daughter to a senseless traffic accident and end up on that lake with the stars bright above where the sapphire woman finds me.

My grief mixes with the horror of what I have done. The steps of my youthful dance were set. Having a child too young. Working a job I hated. A drunken indiscretion tearing it all down. Falling down into the bottle in my sorrow.

Except I had replaced the second act of my life, the one truly worth living, with a shorter, harder second act.

I could feel it. I would die young in a cold alley, an empty bottle in my hand.

"Why?" I ask. I can only get the one word out but hope she

understands. I want to know why this was happening. Why she came to me. Why she let me change things.

She leans down and gently takes my hand. "Come see," she says, pulling me into her liquid dance.

———

FOLD. SHIFT.

The sapphire woman holds my hand tightly as we walk down a hallway, short grey carpet under our feet, the walls painted a soothing pale blue. We pass an open room and in it is an old woman in a hospital bed. Her face is deeply wrinkled like rough desert land eroded by centuries of rain, but there is a smattering of freckles competing for space amongst the age spots. The short hair on her head is a snowy white. I'd know her anywhere at any age. It's my Stella.

A woman in her sixties sits close by her, holding her hand and I recognize the long nose and wide forehead. This is our daughter, the one from when I changed things. A man is standing behind her, a hand on her shoulder. There are other people there. Some of them with the same long nose and wide forehead. Grandchildren and great-grandchildren.

As we pass, Stella lets out a great shuddering breath. Her last breath. I know it. She has let go of her life surrounded by our daughter, our grandchildren, our great-grandchildren.

The blue eyes of the sapphire woman meet my gaze after we pass, and her strong grip keeps me from falling.

"This is her life?" I whisper. "Her life without me?"

She smiles and this time there is no quirk to it, only compassion.

The hallway spins around me and I would have fallen but for the strength of the sapphire woman. "Was... was she happy?" I manage to ask.

The sapphire woman shrugs, it is a flowing, graceful move-ment. "Happiness. Sorrow. Joy. Fear. Grief. All of the spectrum that makes up a life. She wants more. You always want more. But her life was filled with love and purpose."

She pulls me into her liquid dance and the hospice house folds away and... we don't shift.

We are in darkness, but it seems to be a friendly darkness. I can see my dance partner clearly, her thick eyebrows, her blue eyes, but there is no discernable light source.

"Who are you?" I gasp.

She shrugs again as if this question is also inconsequential. "Names are poor markers. I have been called many things over the centuries, every culture impressing their views, their looks, their names on me. Shakti. Shiva. Maat. I am all, but I am none."

In my mind I can feel and remember both lives, where I married Stella first or where I married Stella second. Where I ended up at that lake grieving and disconsolate or where I ended up in the alley with the sharp fingers of winter stealing my life away. Where my life had a meaningful second act and where my life was wasted and short.

They are both real to me.

"Choose," the sapphire woman says, her voice containing a power I hadn't heard before, reverberating in the darkness.

"What?" I ask, my mind struggling with it all.

"Choose which life you live. Choose which life your beloved lives. Choose which daughter of yours is born."

And then I hate her, the sapphire woman. How is this a choice anyone could make? Why had she come to me, why was she giving me this choice?

"No!" I shout, my voice lacking her strength, the void around us absorbing the energy so it sounds weak and hollow.

She smiles, but it is just a small thing, her eyes welling with tears. Maybe this is what it is like to be her. Choosing things that make part of reality disappear forever.

But how can I choose? A good life for Stella but a terrible life for me. A short life for Stella and me there grieving at the lake, trying desperately to avoid falling back into the bottle.

I had my brother drive me up to the cabin. I had supplies but no alcohol. I had surrendered my cell phone for a cheap flip phone just for emergencies. No calling Uber to take me to a liquor store and I was in no shape to walk the two miles to the little General Store. And just in case, my brother had a talk with them on the way in telling them not to sell me booze.

Is that the best life for me? Would there be a third act worth living now that I had no wife and no daughter? My parents gone.

But if I chose the life where Stella came first that would erase the child I had with Angela Ratner as well as the second version of my time with Stella and our daughter.

This is an impossible choice.

Time is different here in the sapphire woman's void. I can feel my thoughts swirling, my mind arguing them back and forth, but I can't feel the passage of time, as if time doesn't matter here, as if it isn't an undeniable force.

And then the arguments settle and my mind knows its choice. I have to choose love. I have to choose Stella. Otherwise neither life makes any sense.

The sapphire woman feels the change, her warm hands taking me and pulling us into a dance. Our last dance.

***

Shift.

The air is cold, but I am past the point of caring. Part of it is the vodka, but even the fire that it lit in my belly is fading. My shivering is starting to stop and I feel strangely and unlikely warm.

The cold has stolen much of the stench from the alley, but I still smell grease and rotting garbage. I exhale slowly a cloud of condensate forming in front of me and I smile.

Stella Young will live into her eighties. She will live to see our daughter grow up and have children. She will live to see our grandchildren grow up and have children too. Her life will be a dance, sometimes with ease, sometimes with difficulty, but it will be a full and complete dance.

The sapphire woman is next to me, kissing me on the cheek, a tingle of electricity passing through my numbing body, the smell of ozone filling my nose. "Well chosen," she whispers, her breath warm in my ear.

And then she is gone and I look up and see a slice of sky, a few stars bright enough to survive the glow of the city. I remember the other life where I made something of myself, where Stella was my second act, where we had a daughter and then I lost them both.

I nod. This is the choice. Although imperfect, this is the right choice. For my Stella. For my daughter that will live and have a full life. For me, using my life in the best way possible.

When the cold takes me, I have a smile on my face.

BACKSTORY—FOLD. SHIFT. GOODBYE

Genre: Fantasy
Type of Time Travel: Bi-directional
Nature of Time Travel: Changing the past and the future

This is a time travel story in the same way *It's a Wonderful Life* is a time travel story, but it has a grittier ending, the protagonist having a very different kind of choice.

As those of you that read my stories know, I write a lot about grief, and grief is all about how things end for us biological beings. For us humans, big things end and small things end, but in the end, all things end.

I've seen the end of the journey of enough of those that I love that I can only hope but wish for a good ending. Not necessarily an easy ending, but knowing that the end makes sense, has meaning, has purpose.

Hiding in the difficult choice that Tim makes in this story is the heart of a romantic. His choice, even though it's not a clean choice, at all, is about love, is about providing the best life he could for those he loved the most, no matter the cost to him personally.

What could be more romantic than that?

What more could many of us want?

PART 10
A GHOST IN TIME

A GHOST IN TIME

DECEMBER 21, 1952

She was humming, just simply humming. No real tune, the sound of it one of plain contentment.

It was late December, but still she was outside behind a modest home hanging laundry on the line and humming while she did. The air was cool, there was a bite to it when the wind kicked up, but it wasn't that cold.

She looked familiar, her long plaited hair, her bright green eyes, her aquiline nose, and strong cheekbones bringing back fond memories. I had seen her at this age in pictures but never in person. Her name was Abigayle Trendall and she was my grandmother.

I could hear the distant sounds of a radio broadcast coming from inside the dwelling and the muffled shouts of children fighting or playing. I never had any of my own so I wasn't always good at telling the difference.

I had never ghosted back in time before and the sensations of it struck me. The scene I was seeing was heightened in a way, the colors so bright, the sounds so clear, that made it almost seem surreal. But it wasn't like being in virtual, the experience had the weight of reality brought home by tiny details like the bits of rust on the poles that anchored the laundry lines, the dirt and wear on Grandmother's clothing, the utter richness and mundanity of all the detail.

Some sensations were distant, like the feel of the cool air and the smell of the fresh laundry, but others were heightened like my eyes had never seen so clearly and my ears had never been so sharp.

Grandmother paused after clipping a sheet to the line and fiddled with her clothing. She wore wool slacks that fit her tall frame well and a fashionable coat, both in navy blue, the ensemble rather nice for the task at hand. She sighed and looked up at the sun, a small, relaxed smile on her face.

It was a moment of contentment or maybe hope, when just being outside, just letting the sun shine on her was enough.

There were three lines strung across the yard, dead grass underneath her feet. She had sheets on the two outside lines creating a little private space for her between them.

She wasn't old, just shy of forty, but her face had the fine lines that showed she was one of those that smoked cigarettes and loved the sun. Crow's feet and frown lines were prominent as well as deepening wrinkles on her forehead that hinted at worry. Her long brown hair was plaited back and shot with streaks of blonde, which was the kiss of the sun, and just a few streaks of grey, the kiss of time.

To me she looked so young and so beautiful.

When she sighed again and tilted her head down and opened her eyes, she was looking right at me.

For a moment I was worried that she could see me, that she could detect my presence here. But the sunshine was bright and what little disturbance my consciousness created in this time would not be visible.

A smile lit up her face and she suddenly seemed even younger. "There you are," she said.

My heart sped up but I resisted the temptation to panic. I was here, at least at a quantum level my consciousness was, but I was also not here. My body was back in the t-chamber and I was just an observer of that which was.

I turned around, as much as any disembodied consciousness can, and saw that there was another woman behind me, a smile lighting up her face. She was short to my grandmother's tallness with black hair that hung to her shoulders dressed in jeans and a dark peacoat that was too big for her. She looked to be around forty, but her face was rounder and lacked the fine weathering of tobacco and sun, pale compared to the face of my grand-mother. She had brown eyes that were at once soulful and intense.

They were in that corridor of privateness, the sheets flapping on either side of them, their eyes locked in a way that spoke volumes.

It didn't feel right to be between them so I moved to the side and watched.

"It's solstice," the second woman said with a smile that looked at once happy and sad. "Winter solstice."

I knew of her, this second woman, but did not know her name. That was one of the things I was here to find out.

"The sun shall return," my grandmother said.

"And so I have returned," the dark-haired woman said.

They stood there staring and it felt like something was passing between them, like unseen electricity sparking through the air, or perhaps feelings and words carried by something other than language.

The breeze kicked up and the flapping of the freshly hung laundry drowned out any other sounds and it no longer seemed like they were in the backyard of a simple house in a dense neighborhood on a winter's day. It felt like in all the world there was just the two of them.

The woman with the dark hair licked her lips like she was hungry or maybe thirsty.

"Thank you for coming," Grandmother said. "I am sorry I couldn't get away. Little Terry is sick again. That girl is always sick, it seems, and the doctors are baffled."

My ears perked up at the mention of my mother. I knew some of those shouts from the home were hers. She died when I was only five and I longed to see what she was like as a child, but that was not why I was here.

"I understand," the other woman said, taking a tentative step forward, but from the pained look on her face, I wasn't sure that she did. "This is our twenty-fourth time doing this together. Twenty-four is the number of family and..." She trailed off, her lips pursing and her nostrils flaring as she blinked back tears.

The air was thick with need and longing and I felt embarrassed to be there. But the number twenty-four was key for me. It meant the first time they did this was in 1929.

"I prepared," Abigayle said, looking away and reaching down to the laundry basket full of damp clothing and bedding and pulled out a small glass mason jar with a red fluid, some seven-day candles that were about halfway burned down, and two old pillows.

"I brought fire," the other woman said, pulling out a lighter. It was silver and etched on the side was a dot with a circle around it, the astronomical symbol of the sun. "And food, gifts from the earth." She hefted the paper lunch bag in her hand.

"You always bring the fire, Terry," my grandmother said with a smile, her cheeks flushing red, her voice almost apologetic.

I felt a flood of relief. I now knew the woman's name and it was so obvious. My mother had been named after this woman.

Terry didn't blush at what my grandmother had said, she

only smiled and nodded like this was something she knew about herself.

They both moved slowly, tentatively, as they arranged the cushions, put the candles and the jar of wine between them, laid out some cheese and crackers on a clean white cloth napkin, and sat down facing each other.

"We shall not be disturbed?" Terry asked, the tone of it making it sound like a half question.

My grandmother nodded to the house, which was shielded from them by the gently flapping, large white sheets. "College Football is on the radio. Even little Terry likes it and she's doing okay today."

Terry nodded and glanced at her watch. "It's 2:42. One minute until the sun starts returning to us." There was a sadness in how she said it, this clandestine meeting, the two of them hiding in plain sight.

"Then, let us give thanks," my grandmother said, her tone deepening, the rhythm of her words steady. "We do not worship the sun like those long ago, but we celebrate its return. The sun is life and its return signals that the depths of winter are here but that the joy of spring and new life shall come."

I knew the words and mouthed them along with her. She had taught me these words when I was young, when she taught me about the Roman's Saturnalia, the Hopi's Soyal, the Lohri festival in India, the Santo Tomás Festival in Guatemala, and more.

She taught me how Christmas was placed at this time of year to redirect the "pagan" celebrations of the returning of the sun to the then burgeoning religion.

"And we give thanks," Terry said, her tone matching Grandmother's, "for each day we have under the sun, for the gift of light and the gift of life. We give thanks for that which makes our very existence possible and celebrate the return of the sun in this, the northern hemisphere, while acknowledging the perfect balance of it as this is the longest day of the year in the southern hemisphere."

Grandmother thought that important too, while this was our shortest day, for others it was the longest. While winter was coming on in force for us, it was summer that was descending for others. This was nature. This was balance. This was what was real.

Terry went to light the seven-day candle closest to her, but the candle was burned down and the lighter could not reach it. Grandmother fished in the laundry basket and handed Terry one of those long stick matches for lighting fires. Their fingers touched briefly, a small shudder passed through my grandmother.

Terry used her lighter and the long match, lit her candle, and gave the burning match to Grandmother who lit her candle.

Together they said, "We welcome back the sun and the warmth and life it brings."

They shared the mason jar and drank wine, they ate, they marked the returning of the sun with their simple ritual, but there was a restraint there that I was surprised by.

A few minutes after solstice was over, the energy of the ceremony seemed to dissipate and my grandmother slumped a little and asked her companion, "How is your life?"

Terry smiled but it was a little twisted, like there was glass in her mouth. "The psychologists, in their infinite wisdom, have declared homosexuality as a mental disorder and my family has disowned me."

Grandmother blinked and looked down.

"Do you think it is a mental disorder?" Terry asked, her voice low, her face puckered like she had eaten something sour. "Do you think your feelings for me are a... disorder?"

Grandmother didn't look up but said, "How can love ever be a disorder?"

A sob escaped Terry. They were both looking down, Terry picking at the dried and dead grass as the wind kicked up and flapped the cloth around them making it seem like they were far away and all alone.

"You do love me," Terry finally said.

"Yes," grandmother said, not looking up. "And I love Gary and my children. I—"

"Do not worry my sweet Abby," Terry said, cutting her off. "I will never ask you to leave them. Not for me. Not for us."

There was silence between them, excited shouts rising from the house and the sounds of cars on the nearby road, piercing the illusion of their isolation.

"But I can't keep doing this," Terry said, now staring at my grandmother who finally looked up.

"No?" Grandmother asked.

Terry shook her head. "No." She moved the plate and the candles that were between them and scooted close to Grandmother and took her hands and squeezed them.

"I cannot touch you but once a year when the sun returns," Terry said. "It is not enough."

My grandmother's cheeks flushed red but she held Terry's eyes.

"Just like the sun returns every year," Terry said. "My thoughts always return to you and my love is as eternal as that sun which is now returning to us."

Grandmother sniffed and nodded. "But...?" she prompted.

"This is love," Terry said. "We know that."

My grandmother gently nodded her head.

"But because of this world it is also a wound," Terry said, and she looked away. "Seeing you, touching you, feels so good. It heals me. Leaving you reopens the wound and it is worse each year."

The wind died down and the football game inside must have gotten boring because there was a sudden, thick silence.

Terry leaned over and kissed my grandmother. It was tentative at first, but then my grandmother put her hand on Terry's neck and drew her close. There was a passion there as strong as the sun that was returning and I had to hold my own tears back.

I have had a long life. I have loved. But I have never loved like this. I don't think many do.

The kiss lasted a long time and a whole book of feelings was carried on it. The wind kicked back up, the sheets flapping around them, and without a word, Terry got up and walked away without looking back.

It was clear by her straight back and the set of her shoulders that she would not be returning.

Silent tears flowed down my grandmother's cheeks.

I stayed with her even though she couldn't know I was here and I couldn't comfort her. The t-chamber had limits, the fabric of reality had limits, and I knew no one else could come back within fifty meters and fifty minutes of my trip here. This was the privacy I could give her.

When the tears became wracking sobs, I couldn't stay and triggered my exit.

DECEMBER 22, 1929

The bedroom was dark, the waning gibbous moon casting a silver glow over everything through the window.

My eyes didn't need to adjust, since I didn't actually have eyes, the quantum machinery of the t-chamber casting my awareness further back in time this time. To the first winter solstice celebration for Abigayle and Terry.

We were in a converted attic space, the off-white plastered ceiling steep. The floor was rough wood with old throw rugs covering over it and I imagined that it would creak when you walked on it.

At first I thought I was at the wrong place or that I hadn't specified the right date, but then there was a giggle and the flaring of a match.

"It's time," Terry said, the lit match casting her face in its warm glow. The last time I had seen her she had been nearly forty, now she was fifteen. Her complexion was so smooth, her face heavier and rounder, but her brown eyes still so intense.

They sat on pillows on a patch of bare wood, a tapered candle between them as well as a mason jar with what had to be wine, some bits of Swiss cheese, some soda crackers, and two fresh seven-day candles. Terry touched the match to the tapered candle and they almost looked like ghosts themselves in the flickering pool of light, the rest of the room hidden in darkness.

They were both dressed in night shirts and swaddled in thick robes with slippers on their feet. My grandmother's hair was more blonde than brown and spilled over her shoulders. Terry's hair was black as the night and long too.

"Are you going to cast a spell on me?" my grandmother asked with a nervous giggle.

It was odd to see her as a girl. She was in her seventies when I was born. I again felt like an unwelcome voyeur, that I shouldn't be here.

"You can count on it," Terry said, her voice bold and a bit loud.

"Shhhh!" Grandmother hissed. "Don't wake anyone up."

Terry looked around like someone was watching and then giggled, covering her mouth and muffling the sound.

It was dark and I was worried my presence would be noticed. It doesn't happen all the time but sometimes ghosts in time are seen, our spectral presences felt. But the two young women were much too focused on each other for that.

When she recovered, Terry handed grandmother a slip of paper and took one herself and whispered, "My aunt says we must follow this, exactly. We must start right before the moment of solstice and be doing it while the sun starts to return to us."

"What if we don't?" grandmother asked.

Terry shrugged and it was a brief, imprecise gesture. "Then the magic won't happen, I guess."

I watched as they awkwardly did the same ceremony they would do for the last time in twenty-three years. Their words slow and stilted, first my young grandmother and then Terry. They toasted the return of the sun with the wine, sharing the jar and laughing. They ate the cheese and crackers, naming them the gifts of the earth and the sun. And then sat there staring at each other.

"So when does the magic happen?" grandmother asked.

"Now," Terry whispered, her voice husky in a way that seemed comical to me because of their youth. She leaned over and kissed my grandmother and it wasn't the kiss I had witnessed in 1952. It was shyer, sloppier, much more tentative at first, but it was powered by the passion of youth.

My grandmother pulled away, putting her hand to her lips. "You don't kiss like Gary does," she whispered.

"Damn right," Terry said, hunger in her eyes.

"We shouldn't," grandmother said, but she licked her lips and stared at Terry's lips.

"You feel it, Abigayle Trendall," Terry said quietly. "I know you do."

Grandmother bit her lip and looked away. Even in the dim

light I could see that her young cheeks were flushing red. "You shall be the death of me, Terry Grandon," she said.

That was it. That was her name. That's what I needed.

I should have triggered the end to this ghosting back in time. I should have left. This was a private moment, the most private of moments.

I knew that t-chamber wouldn't let me stay if things got too heated. This was one of the first modifications to the device as this technology was used in the same way as many new technologies had been, to indulge in our endless fascination with sex.

Despite the intimacy of the moment, I couldn't leave. Not yet.

"But it will be a pleasant death," Terry said, leaning close to her.

"Do you promise?" grandmother asked, smiling in a way that looked entirely too mature for her age.

"I do," Terry said, licking her lips. "Do you promise?"

Grandmother nodded. "I do."

They were young women exploring, teasing, but it sounded strangely like a wedding ceremony.

They kissed again and the youthful passion of it was overwhelming. That was enough. I left.

DECEMBER 21, 2006

This was the hardest jump of all. This is the one that was forbidden. This was the one that was destined.

My grandmother was old, her face as wrinkled as a dried-up apple, her years of smoking and sunning having more than caught up to her. Her green eyes were dim and it was hard to tell exactly where she was in her mind. She was doing a kind of time traveling herself.

She was sitting in an old blue recliner dressed in a brown robe that could not hide how thin she had become. She was in her bland room in the care facility she lived in, facing the window staring out at the courtyard watching the last bits of fading light, the sun having gone to bed extra early this day.

We were in a locked down memory unit and grandmother belonged there.

"Solstice is here," she said, her voice like the whisper of fall leaves in the wind. "The sun is returning. But she never did."

A young man squatted next to the chair holding her warm hand with its paper-thin skin. He was just seventeen, tall and lanky, dressed in jeans and a light blue button-down shirt that if you looked closely you could tell was a woman's shirt. His hair was dark brown and curly, falling past his ears.

"What was her name?" my grandmother asked, turning to the young man. "Can you tell me, Allan? What was her name? She should be here with me."

Grandmother's hair was still long and plaited into a braid but it was pure white with tendrils of it having escaped the braid to frame her weathered face.

"Call me Ali," the boy who did not want to be a boy said. He had asked more times than he could count for his grandmother to call him that.

I knew this scene and I could hear the words coming before either one of them said them. I felt for the old woman whose memory was a fleeting series of soap bubbles that popped at the slight provocation. I felt even more for the young man who didn't feel at home in his own body.

I felt for him, because I used to be him.

And that was why this was forbidden. You were not allowed to be a ghost in your own presence. The t-chamber did its best to detect such things, but this was sixty-four years ago before I had transitioned, before the gene therapy that saved me from the disease that took my mother so young.

"I just want to remember her name," grandmother said. "I just want to see her lovely face one last time." She took a deep breath and it came out in a shuddering exhale. "It was a different era, you understand that, don't you, Ali? I... I..." She trailed off her dim eyes going distant.

The younger me blinked, surprised that Grandmother had used that name.

"Of course," he said.

"You don't think me terrible, do you?" she asked.

"Of course not. It could not have been easy so long ago."

"As it is not easy now for you," Grandmother said. Her eyes went back to the darkening courtyard and my younger self looked at his watch and said, "It's almost time. I have everything. We can do it just like you taught me."

Ali unzipped a backpack and pulled out the jar, candles, lighter, and slips of paper.

"I... I need to remember her name," Grandmother said. "How could I have forgotten her name?"

This was the moment of destiny. This was why ghosting back to yourself was forbidden. You can alter the timeline. You can create a paradox.

But as the ghost in the room, I was relaxed and unworried. This had already happened when I was young and on the cusp of a change that terrified me just slightly less than not making that change.

As Ali pulled up a stool and arranged things on the windowsill in front of Grandmother, I prepared. It was an odd thing. I had no idea how to do it but I knew it had already been done.

Ali sat next to the old woman and held her hand. When he stilled, I moved close and I...

I don't know how to explain this. I was a ghost, a presence, I had no body and I could not touch my younger self, but that is what I thought about doing, putting my hands on the young Ali's head. Touching me in the past.

I have only written about two trips back in time, but I visited many winter solstices with Abigayle and Terry and I had done a lot of research. I poured that knowledge into the younger me.

At first I felt like nothing, but still I persisted trying to feel what I imagined it would feel like.

Ali shook his head, his overlong bangs falling into his eyes. "What...?" he began.

And then I felt it. I don't know how to describe it besides saying I felt a connection. It was like looking into the eyes of someone you loved. I felt the younger me more viscerally than just a memory and the information flowed.

"Her name..." Ali began to say, his words tentative and a bit slurred like he was in a trance.

"Yes?" Grandmother asked, suddenly more energy in her voice, like she could feel me too and knew this moment was coming.

The younger me swallowed, took a deep breath, and said, "Her name is Terry Grandon and you celebrated your first winter solstice together in 1929 in your bedroom in the attic. The ceremony came from Terry's aunt."

Grandmother blinked and then her eyes welled up with tears. "Yes. Yes. Of course. Damn this mind of mine. I named your mother after her, although your grandfather never knew. How could I forget that? But why didn't she ever come back?"

I stayed like that and poured what I knew into my past-self knowing that this would be hard on Ali. It would be over fifty years until the technology to do this would be created and there would be an explanation. And another fifteen years waiting for my chance to use it.

I poured everything I knew about Abigayle and Terry into Ali, and just one other thing. I let young Ali know that there was a way out of the confusion he was feeling—that it was going to be the hardest thing he would ever do. That soon he would give in and start thinking of himself as a her and follow the difficult steps after that and everything would change for her.

It was a strange experience. I was the older Ali pouring what I could into the younger Ali and remembering what it felt like at the same time.

Matter can't travel through time but energy can. Consciousness can. Spirit can. Ghosts have been seen throughout the centuries. We are those ghosts. And while I remember the confusion as to what was happening as my mind was flooded with thoughts and ideas, I also remember the warmth of it. It felt like I was home, for the very first time.

It changed everything.

I stayed and watched as they welcomed the sun back with the same ceremony Abigayle and Terry had first done in 1929. I said the words I knew so well with them. I too celebrated the return of the sun, so glad for a few more moments with my long-dead grandmother even in her greatly diminished state.

I watched the shift in Ali as she stopped fighting being a her and relaxed into what she was. She smiled and, although I knew better than anyone how far she had to go, it was one of those smiles that says you are glad to be alive and makes those that see it feel the same way.

I watched as she used the information I had fed her and found some old pictures of Terry on her phone. I cried with them as Ali told her that Terry had died suddenly of a brain aneurysm in 1954, two years after grandmother had last seen her and that's why grandmother could not find her in the seventies when she went searching for her. I wept tears of joy as the younger me told her grandmother why she wanted to be called Ali.

This interaction between me and my younger self was a temporal paradox, a causal loop to be specific, forbidden and feared. Much like the realities that the world wasn't ready for what my grandmother and I dealt with.

Grandmother's lucidity soon faded, her eyes dimming, and she said to young Ali, "I believe it's solstice today."

"Yes it is, Grandmother," Ali said, and I was so proud of my younger self for not fighting Grandmother's confusion, not taking on a battle that could not be won and had no benefit.

"I used to celebrate winter solstice with the most lovely woman," Grandmother said.

Ali nodded and smiled. "Yes. You have told me about her," she said. "Her name was Terry Grandon and you loved her very, very much."

Grandmother smiled and suddenly all the wrinkles didn't matter and I saw the much younger woman between the clean sheets sighing and looking up at the sun. I saw that sweet moment of contentment and anticipation returning to her.

She wasn't grieving what couldn't have been, what the world wouldn't yet let be. She was just in that sublime moment of love, celebrating her favorite holiday of the year and remembering someone so very dear to her.

BACKSTORY—A GHOST IN TIME

Genre: Science Fiction
Type of Time Travel: Backward only, causal loop
Nature of Time Travel: Viewing and protecting the past

Those of you that have read much of my writing know I write a lot of ghost stories and here I wrote of a different type of ghost, and provided a different explanation for ghosts.

The setup here is similar to "Goodbye Mrs. Hopkins" in that time travel is about observing history, but with some differences, like only being able to go back to a particular point in the space-time continuum once.

If such a form of time travel existed, it would have all kinds of implications to our privacy, and leave us, in essence, with no privacy whatsoever.

What would the proper use of such technology be? In this story a woman uses it to understand her grandmother better, to protect her grandmother's privacy, and to comfort her grandmother at the end of her life.

But more than that, this story explores a series of socially unaccepted practices through time, including creating causal loops.

PART 11
MY LOVE'S PAST

ONE

I know you're not going to believe this. Hell, I have trouble believing it and I lived it. So I'm just going to come out and say it.

Time travel is real.

Yup, real as you or me, but not what you think it is. Or, rather, not *who* you think it is. Or... It's hard to explain, so I guess I'm just going to have to tell you the story. And like any time-travel story, the "beginning" and the "end" are relative, subjective, but I'll start where it begins for me.

My name is Ashton Bach, but everyone calls me Bach. When I was in junior high, I lobbied for the nickname of "Ash," which I thought was cool, but that fell flat next to my last name, the same name as the famous German composer. Which is ironic, seeing how I am the least musically inclined person you will ever meet.

I just turned fifty years old and after what I've been through in the last few... well, I want to call them days, but we *are* talking time travel here, so let me try that again. After the last few days of my subjective experience skipping around the timeline, I feel a hell of a lot older.

Well, older in that I am tired and worn out, scratched and bruised. But I also feel younger, like I'm seeing the world as it really is for the very first time.

It's much weirder and much more wonderful than I imagined.

And while it may seem like I'm meandering a bit, trying to find my way into the story (spoiler alert: I am) those pieces of information are actually important. I am a fifty-year-old geek who everyone calls Bach but wished he was called Ash.

Got it?

Okay, here we go.

It started on a Saturday. I was at home working. It's what I do. Well, I play a lot of video games and I go bowling on Sundays (kind of my church), and I volunteer at the humane society helping to take care of dogs on Monday. You know, since I work on Saturdays, I take Mondays off.

Yeah. I am a bit out of sync with the world. I bet you are getting that about me already. Another important thing to remember.

Anyway, I was working on a Saturday afternoon. Which I love. No one calls me. No one bothers me. I had Journey cranked (remember, I'm not a kid although I can sure act like one) on my smart speaker and was standing at my desk typing away.

Well, programming. That's what I do. I make electrons dance and people pay me to do it. I'm a programmer for hire helping corporations fulfill their avaristic dreams via technology. It's kind of like getting paid to play video games—except for all the damn meetings, copious messages on Slack, phone calls, and endless emergencies and... well, you get the idea. I may love my job, but it's still a J O B.

Okay, so middle-aged dude (me) at a standing desk, long greying hair pulled back into a ponytail dressed in shorts, a faded Bob Seger concert T-shirt, and some cheap flip-flops.

My office is an ode to my era of geek with things like a vintage *Star Wars* poster of X-wings battling in front of the death star, and an original *Raiders of the Lost Ark* movie poster. Also bookshelves filled with first-edition hardbacks with names like Tolkien, Heinlein, Asimov, and the like. Other shelves with DVDs, Blu-rays, and games. It's all a bit messy and a bit chaotic with no unifying theme except for "middle-aged geek" and that's the way I like it.

I'm typing. I'm mouthing the words I've been hearing Steve Perry sing for decades. It's my fun Saturday everyone-leave-me-alone groove, when a bunch of things happen at once.

During a break between songs, I hear some honking outside. My desk faces away from the window, so I turn around and glance out at the busy road and see a tall homeless guy standing there on the sidewalk, swaying like he's having some kind of religious experience... or maybe he's just starving. He's way overdressed for Phoenix in a dirty and tattered trench coat, but at least he's rocking a ponytail, a mess though it may be.

Right as a new song starts up, my smart speaker goes mute and I turn back around.

I hear my front door open.

A dog barks loudly, an urgent "danger danger, Will Robinson" kind of bark, and I hear the telltale click of nails on my laminate floors.

I take a step to the side so my monster monitor is not occluding my view of the door.

And then the dog is in my office. A corgi with pointed ears, short legs, and a lovely tan-and-white coat. Its big brown eyes connect with mine and I swear the dog knows me.

I know dogs. I love dogs. I'm currently living in an apartment, having recently moved to Phoenix to keep an eye on my aging parents, and I can't have one here.

That's the other thing I do a lot. Help my parents out. Yard work. Doctors' appointments. Making sure they are okay. I'm their only child and it's the right thing to do.

But back to our story and that corgi in my office. So I know what it feels like to look into the eyes of a dog. You can connect instantly. It can be deep. And this is that and a whole bunch more.

The corgi is panting, looking like it's been running as fast as it can on those short legs.

I open my mouth, planning to say something doggy-adorable like, "How'd you get in here, you beautiful boy?" but the dog beats me to it.

He barks and then says....

Wait. It's about to get weird, but stay with me, okay. Remember that I said time travel is real but it wasn't what or *who* you thought it was.

So he barks, opens his mouth, and says, "Come with me if you want to live."

Well, the dog doesn't exactly "speak," no moving of the mouth, but I hear those words in my head.

And no, the dog doesn't sound anything like Arnold Schwarzenegger in *Terminator* 2. In fact, the dog's speaking voice sounds more female than male, the kind of voice you would expect from a young, well-educated woman with a high-brow English accent.

So I assumed wrong. The dog is a girl. I also assumed that the dog wasn't telepathic, so zero out of two for me.

And yeah, T2 is something of a landmark movie for me. I

was twenty-two when it came out. It was the best movie I had ever seen. I've probably watched it fifty times by now. I can say a lot of the lines from memory.

And I am geek enough to know that the phrase originated with *The Terminator*, but I think it was Schwarzenegger's robotic delivery of it that embedded it into our cultural zeitgeist.

So, I'm confronted with a telepathic corgi uttering the ultimate movie catch line (for a dude my age, that is), so what do I do?

I follow the dog, of course.

And as I do, I clearly hear the honking of horns and then the crunch of metal. I'm in my modest living room, which is not much more than a comfy brown couch, huge flat-screen TV, and a gaming rig. I glance back into my office to see an old red Chevy pickup crash through the wall and take out my standing desk, my computer, and my beautiful, ultra-wide 49" monitor.

Remember, my desk faces the room, not the window.

I wouldn't have seen the out of control truck hop the curb and head towards my building. If the speaker hadn't glitched out I wouldn't have heard it over Steve Perry telling me "Don't Stop Believin'."

And as much as it hurts to see my beautiful desk and monitor and computer turned into so much garbage, I realize the talking dog had been speaking the truth and had just saved my life.

I didn't need any more convincing than that. I followed the dog.

TWO

I don't like Phoenix. It's hot. It's a sprawling wasteland of strip malls and suburbia that has taken over the hot desert floor of the Valley of the Sun.

My last place of residence was Seattle. Yeah, the constant clouds take some getting used to, but there is water and you can grow things, and the city, while sprawling, has its own funky vibe that is so much fun.

Phoenix is where I was born. I only came back to take care of my parents.

Okay, well, maybe it was more than that. Like losing my wife to cancer and having everything about Seattle remind me of her. We had met there, fell in love there, and lived there for over two decades.

So, yeah, while I was taking care of my parents physically, they were taking care of me emotionally.

I'm a gangly geek who spends his days on a computer making a living and loves to spend his nights on a computer shooting zombies (or aliens, or anything, really). How am I supposed to find another woman like Mia that will embrace my geeky self?

And even that feels foreign to me, the "find another woman" part. That is there, but I'm more in the phase where I can't imagine being happy—or truly functional—without her, even though she's been gone for two years.

All of this is just more salient details about me that you need to know.

So, back to the telepathic corgi that just saved my life with the Terminator series catch phrase.

I find her on the grass outside my apartment complex looking like any other dog. She is sitting there panting in the hot sun and scratches at her pointy ear with her back claw.

I can smell oil and my ears are still ringing from the sound of the crash.

And then I smell smoke.

Shit.

The apartment complex isn't at all inspiring. Three long buildings two stories high encased in faux adobe with a pool nestled between two of the buildings. The place is about to burn down. I should do something about that, right? But what about this dog, I don't want to lose her. I mean, she's a telepathic dog that just saved my life. But my neighbors.

"Don't go anywhere," I say to the dog, holding my palm up. "Please. I'll be right back."

I pull my phone from my pocket, dial 911, and run into the apartment complex and start banging on doors.

I could afford a house, being a bit slinger for hire pays me pretty well, but I don't want to put roots down. Although I have discovered that I may be a bit too old for apartment living. Too much noise. Too many people. But it is what it is, and I would hate myself if I didn't try to help my neighbors.

Twenty minutes later, the fire department is on site and my whole apartment building is engulfed in flames and the neighbors are warned and the corgi is gone.

For a moment there, a thin little moment, I thought this was the universe's rather twisted way of making up for what happened to Mia. Like it was saying, "Sorry about the love of your life and her cancer, but here's a telepathic dog that just saved your life for you to hang out with."

But not even that.

And what if it had all been my imagination? Maybe I hadn't closed my door properly and the dog had wandered in at the same time my smart speaker glitched. Maybe the dog had barked and my subconscious had heard the wreck happening and made me think the dog was talking so I would move my ass.

And that made it even worse.

Not finding the dog, I look around and it's a scene, I'll tell you that. Three engines spraying water and an assemblage of about fifteen firefighters. There's half a dozen cops trying to corral the civilians and deal with the snarl of traffic on the road, the fire engines blocking a lane, and the lookie-loos slowing down to gawk at the tragedy.

I flop onto the grass and watch the fire department spray water on what used to be my place of residence. The heat from the fire is like a wall of hot that is much worse than the summer sun. I'm twenty yards away and it's like I just stuck my head into an oven on broil.

Other neighbors are wandering around, a glazed look of shock in their eyes. And if I looked in the mirror, I'm sure I'd look that way too.

As I stare at the flames, I realize that my life is in ruins. Again. Not only is my desk and computing rig gone, but my vintage *Star Wars* poster, my antique Tonka truck collection—the awesome old metal ones—, my DVDs and Blu-rays, my—

And then it hits me. I had kept a stash of Mia's favorite clothes. When it got really bad, I would unseal the big Tupperware tub I kept them in and just breathe in her scent, a bit musky and a bit flowery. For a second it would be like she was not gone, like my life was not ruined, like I was not alone.

It was only a moment and only a trick, but the fire would take that from me too. The desk and other things were replaceable, just things, but what I had left of Mia was not.

I twiddle with the gold band I still wear on my left hand. At least I still have that.

The sun is setting to the west and I figure I'd better call my folks, tell them what happened, go stay with them until I can find another place, but I hesitate.

While I have a fertile imagination, there was something about that corgi. Something about her eyes. I didn't really imagine it, did I? As I think on it, I can't remember her mouth moving. I connected with those eyes and heard her voice but she looked like a dog the whole time.

And then she is there nuzzling her way under my arm, panting, her doggy breath smell filling my nose. Suddenly things aren't so bad anymore.

"There you are," I say with a smile, petting her silky fur. I don't care if I had imagined her talking or not, it is clear what I need in my life is a dog. One that needs a home.

But this corgi is well cared for. I get on my knees and look her over and see a few things. First, that look of deep intelligence is still there, like she is seeing into my soul, like she knows me. Second, she isn't wearing a collar.

"Who are you, girl?" I ask.

Those penetrating brown eyes look deep into my soul, she stops panting, and I hear a female voice in my head say, "My name is Angelica Huston. Come with me if you want to live again."

She starts panting again and trots off, away from the flashing red lights and the heat of the fire.

I follow. Of course I do.

THREE

"Like the actress?" I ask, catching up to the corgi who is trotting down the sidewalk away from my burning apartment complex, the heat from the fire rapidly fading. She may have short legs, but she can move when she wants to. "Like from *The Grifters* or *Prizzi's Honor?*"

Right. I've got a telepathic dog that just saved my life on my hands and all I can think of to ask is about her name.

She gives a sharp bark and starts trotting faster down the sidewalk. We've passed a couple more apartment buildings similar to mine and are now walking past homes that were probably built in the nineties with stucco walls and terracotta shingles in mute earth tones. The yards are desert-appropriate with mostly gravel and a few hardy trees and some cacti.

"I knew I liked you, Ashton Bach," she says. "While my real name is unpronounceable by apes like you, I am glad the great actress's—whose name I adopted—more significant works are known to you. Except, I do spell 'Angelica' with a 'g' not a 'j'. Just seems more sensible."

So the dog is telepathic. She knows who I am. And she watches movies and has a thing for Anjelica (with a "j") Huston.

What...?

I've been known to imbibe at times. A beer here and there. A joint now and then. I even tried magic mushrooms once—spoiler alert, too much vomiting for me—but I had never hallucinated a talking dog.

Because I must be hallucinating this, right?

I mean, I get it. Angelica Huston is a fine actress and under used. She is best known for her portrayal of Morticia Addams in *The Addams Family* movies, which is clearly not her best work, but I am by no means the kind of fan this dog seems to be. Or maybe I have some subconscious thing for her that I never real- ized and the stress of this accident and losing my last remnants of Mia has forced a little psychological break and I'm really running around Phoenix after a stray corgi, all the good parts just going on in my mind.

I shrug my shoulders and walk fast to keep up with the dog. We leave the nineties houses behind and turn onto a smaller street with older homes that are more varied, and then turn down a narrow alley. The dog slips between two broken boards in an aging privacy fence and I'm alone.

I can hear the distant sound of traffic and smell the heady scent of flowers from someone's yard, but that's it. I'm alone in an alley wondering whether I should trespass onto a stranger's yard to follow my hallucination.

And I just stand there.

This is trauma, pure and simple. This is unresolved grief and me living too isolated a life in Phoenix. Corgis don't talk to humans telepathically.

The second time, she had said, "Come with me if you want to live *again*." That's not the line from the movie. What had she meant by "again"? Or rather what had my subconscious meant by "again"?

I have no idea where I am. Why would my subconscious bring me here unless I am so far gone that I need serious help?

"Well, come on then, ape," Angelica Huston says in my head, her head sticking through the hole in the fence. "I don't have all day." And then those eyes seem to be looking deeper into me and she does this bark that sounds way more like a laugh than a normal bark.

Her head disappears and I stand there chewing on my lip, looking around, making sure no one is coming, and then I do it.

Well, "do it" makes it sound like I'm some well-muscled dude from a Nike ad. I'm not. I'm tall and skinny and have the upper body strength of someone who spends their days on a computer.

What I do do is climb over the fence, managing to scrape my knee, cut my hand, and rip my shorts, but I make it over and only land hard enough to jar my teeth and not break anything.

I open my mouth to speak but see the spaceship.

Well, it's either that or a giant silver dog bone sitting in the half-dead, half-weedy yard of what must be an unoccupied house.

The dog is standing by the bone or ship or whatever it is. It dwarfs her and is about fifteen feet long and six feet wide where it flares out at the ends. It is reflective, looking like it's made out of metal, and I can see a distorted version of myself gawking.

I'm squished so I look short, and the dog, who is closer, looks giant next to me.

There are so many questions. I mean, could I really be hallucinating something this bizarre without some kind of chemical aid? But on the other hand (or paw, as it were) can this be real?

"I... Umm... You...." I mumble like an idiot, sounding like I don't know how to talk and am not a well-trained engineer. "What is going on?"

As I write this, I don't even know how to refer to my companion. If I call her "the dog" or "the corgi" that seems to fall short of what I am experiencing with this creature. If I call her by her name, Angelica Huston, then you might summon the image of a woman with black hair, prominent cheekbones, and her ever-present bangs.

Suffice it to say that in the moment I am way more confused than that.

"Are you an alien?" I ask.

Okay, with all the sci-fi movies and books I've inhaled, that took me way longer than it should have.

"Duh," Angelica says in my head. "I'm from Sirius. The dog star, you know."

"And... what... why...?" I'm back to incoherent mumbling.

She pads over and licks my scraped knee and sits down and I find myself sitting down too. Did she make me do that? What remains of the grass is dry and poking into my legs quite uncomfortably.

"Can you please just come with me?" she asks, her feminine voice crystal clear in my head although she is just sitting there panting in the heat. "I will level with you, Ashton Bach. I just got promoted and you are my first mission in my new role. I promise things will become clear, but for now we need to go."

I nod. I am not really signaling my agreement, it's more like my head isn't on properly and it bounces up and down because there is nothing else it can do.

An iris opens in the side of the ship and the dog trots in, jumping up and landing inside the ship and disappearing.

There is a brief pause while I sit there quite convinced that I have lost it and will soon be spending the rest of my life as a ward of the state. I mean, my hallucination is a talking dog that just got promoted and I am her mission. If that isn't the kind of thing you get locked up for, I don't know what is.

But then I can see her looking at me, those deep brown eyes look more than a little sad.

"This will help you, Ashton Bach," she says. "And I've got air-conditioning."

"But... but my parents," I say, suddenly thinking of my responsibilities here. "I need to check on them tonight."

Angelica cocks her head and I swear she has a smile on her doggy face. "Don't worry, Ashton Bach, I will get you back in time."

And something clicks in my head. If I'm crazy, I might as well see how deep the rabbit hole goes. If I'm not crazy, it's a freaking telepathic alien dog with a spaceship.

I move and I move fast.

FOUR

The inside of a dog-star alien's spaceship is all rounded corners and soft surfaces. Which is good because there is plenty of crawling for someone my size. This spaceship is definitely built for those with four legs, not bipedal apes like myself.

Wait. When did I start thinking of myself as an ape? Alien telepathic dogs can really get in your head. Literally. But I guess I see the rationale from her perspective. We evolved from apes. She evolved from canines. I'm an ape. She's a dog.

But still, it's strange, isn't it?

The surfaces inside that dog's spaceship are grey and undecorated. The ship has this loamy, earthy scent to it that is rather pleasant. And, I am happy to report, there is air-conditioning, although I never see any vents or any delivery mechanism for it.

Angelica Huston leads me to what must be the bridge. It's just tall enough for me to sit comfortably and just big enough for me and this low platform in the middle of the room. It has four small holes in it and she climbs on and inserts her paws, sniffing at a stalk that rises in front of the platform.

The scent of the room changes, but I can't really tell you

quite how. It's loamier maybe, definitely more intense. I get the distinct impression that the stalk she is sniffing is emitting odors that are more suited to canines than apes.

The curved front of the room changes from bland grey to a grainy black-and-white view of the single-story home in front of the ship.

I don't feel anything, no movement whatsoever, but the black-and-white image changes and soon we are looking at the roof of the house and then the house is far below us and then Phoenix is laid out in an orderly grid that is barely disturbed by the occasional craggy hill, and then the view of Phoenix is sliding down off the screen and is gone.

"Where are we going?" I ask.

Angelica seems to be busy, her paws making small movements in the holes, her nose twitching rapidly, while her eyes take in the view of the Earth below us.

She is flying the ship. Obviously. That is what that platform is all about. No hands. No fingers. So these dog aliens developed technology that they can use with their paws. And the smells, well that must be since their olfactory senses are way better than ours, they have technology to communicate information via smell.

She turns and glances at me, her eyes looking intense this time and I feel my stomach tighten. I'm no longer considering hallucination. I'm all the way in. This is real. And with that look, I'm wondering what the hell I got myself into.

"We are going to Seattle," she says in my head. "But 'where' is not the right question to ask, Ashton Bach."

We must be high now because the view below us is partially occluded by clouds and even more toylike than from an airplane.

"What is the right question?" I ask.

I swear she smiles again. "'When' is the right question."

It takes a moment for my strained brain to put it together.

She used the terminator catch-phrase. She just told me she would "get me back in time." She's taking us to Seattle.

"You are a time traveler," I gasp.

She gives a joyful bark and wags her tail. "My species are the *only* time travelers."

We're going to Seattle. In the past. She also said, "Come with me if you want to live *again*."

"Mia," I say, tears forming in my eyes, but Angelica Huston isn't paying attention to me anymore.

We are so high, I can see the curvature of the Earth. If I'm not hallucinating, I just became an astronaut. And then I can't even think about that most geeky of milestones because the view of the Earth changes.

It's hard to explain. It's not like when in the first Superman movie, Christopher Reeve's Superman made the Earth spin backwards to turn back time, it's more like the Earth shudders, goes out of focus for a few breathless moments, and then shudders back into focus.

While this is happening, I feel like I'm shuddering myself. Like I'm going out of focus and then I'm shuddering back into focus. It smells like plastic is burning and my skin prickles like a bad case of the hives are about to descend. My already rattled brain is further rattled and I'm glad I skipped lunch, otherwise it would have been all over the soft grey floor of Angelica Huston's spaceship.

And then we are plunging down towards Seattle, the verdant land and so much water, the city bracketed by Puget Sound and Lake Washington with Mount Rainier to the south, the land around the city thick with forests. Even on the grainy black-and-white display it's spectacular, but all I can think of is my beloved Mia whole and healthy.

FIVE

"When are we? What is our mission? Why me?" I ask. I had more questions. Believe me, I had more questions, but sitting on the bridge of the alien dog's spaceship watching the Earth rise up, getting a glimpse of the Space Needle, watching as we plunged into a rather plain Seattle suburb just west of Lake Washington, and watching as we land in someone's backyard was enough to stifle all of those other questions.

I didn't feel motion, ever—except for that shudder thing when, I presume, we were time traveling. The ship must have inertial dampers or something—either that or I was hallucinating.

No. Not hallucinating. Let's see how deep the rabbit hole goes.

So, as we descend, I did my best to collect myself and came up with my oh-so-obvious when/what/why question.

Angelica Huston, still on the canine control platform, turns to me and says, "1984. Getting your life back. Why not?"

It takes me a moment to unpack that.

We had time traveled back to 1984, which gave me a bit of a

shudder. George Orwell's dystopian future did not come to pass, but a sci-fi geek like me is going to notice a date like that.

Our mission was "getting my life back" and I had no idea how we could do that in 1984.

And as to why me, the answer was "why not?"

By the time I had unpacked it all, I'm outside the spaceship chasing a corgi through a damp Seattle evening, quite under-dressed in my shorts and Bob Seger T-shirt. But hey, at least folks these days will be a lot more familiar with the marvelous Mr. Seger.

But how do I get my life back in 1984? Mia will be all of twelve, and if getting my life back doesn't have something to do with her, what kind of world is this?

The neighborhood looks like an old one, with smaller single-story homes, some built out of cinderblocks, some stick built, most with attached one-car garages. But then I have to twist my mind around. It's 1984. These could be newer homes. This is Seattle, so trees are large and verdant, hedges abound, and the perfumed scent of flowers fills my nose.

I take a deep breath. I may have been born in the desert, but this is what hope smells like to me. My skin drinks in the damp air and I feel more energy in my limbs than I have had in a while.

A few minutes later, I'm in an alley that runs between two rows of houses faced with wooden privacy fences, tree branches are arching over, and a sudden bit of mist descends, making the rather mundane feel rather mystical.

I can't see Angelica and I speed up my pace and then suddenly I'm kissing the gravel of the alleyway, my vintage Seger T getting rudely roughed up.

I curse and sit up and delicately pull some small rocks out of my right palm. What's another scrape or two in the scheme of things if I get to time travel?

I'm telling myself that, but I'm not leaping up to go catch the alien time traveler. I take my time. Assess the damage—something one must take more seriously as one gets older.

Okay, not "one," "me."

I must take this kind of thing more seriously because I am older. The body changes. It hurts more. It recovers slower. But then again, I have a body and my wife does not, so this is an observation not a complaint.

I take a deep breath and sigh. My wife doesn't have a body and that means I don't have a life.

I think I would have sat there for too long were it not for the sound of crying. It sounds like a girl, a soft sobbing coming from close by. It pulls at my heart and I'm not thinking about my aging body or my dead wife anymore.

I get up and move slowly forward and find a girl huddled into the narrow space between two aluminum trash cans, as if that will provide shelter for her. She's lanky and has light brown skin, dark hair, and brown eyes even more soulful than the dog's.

Her wavy black hair is pulled back into a ponytail and she is wearing a nightgown, dark blue with yellow stars.

My heart skips a beat (or ten). I know who it is. I know this story. It's one my wife told me after we had been a couple for a while about a mystical Seattle evening when this stranger came and told her she would be okay.

"Hi, Mia," I say, feeling my eyes fill with tears. "My name is Ash, and it's going to be all right."

She looks at me, her smooth brow furrowing and her turned-up little nose wrinkling. "Ash? That's a strange name."

"Well, I'm a strange person," I say. "I'm from the future and I'm here to tell you that what's going on inside between your parents, even though I know it's hard to see them fight and it's scary, is going to bc okay."

"Future?" she asks.

I nod and sit down on the gravel in front of her. This girl is so young. She's not my Mia, not yet, but I can still see pieces of her. The mole on her left cheek. The way she bites her lower lip. Her insatiable curiosity.

"Yes. I've time traveled back from 2019," I say.

"How? Tell me." She is leaning, her troubles forgotten for the moment.

"A talking dog brought me here in her bone-shaped spaceship," I say.

She leans back, her forehead furrowing again. "I'm not stupid. I've seen the Mr. Peabody and Sherman cartoon, you know. I suppose your dog is white and wears glasses and likes to give history lessons."

I laugh because I hadn't realized how similar this all was to a cartoon that started around 1960. "No," I say. "My dog is named Angelica Huston and she's a tan and white corgi, and not one lecture so far. And as you can see, I'm not a boy named Sherman."

She shakes her head rapidly, her ponytail flopping back and forth. "No. You are an old man." She wrinkles her nose again.

Although Mia told me the story of this encounter from her perspective with fifteen years between, I don't worry about it. About if I'm saying the right thing or doing the right thing. I can't. I can only be who I am with this version of Mia.

And if Mia and I have done this before, can I really screw it up?

"I am old, so that makes me wise, right?" I ask.

She shrugs tentatively.

"You are a smart one, aren't you?" I say. "Age does not equal wisdom, but since I'm from the future, I know what's about to happen."

"You do?" She leans forward a bit.

I nod. "Right about now your parents have realized you are not in your room. They are starting to look for you. Soon they will get frantic. When you go in, they will act angry, but that's just because they are scared and they love you so much. And hidden behind them being scared, they will feel ashamed of their fighting and how it affects you."

She's biting her lip and nodding for me to continue.

"I know you feel like it's your fault," I say, "but your parents fighting is not about you. They are unhappy, that is all."

"Why can't they just love each other?" she asks.

And this one is hard for me to answer. My own marriage with the grown-up Mia was a good one. We fought, but not often. I never really doubted she was with me. "Sometimes people love each other but just can't get along," I say.

She nods slowly as if thinking about it.

"Look, a year from now everything will be very different, but everyone will be a lot happier," I say. "Can you trust me on that?"

She gives me another weak shrug and it's uncanny. It's one of the gestures she retained as an adult. It was always a signal that I hadn't gotten through to her.

"When you go in," I say, "your mom will see you first and she will say..." I take a moment, because this bit I have to get right. "She will say, 'Mia, you are my heart, and my heart can't take this.'"

Her brow furrows again. "That doesn't make any sense. How can I be her heart and her heart can't take it?"

There are shouts coming from the house on the other side of the fence. I can barely hear them, but Mia turns to look and then looks back at me, her eyes wide.

I get up and brush myself off. "Remember, Mia. If your mom says that, then you know I'm a time traveler and you know that in one year things will be different but a lot better."

I hear a muffled male voice calling out Mia's name.

She nods, getting up and peering timidly back towards her

house. "Thank you, Mr. Ash," she says and then moves to the gate, opens it, and walks in without a second look.

I stand there listening. I can't hear the words, but I can hear the tone shift when they are reunited.

They've got a hard year in front of them, that is for sure.

"Ready?" Angelica Huston asks, panting next to me.

I'm not surprised that she is here. I don't know that anything will surprise me again.

I don't speak right away. I remember Mia telling me about the encounter, about how the "old man" was too skinny and too old to be creepy. About how her mother said exactly what he said she would and that helped her through the year, through her parent's ugly divorce. She told me the man had a funny name but she couldn't remember what it was but that he really helped her.

I met Mia at a party some long-gone Seattle tech startup was having in 1996. I wouldn't have even gone and talked to her—she was way out of my league. Tall and hauntingly beautiful with straight hair just brushing her shoulders—she didn't like the waves and spent hours straightening it in those days. And she had these beautifully intelligent eyes. It was no surprise that I kept looking at her, but the surprise was she kept looking at me.

Believe me, this was not my experience with women. Ones that looked like Mia didn't ever stare at me. I remember going up to her and introducing myself.

"Have we met?" she asked. "You look so familiar."

In that misty alley in Seattle I squat down and look at the corgi. "If not for tonight," I say, "Mia and I would have never gotten together."

The dog licks my scraped hand and I hear her say, "You're smarter than the average ape, Ashton Bach. Ready for more?"

SIX

The mind is a strange thing... or, rather, *my* mind is a strange thing. I don't know about yours. I keep thinking about Mia and time travel and how Angelica Huston said her species was the only one with time travel.

And I think about this saying I've heard. I don't know if it's a saying or a thought experiment, but it goes something like this. If there was time travel, we would know it because the time travelers would be here. No matter how far in the future time travel was invented, they would be back in the past making their presence known.

But maybe they are and the time travelers are dogs, and it's our ape-centric view of the world that keeps us from seeing it. Maybe our ape-centric view of the world keeps us from seeing a lot of things. Important things.

"Only canines time travel?" I ask, following Angelica Huston through the quiet Seattle neighborhood. It's dark enough now that streetlights have come on and twinkle through the mist of the damp evening. I breathe deeply of the moist air, savoring the scent of flowers and growing things.

"The felines want it," she says in my head, "but that would be 'catastrophic.'"

She stops and looks at me, her head slightly cocked, and it takes me a moment. I'm still steeped in twelve-year-old Mia and this train of thought is largely a diversion. I chuckle when I get it. "Cat-astrophic. Good one. But why?"

She cocks her head to the other side like she's reevaluating my base intelligence level. "You ever heard of a seeing eye cat or a drug sniffing cat or a rescue cat?" she asks.

I shake my head, not sure where she is going. "No…"

"Dogs serve. Cats want to be served. Who do you want in control of the most powerful technology the universe has ever seen?"

With that she's trotting forward down the suburban sidewalk and I am walking fast to keep up with her.

My mind is thoroughly distracted by that. The most powerful technology in the universe is time travel. Because a small change can make a big difference. Which makes me wonder why the hell the universe's most powerful technology is being deployed to make sure Mia and I meet. She's dead. We didn't have any children. I haven't made any great contributions to the world.

"Why me?" I ask even before I've thought it through.

Angelica doesn't turn. "Why not you, Ashton Bach?"

"But… I… I'm nobody," I say. "I'm just a guy with a broken heart. Why does it matter if Mia and I meet? Why would you be using time travel for my benefit. Why?"

We're in front of the house whose yard the spaceship is parked in. Angelica sits and nods towards the low wall that fronts the overgrown green yard, right in front of the for-sale sign. Apparently, time-traveling dogs have a database of vacant houses with large enough backyards to park their spaceships in.

I sit and those kind brown eyes are hard to look at.

"How do you feel after seeing her?" she asks.

I take a deep breath and sigh. "Well... it's complicated, but I... I feel..." A small smile creeps onto my face. "I'm so glad I got to meet her like that, to help her. It makes me understand her in a different way."

The dog nods. "And isn't that reason enough? Remember the whole dogs serve cats want to be served thing? Besides, there's time enough for—" She stops, her nose working and her pointed ears swiveling like a radar. And then she is barking with such intensity you would think the world is about to end. She tears around the side of the house towards the backyard barking even louder.

And given that canines control the universe's most powerful technology, maybe the world is about to end. I run after her and find her facing off with three cats in front of the silver bone-shaped spaceship, growling and her hackles raised.

The small yard is a tight fit for the spaceship with a couple of big maple trees leaning over it, the grass back here even longer than the front yard, a small covered patio with metal furniture attached to the back of the house.

At this juncture it is appropriate to say that I am not a cat person. I don't dislike them, but most cats seem to dislike me. I'm the one who will inevitably get scratched at almost any cat encounter.

While it's now clear to me that dogs are aliens, that is something I have always thought of cats. They just don't seem to be from around here. It's like they are all royalty banished to our primitive planet looking for a properly cushy place to live.

These three cats are hissing, their fur up and their backs arched. They are close to where the spaceship's hatch irises open. The one in the center is big and black and flanking it are two tabbies, and it kind of looks like Angelica Huston is outgunned—well, out-clawed for sure. The black one is holding her attention while the tabbies move to flank her.

Well, I don't know Angelica Huston well, but she just gave me the kind of gift you can't repay. I grab a rake leaning against the fence and with a shout, I charge the big black cat.

Much to my surprise, it doesn't run away. It dodges my clumsy thrust of the rake, lets out a snarl, leaps, lands on my chest, and knocks me flat onto the damp weedy grass.

There I am with one of the biggest, fiercest cats I've ever seen sitting on my chest hissing, its yellow eyes making it look positively wild.

For a moment, things seem still and quiet. I don't hear Angelica's barking or the hissing of the tabbies. I hear my heart beating in my ear, but slowly. The cat raises its paw, its claws bared. Time is slowed, like it's all in slow motion. The cat's mouth opens, showing fangs and saliva, and I swear it is enjoying this.

The cat can't kill me. Not with one blow. It's not a panther or something. A dim part of me knows this, but the look in those eyes convinces me otherwise. Still in slow-motion, my heart thumps, the claws extend farther, and the paw swings for my face.

Yeah, my face is nothing to write home about. I'm sure when Mia and I started dating she didn't say to her girlfriends, "Oh, he is soooo dreamy." It was probably something more like, "He's kind and smart and that makes it okay that he has a huge nose and kind of a braying laugh."

But it's *my* face, you know? I see it every day in the mirror and I am not wanting to look in the mirror and see scarring that makes me look like some kind of Bond villain.

So what is an under-exercised, middle-aged geek supposed to do?

I scream. Like a girl. It's a shrill expulsion of fear and all the emotions of what I've just been through. It's full of the confused feelings I have about meeting twelve-year-old Mia. It's powered by the world-shattering realization that cats and dogs are aliens and time travel is real.

Time speeds back up and that cat freezes, its paw cocked back, claws fully extended.

I bought myself a moment with that scream. Less than a second. Sound descends again and I hear Angelica barking and the tabbies hissing and yowling.

I don't have time to think during that thin moment. I just react and swat at the cat like it's a mosquito or something.

Yes, that's right, ladies and gentlemen, Ashton Bach, while helping to defend the world's most powerful technology from a determined feline force, screams and swats.

My hand connects with the big cat as its paw comes crashing down towards me.

And yeah, I'm skinny and old-ish and don't do anything in the way of upper body exercise and it's a big cat, but I still outweigh it by over a hundred pounds.

The swat works, the cat is unceremoniously removed from my chest and I collect a few painful scratches on my hand.

I surge up, brandishing the rake and the cat hisses and swats at it.

Angelica's barking is moving away as well as the hissing of the tabbies.

"That's right," I say, thrusting the rake. "It's just you and me now, kitty."

And then for the second time today I hear a voice in my head. But this one is hissing and deep. "This is not over, ape-man."

Well, that rattles my already very rattled brain. Both dogs and cats are telepathic? Why have they been holding out on us for so long? What does any of this mean in the larger scheme of things?

And that cat has an English accent too. Do all aliens learn to project the English language in London or something?

The cat is lunging, but I return to my senses in time and block it with the rake. "I won't be here long," I say a bit too smugly. "Time travel, you know."

The cat backs up a step and those yellow eyes of his just drill into me. "I smell you, ape-man. I know you. And my ancestors will know you too. You will know no peace from my kind, mark my words."

And then Angelica Huston is here and barking loud enough to wake the dead and the black cat is running off.

Well, at least I know why every cat on the planet seems to hate me.

SEVEN

After the big black cat is gone, I find myself sitting on the moist overgrown grass in the abandoned backyard staring at my reflection in the dog bone-shaped spaceship.

My mind is reeling. This rabbit hole is deep, way deep.

Angelica Huston licks my wounds and I feel unaccountably better. She is always doing that, like a dog will do, and every time she does, I feel better. Like there is something magical in her alien doggy saliva.

She licks her own wounds, too, but mine come first. She is a good dog.

I feel calm. I feel like the world is a good place and everything is going to work out. I don't really care about all the scrapes and scratches. I'm not so freaked out that I saw my apartment burn down, time traveled back thirty-five years, met the girl that would become my wife, and got in a fight with a big black cat that basically cursed me to have all his descendants know me and hate me.

"So... this is your first mission?" I ask, my mind wandering back to something Angelica Huston told me about getting promoted.

"Yes. I used to be on the catch-and-release team," she says in my head, her English accent taking on an unmistakable note of pride. "Reached the highest ranks there. Was chief human abductor for English speaking countries."

I smile and nod. That doggy saliva is good stuff. "Why did you abduct people?" I ask, rather innocently.

She pauses licking her wounds and stares at me, her adorable head cocked to the side. "We have been studying you apes for quite a long time now," she says. "My team was in charge of physical sample collection."

I nod again. I mean, my brain is processing this, correlating it with all the alien abductions stories that have been going around, but it doesn't bother me. The dogs are aliens. They've been studying us. Abducting us. Okay.

What is all of that against the backdrop of time travel and the canines from the dog star Sirius being in charge of it?

Soon we're back in the ship and I'm sitting on the soft grey surface of the bridge and Angelica Huston is on her pedestal. Seattle falls away below us, and when we can see the curvature of the Earth, there is that stutter, out-of-focus, stutter, in-focus thing going on and I feel sick and strange, smell something akin to burning plastic, and am so very fascinated by it all.

"When are we going?" I ask, after all this is not my first time jump and I know the question is always "when" not "where."

"1989," she says.

I rack my brain. 1989. George H. W. Bush was president. The Soviets were at the end of their mess in Afghanistan. Pan Am Flight 103 was blown up. The first Batman movie as well as the second Back to the Future movie came out. And Mia turned seventeen.

A pang of guilt hits me as I sit on the soft floor of the spaceship. There are things that could be done, things that would help the world, and I am thinking only of myself.

Maybe I should be more like a dog and focus on how I can serve.

And then it hits me. I have no idea what model of time travel we are operating on, so I have no idea what kind of actions might actually be of service.

Can the future be changed? Does each intervention result in a new parallel universe isolating your change to the new one? Is time fixed and are we just looping through time doing the things we have already done like I just did with Mia?

This is important stuff.

I mean, if you are going to time travel, you've got to know the science behind it and what the stakes are.

And, yeah, I get that science says time travel isn't possible, but I have evidence to the contrary.

Unless, of course, I'm still falling down the rabbit hole of my own psychotic break. Using the story Mia told me of the strange man that I reminded her of when we first met that helped her in 1984 and seemed to predict the future and inserting myself into it. But even if this is a momentary lapse of reason, there is no reason that my psychosis shouldn't make sense.

I babble to Angelica Huston asking her about how time travel works and she turns from the pedestal, the grainy black-and-white view at the front of the bridge showing our descent back towards Earth.

"Don't be so binary, Ashton Bach," she says in my head.

I blink and rack my brain. "So... we do and don't create parallel universes when we change things and we can and can't change the past?"

She gives me a short bark. "Closer."

Closer? Closer to what? Me having a psychotic break? That is, provided I haven't already had one and then it would be a psychotic break within my psychotic break. Lovely.

But the calming effect of Angelica Huston's lick flows over me again and my thoughts become more orderly.

I just saw Mia and did something that had already affected my life. So, in this case, time travel has an effect, but since that effect had already happened, you are changing and not changing the timeline. At the same time. Cause and effect are not so linear anymore.

Yeah, that calming doggy saliva is good stuff. Maybe what this world needs more of is to be licked by a friendly dog so we can all calm the hell down.

And then I have to wonder that if something drastic happened on a time-travel journey, something that hadn't happened before, maybe that would cause the timeline to fork and a parallel timeline to be created.

The whole "many worlds" thing I always found to be rather exhausting. Saying that for every possible choice being made at every point, a new parallel universe is created just because of that choice just sounds bonkers to me. So many universes and no real choice.

It's not like I quite get what Angelica is getting at, but it feels much more reasonable.

I babble on some more about this as we descend toward the Earth and she barks again and says, "Closer."

And then I see that we are approaching Seattle again. The clouds are thick, but I can see them tattering around the west coast and Puget Sound, making it clear where we are going. To the east, the white tipped peaks of Mount Adams, Mount Rainier, and Mount Baker poke through the blanket of clouds like the spine of some enormous creature moving below, the sun heading towards the horizon casting it all into sharp relief even on the grainy black-and-white display.

We plunge into the clouds and all thoughts of time travel and parallel universes and feline foes are erased, and all I can think of is Mia.

EIGHT

It's dark and damp and I feel like a real creep.

The sun is well down and I'm freezing in my shorts and Seger concert T-shirt. The Seattle high school across the street is fairly typical of a suburban eighties high school, a bit sprawling and rather plainly built out of cinder blocks painted in green and black, undoubtedly the school's colors.

I'm squatting behind a hedge of yet another vacant house watching the comings and goings of the school's teenage students. They move in small clumps, their young voices echoing in the damp air. A few are alone but most of the groups are three or four.

They spill out of the school in small groups, done with some kind of extracurricular activity, some going to cars, others walking off.

It's that I'm the middle-aged guy spying on teenagers that makes me feel like a creep. I mean, what reasonable explanation is there for a man of my age to be squatting behind a hedge watching the school?

Angelica Huston dropped me off here and trotted off, not

telling me what's going on or what I am supposed to do. She left me with an enigmatic, "You'll know, now buck up and be a good ape."

With my luck, I expect the cops to find me at any moment and throw me in jail.

And yes, I'm looking for Mia with her long limbs and wavy black hair. I want to see her, just a glimpse. Maybe that is all I'm here for, just a look at the love of my life at another age and then I can go.

I rack my brain, but I can't remember much about her high school years. She didn't talk about it, really. I knew she played the clarinet, so there was probably band practice, but beyond that, I have no idea.

"What. The. Hell."

I turn and there she is, Mia at seventeen. She's even taller and more gangly than at twelve, dressed in tight jeans and a blue sweater with a letterman's jacket over it.

Pimples decorate her face, and her brown eyes are wide.

She had been walking down the street and I had been so focused on the high school, I hadn't noticed her.

I am a geek, after all, not a spy, and I've had a hell of a day. I mean, technically speaking, this is my third day in my third different year, but it is still a single subjective day.

"Hi, Mia," I say, a sheepish grin on my face. It slips out, what else can I say? I was worried that the police would find me trying to catch a glimpse of my future wife, but it's her that finds me.

"How the hell do you know my name?" she asks, her hand going into her jeans pocket.

I slowly stand up and back up a few steps, my sandaled feet cold on the damp grass.

"What the hell are you doing here?" she asks, her hand coming out of her pocket holding a small cylinder.

And how am I supposed to answer that? I don't even know. I

can't tell her that an alien time traveler dropped me off with no instructions and that time traveler is a telepathic dog who has taken the name of an American actress.

So, I once again do what any self-respecting geek would do in such a situation. I run.

Any thought of my "mission" here is gone. It's clear I'm not going to have a nice heartfelt conversation with her and that anything I could possibly say will just turn me into a bigger creep in her eyes.

At the same time I turn to run, she sprays. That was a can of pepper spray she pulled out of her pocket and she knows how to use it.

I was turning so I only got a little in my eyes. Just enough to make them feel like they are on fire and make them water like Niagara Falls.

So, I'm running, my eyes watering, but at least I can see, kind of. And the benefit of being an out-of-shape desk jockey and running as fast as I can is that I am soon warm... and have a hell of a stitch in my side.

I stop, leaning against a tree trying to catch my breath. I seriously need to add some aerobic exercise into my daily routine.

I ran up a side street away from the high school, but it is still in view. Through the tears, I can see Mia staring in my direction, shaking her head, and then turning to step off the curb and walk across the street.

At the same time, there is a screeching of tires as an old Dodge Charger comes careening around the corner.

Wait. Not old. This is time travel and it's 1989, so the Charger isn't that old, it just looks old to me. Just like the houses.

The car is weaving down the street, heading towards Mia and the high school. I open my mouth to scream at her to watch out, but the car is past before I get the chance.

And then I do the math in my head. Our encounter was short, but I delayed her maybe fifteen seconds.

Those fifteen seconds just saved her life.

And my future.

And that's worth the embarrassment and the pepper spray in the eyes.

NINE

IT'S GOT TO BE THE SAME CAT. THE VACANT SEATTLE HOME has motion-sensor security lights and swaths of harsh bright light illuminate him. Big and black with yellow eyes, hissing with his back arched.

I know, I know, there are about a million black cats, how can this be the same one?

Well, it was sniffing at where the portal is in the dog bone-shaped spaceship, and when it turns and notices me, I can see the recognition in its feral yellow eyes.

The scratch on my hand the cat delivered five years earlier is still fresh, still burning.

"I don't want to fight," I say.

After the incident with Mia, I kept going. This time I had paid attention to where Angelica Huston parked the spaceship, and I came back alone to the vacant house and the backyard where the spaceship is.

I have no idea where the dog is or what she might be up to.

"Well I do," the cat says in my head with the same British accent I remember. He stalks a step forward and hisses at me.

Yup, that is that cat. It had been five years for it and it didn't look any older, in fact, it looked bigger and stronger.

So, I'll admit, I want to run, but then I think about the whole "most powerful technology in the universe" thing. About the feline desire to acquire it.

But then I think—and yes, I do have the tendency to over-think absolutely everything—that because of my own strange relationship with cats, which I finally understand, that maybe I was off. I know what Angelica Huston said, but I don't know if you can take a dog's word when it comes to cats, or vice versa for that matter.

"*When* do you want to go?" I ask and feel pretty proud asking a casual question in time-travel speak.

"None of your business, ape," he says, taking another step forward. Well that confirms that is what they are after.

Now, I haven't picked up the animal and examined its genitals, as is common—and quite rude—when wondering at the gender of a pet, but because of the deep rumble and size of this one, I have determined that the cat is a he.

He is stalking around me, getting behind me so I have a clear shot of getting to the ship. I glance around for a weapon, but there is nothing in this grassy backyard. A swing set on the other side of the spaceship and some nice overgrown flower beds against the wooden privacy fence, but no handy rakes or bats or rocks or anything.

He yowls and in a few moments three other cats join him. Two tabbies, probably the same from our encounter five years ago, and a big Siamese with haunting blue eyes.

They hiss and slowly close in on me and I have nowhere to go but to back up to the ship. Where is Angelica Huston?

"Nice kitties," I say, my voice almost breaking.

I have a lifetime of getting scratched by cats for no reason— well, there is a reason, but I just found out—and now I have four determined aliens with claws and I know that this is not going to end well.

They are closing in. I am backing up and bump into the cool, smooth metal of the spaceship, nowhere left to go. The black cat out half a step in front of its companions, determined to strike the first blow.

This is going to get bloody and this is going to get painful, so I do the same damn thing I did in 1984. I scream. At the top of my lungs.

It isn't manly. It isn't dignified. But, apparently, my wimp scream is not enjoyed by cats. They back up a step. I see an opening and I run.

I feel a scratch at my ankle but otherwise get out of the yard unscathed. But I'm mad. I had tried to be reasonable. I had tried to have a discussion, and they had insisted on violence.

I am huffing on the sidewalk two houses down thinking this through. They hadn't followed, and I notice a hose setup on the side of the yard the spaceship is in.

I sneak back. I slowly turn on the hose, cringing at the squeak, and then peer around the corner and see the four cats still sniffing around where the portal opens into the ship.

With great pleasure, I leap out and hose all four of those cats down.

They hiss. They screech. They are quickly soaked and then they are quickly gone.

"Well done, Ashton Bach," Angelica Huston says in my head as she trots into the backyard. "I was wondering how you would handle them."

I'm sputtering incoherent syllables. She knew. She left me to face them alone. She put me in that terrible situation with the seventeen-year-old Mia instead of letting me just delay her in a less embarrassing way.

"You coming?" she calls from the spaceship portal. "Or do you want to stay in this time?"

TEN

If this were a movie, now would be the time for a montage. The one in which Angelica Huston and I go up into the atmosphere in her spaceship until the curve of the Earth is visible and there is the shudder, out-of-focus, shudder, in-focus thing as we change times. I smell that burning plastic smell and I feel sick and my skin is hot and itchy and then we are back in Seattle where we deal with an annoying, and growing, band of cats and I have odd encounters either directly with Mia or tangential to Mia.

It's all about her. Every single jump. I get to see a different version of her, every single time.

I'm there to stop her tripping and falling down the stairs her first day in college.

I'm there to keep her from walking out into a crosswalk and getting creamed by a drunk driver running a red light.

I'm there to say "You're crazy if you don't offer her the job" to the woman that hires her right out of college after their interview over coffee.

I'm there to see what she looks like after she cuts her beautiful long hair off after a bad breakup.

I'm there to see her brief college hippy phase and her post-college yuppie phase too.

This montage would be interspersed with cat encounters that involve me facing a growing band of cats led by that big black one.

You would also see me acquiring some clothing at a second-hand store and start having my encounters with Mia in disguise. The prize of this being a long black duster similar to what Neo wore in *The Matrix*.

You would also see me find and carry several water pistols and care for them like many people care for real guns. You would see me deploy them repeatedly in defense of the bone-shaped canine spaceship. You would see the pistols working at first, but after a few encounters the number of cats would become too much and you would watch me buy and deploy a long water blaster rifle that I carry slung under that glorious duster.

I'm not the time-travel neophyte I was for those few trips. I walk with confidence and I carry a lot of water guns.

And when thinking about music, the whole thing would likely be backed by The Police's 1983 hit "Every Breath You Take."

Because weirdly, and maybe creepily, I was there watching and taking care of Mia. Time after time.

Oh, wait. Let's switch that backing track to Cyndi Lauper's 1983 hit "Time after Time." Much better.

So, jump after jump, I am there with Mia providing the guardian angel nudges in her young life interspersed with cat battles involving squirt guns while I'm rocking a black duster all to the earnest sounds of Lauper's "Time after Time."

After eight total jumps, we're back in the ship and I am

exhausted. I look cool in my shades and duster, but the constant pace is getting to me.

"Can we take a break?" I ask with a yawn. Angelica Huston has hopped onto the little control pedestal and is about to put her paws in. "And maybe we should get some food. This is time travel, isn't there time enough for food and rest?"

She turns, her head tilting and her radar ears pointing right at me, and she just stares, panting. Our last cat battle was vigorous, but now that I am fully clothed, I escaped without any new scratches.

"But Mia needs you," she says in my head.

"You're kidding, right?" I ask. "Time travel. We go somewhere, fill our bellies, take a shower, sleep for twelve hours and we'll still be back in time."

The corgi turns from me and puts her paws into the pedestal's holes and the front display comes to life. It's not a grainy black-and-white view of the Earth this time, but a twisting 3D view of bright lines dancing through a dark void with an odd script written on them.

The view is black and white still and grainy still, but as Angelica Huston stands there, we zoom out and see how these lines are really just threads in a much larger tapestry and then we zoom in and are looking at a single thread, much thicker and brighter, and how it interacts with all the threads around it.

That has to be Mia.

And there is another thread that comes in from far away and keeps crossing her thread at a sharp angle.

That must be me.

It's a tangle and rather hard to discern much, but soon I see a third thread that must be Angelica Huston and a tangle of other threads that must be our cat nemesis and his gang.

All these lines weave and interact diving in and out of proximity with each other in ways that even look complicated on this display. I have to imagine that this being just a representation of how we interact through time that the reality is much more complicated.

And what is this technology that can track this? Exactly how sophisticated are these canine aliens? Now I am really starting to appreciate that "most powerful technology in the universe" thing.

This is with me just barely grasping what I am seeing.

The lines, timelines I guess, are bright until they hit an invisible marker that is slowly moving and then they turn dull and ghostly for a bit and then they diffuse into incoherent vapor. That must be the line of "now" as time slips by. The tangle of lines that is the cats had moved away but are moving back closer to us. The line of Mia is barely in the view; her line is interacting with other lines now.

"We have to go now," Angelica says.

And the display shifts and I see the Earth falling below us. I miss the lines, the timelines. There was something lulling and comforting about them.

"One more stop and we'll be done," Angelica says. "Buck up, my ape friend. I'll have you home soon and you can sleep all you like."

I lie down on the soft floor of the ship and take a little cat nap while she takes us up, while we jump in time, and while she takes us back down.

ELEVEN

Any time-travel story you watch or read will warn you about meeting a past version of yourself. You might tell yourself something you shouldn't know. You might hurt yourself or keep yourself from doing what you should have done.

What they don't tell you about is the utter horror you might experience on seeing your past-self.

Remember that fancy startup party where I told you I met Mia? Well, I'm there in my black duster and I can see the dork that is the twenty-something me standing alone in a corner nursing a rum and Coke.

It's 1996 and my past-self is wearing a sweater vest, for God's sake. A plaid sweater vest in black and green!

I have no recollection of this. Zero. I mean, I am no fashionista, but a sweater vest? How did I get Mia's attention in the first place? Was that the reason she kept looking at me? I desperately want to go up to myself, rip that damn sweater vest off, and kick myself in the ass.

Not to mention the shaggy brown hair that slumps into my face. That, at least, I understand. I was growing my hair out, feeling confident enough in my job to know that no one really cares what the geek looks like as long as the code gets written.

But that middle stage is just terrible. It's like a furry brown helmet squatting on my head.

The party's location is a bar in a renovated industrial loft with aged brick walls, exposed ventilation, lots of little round tables, and a long wooden bar. The lights are soft and the music is a bit loud and way too nineties for me with milling young people that will soon be known as hipsters in their skinny jeans and beanies, expensive drinks in their hands.

And then I see Mia and... well, I can hardly see anything else. She's tall and slim, her black hair straightened and grown out enough to hang to her shoulders. She has a shy smile on her face that lifts up the mole on her left cheek. She's wearing a simple black sleeveless dress with a short skirt and a fit that accentuates her graceful form and her long limbs. She has a silver clutch in her hand.

She walks in with a dark-haired man that I know is a friend from college and looks around with a smile. She merges into the sea of people with a confidence I could never manage, saying hello, chatting, smiling, eyes following her when she moves on.

My younger self stays put with that rum and Coke, having several conversations with some people who float by. It looks like the rum and those conversations are relaxing the younger me.

Not that I look any better relaxed in that damn sweater.

And then I remember. The sweater was a gift from my mother and I had worn it knowing there would be pictures taken and then I could show her I wore it and she would be so happy.

A nice thought but a terrible look.

And this is the guy that currently lives in shorts, T-shirts, and sandals most of the time speaking. It's not like I know what good fashion is, but I know that a sweater vest is never in fashion.

Angelica Huston is waiting outside. She sent me in with

very specific instructions. At 9:03 PM I am to walk over to my younger self, deliver my line, and then leave.

And then my life will be on track—again? For the first time? —and Mia and I will fall in love and...

Well, that is where it gets sticky. What about that "and"? *And* we will have a nice life together, *and* Mia will end up with pancreatic cancer. *And* she will have a very difficult end. *And* I will be by her side for it all. *And* end up a husk of who I once was.

As I watch Mia circulate effortlessly and I watch my awkward younger self in his sweater vest, I have to wonder about it all. What if I don't deliver my line? What if Mia and I never get together? Surely, I would meet someone else. Maybe someone who didn't die tragically young.

Or maybe I should talk to Mia, warn her of the coming cancer diagnosis, maybe if she sought treatments at first symptom, the back pain and fatigue, maybe she could have beaten it, could have survived longer.

The other things I did as Mia's time-traveling guardian angel were clear and easy. Comfort her while her parents argued. Stopping her from getting run over by a car, several times. Helping her get a job. All of that was clearly worth doing. This... I just don't know.

And I had too much time to think. The hipster/yuppies swirl around me, most of them giving a wide berth to the tall old guy in dark shades and a long duster. Little do they know that in three years when *The Matrix* comes out, this will be as cool as you can get.

And then it is 8:30 PM and Mia has settled at the bar with a group of friends and keeps looking at my younger self.

Of course she is. Me, the twenty-three-years older version of that sweater-vested geek has been in and out of her life since she was twelve. A few times quite recognizably. The difference in ages and the long hair will keep her from putting it together, but the recognition is clearly there.

And then I'm freaking out about how this time travel works where you apparently can and can't change the timeline and you do and don't create new parallel universes.

If I don't do my part, will I disappear, fork the timeline, cause all of reality to implode because of the paradox? Okay, that last one is silly, but you get the picture. My mind is running amok.

And then a woman is standing in front of me, a smile playing on her red lips. She is tall, almost six feet, with short blond hair, light blue eyes, and generous curves dressed simply in black jeans and a black sweater with a rain jacket draped over her arm. "Let's go, Bach," she says. "You know you can't do this."

My jaw drops and just hangs there. If you were looking at us, you'd figure I'm a lonely weirdo who never gets this kind of attention. But I'm really just trying to figure out how she knows who I am.

"What... I... Who...?" I stammer.

She smiles, showing off white teeth and rather pronounced canines. Like, not a vampire, but noticeable.

"You say hello," she whispers, nodding at Mia and moving so her side is pressed to mine, "you say goodbye." Her movements are graceful, sinuous even, like she's a dancer or something. She has enough perfume on for me to smell it and it's almost too strong, the floral note filling up my nose and chasing away the smell of alcohol and too many bodies.

I take a deep breath and get my brain engaged. She knows what I am doing here, so that means that either Angelica Huston sent her or...

"Let me guess," I say, trying to sound as cool as I look. "You are a *cat* person."

She laughs—it's a bright sound and fills my ears. "You're not as dumb as he said you'd be."

He being the big black cat with yellow eyes that keeps trying to get into Angelica Huston's time-traveling spaceship.

And then she stands on her tiptoes and whispers in my ear, her breath warm. "Let's get out of here. I'll make it worth your while. I promise."

A shiver runs down my spine as my body responds to her presence and her offer. It has been a long time for me. Since Mia got really sick. I may be over fifty, but I am still quite human. And she is quite lovely.

But I'm not that shy geek in the sweater vest anymore. I know what a real relationship feels like and I know the power of love beyond attraction that lifts up and makes passion all the better.

And besides, Mia is here, young and beautiful and so full of life. My body may respond to this cat person, but the rest of me does not.

The doubts I had about doing my part here, ensuring that my younger self ends up talking to Mia, evaporate. Time travel may be the most powerful technology in the universe, but love is the most powerful force. Mia and I had love. Not long enough, true, but it would never have been long enough, even if we lived to be old and wrinkled and died together in our sleep.

"While I appreciate the offer," I say. "I'm good right here."

I feel something hard press to my side. My heart leaps and adrenaline flows through my system. The cat person has a gun hidden under the raincoat on her arm.

"I'm afraid I have to insist," she says.

I feel like such a fool. Thinking I'm Neo-cool in my black duster, but all I have hidden are squirt guns which work fairly well in chasing off cats but are nothing compared to a real gun.

Not that I would know how to shoot a gun in real life. Sure,

I've done it so many times in video games, but that's not like dealing with a real weapon and real bullets and real blood.

"Now," she says, her voice still sweet, shoving the gun painfully into my ribs. "We go right now, and I'll leave your beloved Mia alone. Delay one more second and I'll come back and shoot her after I deal with you."

I've seen enough movies to know that time travel often gets tricky, that the heroes must defend time itself from being tampered with, that the stakes are always sky high.

But those are movies and they don't involve intelligent alien canines and felines. What once was a fun, if exhausting, jaunt has turned into something different. Something serious.

I don't argue. I walk out the door with the cat person behind me.

TWELVE

"Why are you doing this?" I ask. She has been marching me towards where the spaceship is hidden in the back of another vacant house just a few minutes' walk from the bar.

The clouds have cleared and a few stars are bright enough to outshine the lights of the city. The sidewalks are wet from the recent rains and the cars make a hissing sound as they pass by on the wet road. The city smells fresh and alive—this was my favorite time when I lived here.

She doesn't answer. She hasn't spoken more than necessary. As I think about it, I guess I shouldn't be surprised that the cats recruited a human. Angelica Huston recruited me with the "come with me if you want to live" line and saving my life.

We quickly walk from the industrial neighborhood in the midst of gentrification to an older neighborhood with modest houses built of brick.

In the small backyard, I see Angelica Huston, her paw held up as if injured. She's got her back to the silver bone-shaped spaceship, blood on her face, surrounded by a dozen cats.

"Any luck?" the woman asks when we are all in the yard.

The yellow-eyed big black cat turns slowly. He is clearly old now, his fur matted down but his yellow eyes still bright. He swishes his tail staring at the woman.

"That's too bad," she says.

Well, that tells me something about these aliens and their telepathic communication. It is, or can be, just person to person.

"You okay, Angelica?" I ask.

"Run, Ashton Bach," she says in my head, her own head hanging down, dejected. Even in defeat, her tone has that British sense of dignity. "I have triggered the self-destruct sequence. The felines must never capture our technology. It looks like I just don't have what it takes to make it in this time-travel business."

Running, well, I'm good at that, but the woman still has her gun pointed at my chest and I have to figure that dying in an explosion is a better way to go than a bullet in the back. And besides, can I abandon Angelica Huston, the dog person that I am?

And then my geek brain goes into high gear asking questions like, what would Neo do? What would Schwarzenegger's benevolent T-800 do? What would Marty McFly do?

Now that last one is way more my speed. In *Back to the Future*, Marty would grab a hoverboard and outwit the bad guys, but no one had a gun in that movie.

And all I've got are squirt guns.

"Seriously?" the woman asks, taking a step forward, continuing her conversation with the black cat. "But you promised this would work. That I would get to go back to..."

A squirt gun is still a gun. It doesn't deliver a bullet to tear through flesh and blood, but it does deliver a stream of water and I've gotten to be pretty accurate and pretty quick on the draw. And these squirt guns have been doctored a bit. The cats had come to care about them less so I added some cayenne pepper to the batch that is on me.

So in what I like to think is a nearly perfect merging of Neo and Marty McFly, I sweep back my duster, pull the two large, black squirt guns holstered there, and fire.

The woman dressed in black isn't expecting me to do anything but stand there and cower like a big ole geek. Her mistake.

And it may be only water with a little cayenne in my guns, but I hit her square in the face and refine my aim so my two streams of water hit directly in her eyes.

Squirt guns with their relatively slow trajectory and issues with wind and the like are actually tricky to use. The farther away you are the more disorganized the water streams are. I chose the pistols because, while they don't have a lot of capacity, they are accurate to about twenty feet.

She curses, cries out in pain, closes her eyes, and shields her face with her arms. The cayenne is working. It may not be pepper spray, but it's not just water anymore.

I drop the empty guns, run two steps, and tackle her. She drops her real gun and goes down. We wrestle briefly and soon she is on top of me and she punches me in the face.

Okay, well, I guess I should have seen that coming. Clearly this cat person does some sort of upper body exercise. I'm not much taller than her and certainly not as strong as she is.

At the same time the squirting, wrestling, punching is going on, I hear hissing and barking from the direction of Angelica Huston and the cats. The barking is at first sharp and defiant, but quickly becomes a yelp. She doesn't stand a chance with that many cats.

The blond woman is groping around for her gun when I get up, just a little bit dizzy, tasting blood and my mouth hurting like hell. Did she loosen a tooth?

She can't see very well, which has delayed her, but I don't know if it will be enough. She's a couple of steps away from me, her hand almost to the sleek black gun.

The duster and the Neo ethic serves me, and I pull two more weapons from under my duster. These are sixteen-ounce spray bottles with way more capacity than a squirt gun, and fancy ones at that. The bottle is made out of stainless steel and contains my water/cayenne mix. They are not as accurate as the squirt guns I started with but have a lot more firepower.

I step towards the cat woman and start squirting into the mass of undulating fur, hitting a few cats.

The woman has found her gun and is standing up. Her eyes are red-rimmed and she appears to be having trouble focusing.

I redirect my stream to her face as I close in and don't slow down. I barrel into her and knock her over and find myself in the middle of a roiling mess of cats and dog.

Angelica Huston's jaw is snapping, the cats are howling, their claws tearing at anything they can find. I'm squirting and yelling and kicking, my long duster serving to parry most of the swiping claws.

It's chaos, glorious chaos. This is no video game, and the stakes are sky high, the most powerful technology in the universe falling into the wrong paws, but that doesn't mean it can't be fun, right?

Angelica and I are taking hits but we are making progress. It's ten cats on us and then six and then five.

At that point we are side by side, our backs against the spaceship and my spray bottles run dry.

The five cats stop, ringed around us with the old black cat in the middle and the cat woman steps forward. Her eyes are red and watering, but she looks like she's recovered from the spray and levels her gun at me.

"Open the ship or your pet human dies," she says.

"Don't do it," I say to the corgi.

"Well, to tell you the truth, Ashton Bach, I wasn't going to," Angelica says in my head with more than a dash of British derision.

"Really?" I ask. Yeah, not my finest moment there after all that Neo-inspired spraying of cats and disabling of a human.

The corgi looks at me, so much empathy in those big brown eyes. "No way, bub," she says. "We are talking about the most powerful technology in the universe. You and I don't really matter compared to that."

I nod and sigh. And then I remember Mia and my sweater-vested self still sitting in the bar. I need to get back there. I need to make sure I meet her. Love is the most powerful force in the universe and that younger me needs to experience it, and all the heartbreak that will eventually come after it.

There has to be a way.

I feel the plastic water cannon hung inside my duster bang against my hip and I have a plan. A bad plan. A sure to fail plan. But if we are going to die, why not?

I sink to my knees in defeat and turn to the spaceship, my shoulders hunched. "No!" I cry out.

I'm no actor and I need to cry, how am I going to do that? My hands are wet with cayenne water so I wipe my eyes, feel the burn and soon my shoulders are heaving and I am crying. For Mia. For my soon to be death. For my stupid, desperate plan.

"I am so sorry, Ashton Bach," Angelica says in my head as she nuzzles against my side. "This is most definitely not the result I was expecting. Even an ape like you deserves better than this."

"Distraction," I hiss in between sobs. "Do something."

I hear restrained British laughter in my head and then she turns and starts howling.

Now this is not some domesticated howl of a well-cared for

pet—this is the lonesome howl of a being about to lose everything they care about, about to lose their life. It pulls at my heart and it strengthens my resolve.

The woman is shouting at Angelica to stop. The cats are yowling. I unclip the water cannon, hold it to my chest, roll on my back and fire. Right into the woman's eyes.

This thing is just a long tube with a plunger you press down. It doesn't have much life, but it does have quite the powerful stream.

The woman sees my movement and shoots her gun just as I fire the water cannon.

The bullet, being faster than the stream of water, lands first, thunking into the spaceship where my head had just been.

The cayenne laden stream hits next, finding its mark and filling her eyes up. She screams, drops the gun, her hands going to her face.

At the same time, the corgi turns into a whirling dervish of lunging, snapping jaws, and wolf-level growling. Cats screech. Fur flies. And I make a mental note to never piss off Angelica Huston.

I get up and the woman is once again feeling around for her gun, but I get to it first. I don't like the feel of it, all black and heavy and full of death. Squirt guns are, honestly, much more my speed, and I say that without any shame.

"What did he promise you?" I ask after backing up a few paces from the woman. Angelica's bark and the hiss of the cats are getting farther away as she chases the rest of them off.

The cat woman looks up at me and she is a pitiful sight, her face red, her eyes swollen, and snot leaking from her nose. She looks older than she did in the bar. She's in great shape, clearly with her being a lot stronger than me, but she's got to be in her mid-forties, that short blond hair chemically enhanced.

"My dad," she says. "He promised to let me see my dad one more time before he dies."

I feel for her. I would give just about anything to see Mia again, to have a few more moments with her even though I've just been in and out of her young life. What I really want is to see her again when she knows who I am and what we mean to each other. I want to tell her that I love her one last time.

And then I remember Mia and I look at my watch. 8:59 PM. I have four minutes to go deliver my line.

I holster the real gun and say, "Stay here. Tell Angelica Huston when she comes back. Maybe we can help you."

"What?" she asks, her red face full of surprise. "You would.... Wait. Who the hell is Angelica Huston? Do you mean the actress from the Addams Family movies?"

"No!" I shout as I run away. "I mean the dog! And don't mention that movie."

THIRTEEN

As I stride across the crowded bar with its clusters of hipsters and geeks with loud music playing and my heart beating even louder, I try to look cool but my breath is labored and my body sweaty and my mouth hurting from being punched and my new scratches bleeding from the fight with the cats and my eyes still burning from the little bit of cayenne water I got in it.

Kinda hard to look cool with all that going on.

As I stride across the bar, I remember this moment from twenty-three years ago, standing in the corner alone, my second rum and Coke just about gone, seeing the old homeless guy stride toward me. He's in a long dirty coat and has ripped jeans and reeks of sweat and spicy food. He's wearing sunglasses and his hair is kind of in a ponytail, but many strands are pulled out and haloing his face. I remember thinking the homeless guy must have really liked Corey Hart and his "Sunglasses at Night" song.

I am remembering the moment from my younger self's point of view and living it from the other end for the first time. It's this strange feedback loop that is quite disorienting.

But my line is simple and it echoes in my memory as I say it to my younger self. I nod toward Mia at the bar who is, thankfully, not looking at us right now. "She's been watching you all night," I say. "You'll regret it forever if you don't at least go introduce yourself."

My sweater-vested younger self had noticed Mia, of course. With that beautiful black hair, those long graceful limbs, those soulful brown eyes, how could I not? I had wanted to do something but lacked the courage. That old homeless guy had pushed me over the edge.

I walk away quickly and glance back before I leave the bar and see my younger self introducing himself to Mia. The spark is obvious, despite the damn sweater vest. I know that spark will turn into the flame of love and that love will outlive Mia's biology.

I know that because I still love her and I would not trade my time with her for anything in this world.

FOURTEEN

Her name is Jessica Cole, the cat person, that is, and she wants to say goodbye to her father.

I dumped the real gun into a trash can on the way back, and while I know she is physically stronger, the spaceship needs four paws to operate, so I think we are okay.

The battle is over. My future with Mia secured. We're in the vacant backyard which smells vaguely of cayenne and shows signs of the battle with areas of the overlong grass stomped and crushed.

Jessica is apologetic and kind now that she thinks we can get her what she wants, but Angelica has a different thought.

"Tell her to come back here in one week, unarmed," she says in my head. I relay the message wondering why Angelica doesn't do it herself. Is this telepathic ability limited in some way, or is the dog just mad?

I can see the wheels turning behind Jessica's bloodshot blue eyes. She's calculating, considering her options, and then her shoulders fall. "Thank you," she says meekly and walks away.

I look at the corgi, her radar ears rotating in the direction of the receding woman. "What was that all about?" I ask.

Angelica tilts her head, her big brown eyes studying me, evaluating me. "Just buying some time." She turns and the spaceship irises smoothly open and she jumps in. "I told you I'd get you back in time, so let's get to it, eh?"

A short trip up, a nauseating time jump, and a short trip down and we are back in Phoenix, Arizona, and I'm trotting after a corgi, overdressed for the desert in my Neo outfit.

It looks like 2019 to me, but I could be wrong. The sprawl of Phoenix has looked this way for a long time. Angelica isn't saying much.

We wind through the residential neighborhood and end up out in front of my apartment complex, except there is no fire, my apartment whole and undamaged.

"Stand here," Angelica says, sitting on the grass at the edge of the sidewalk near the busy street with two lanes of traffic buzzing in each direction.

"Why?" I ask.

"Because it is important, Ashton Bach," she says.

I shrug and stand there next to the corgi, sweating in the duster and the ripped jeans, grateful for the sunglasses.

"Why don't you call me Ash," I say, finally feeling confident enough after defending the world's most powerful technology against a determined pack of cats and an armed cat person to ask for the nickname I want.

"Very well, Ash," she says. "You may call me Angelica Huston."

I smile. At least I could get a dog to use my preferred nickname, almost forty years later. Well, not a dog, really. A technologically advanced, telepathic alien. Now that is something. And Ash makes me sound tougher than I really am. As if the corgi is the nice one of the two of us and I am the badass. That's not true, of course. I played my part, but Angelica is the one with the time-traveling spaceship and the plan.

It's been a hell of a subjective day... or two ... or three? I have no idea how long it's been in terms of hours since the corgi saved my life, but I do know I haven't eaten in that long. A wave of dizziness hits me now that all the craziness is over and I sway there on the sidewalk next to the busy street.

I really need to eat. I really need to sleep. The traffic is mesmerizing and time slips by me and I have no idea how long I've been there.

Another wave of dizziness hits me and I step off the curb and jump back when the blaring of a horn nearly scares me to death.

There is the screeching of brakes, more horns, and then a loud clang as an old red pickup truck jumps the curb right in front of me and goes barreling towards my apartment building.

As the truck bounces over the grass going right towards my office window, I realize something. That homeless guy I had seen out my windows was me.

I had caused the accident that Angelica Huston used to "save" my life and pull me into all of this. I *am* causing that accident.

I stumble back and trip and fall heavily on the rough desert grass on the other side of the sidewalk, the corgi nowhere to be seen.

The truck slams into my apartment, crashing through the window and into my office. I just stare. I can't look away. Moments later I see myself in shorts and a Bob Seger concert T-shirt on the grass in front of the building, the past Angelica Huston with me.

Now I'm really dizzy, but I lever myself up and walk in the other direction. I don't want the police talking to two versions of myself, and I can't let my past-self see me up close.

I glance back and see myself looking at the dog and then

looking back at the apartment building, the scent of smoke just reaching me. I know I'll do the right thing and warn my neighbors and still have the adventure of a lifetime.

And then I smile. The second time Angelica Huston used her line on me she said, "Come with me if you want to live *again*." And I do feel like I am living, really living, for the first time in years.

See, I told you it would get weird. Time travel is real, but it's the canines not the apes that have control of the technology. Dogs are aliens and so are cats and both are telepathic—or at least some are. And sometimes squirt guns are better than real guns.

Sure, that time-traveling dog seemed to have used me, but I got to know my beloved Mia in ways I never imagined. She may be gone, but my love for her is not.

Wait. This is time travel we are talking about. Mia is back there alive and well in the past, if I can just find Angelica Huston and get her to take me back in time.

BACKSTORY—MY LOVE'S PAST

Genre: Fantasy
Type of Time Travel: Bi-directional
Nature of Time Travel: Causal loop

The origin of this story is pretty interesting (as I bet you can imagine), but I don't have room to write about that here. I will give you the very short version: It was on the rim of the Grand Canyon in January of 2019. It had snowed eight inches the night before and the canyon was at its most spectacular. My wife and I, grieving the loss of our spaniel Madison, met an older corgi named Aspen trying valiantly to keep up with her person on her short little legs on the hard-packed snow. That environment and that dog led directly to the creation of Angelica Huston. Intrigued? There's more on my website at *RobertJMcCarter.com/AngelicaOrigin*

Angelica Huston made her first appearance in a short story called "Dog People" written for *Snot Nosed Aliens: Stories from Pulphouse Fiction Magazine*. That is a story featuring Angelica Huston before she was a time traveler. The anthology has a lot of other fun stories and "Dog People" features the Grand Canyon as my wife and I saw it that January.

From there, needing more Angelica Huston in my life, I wrote this story as a stand-alone time travel adventure. But as is the case with twisty time travel stories, there was more to tell and this story became the first part of a novel full of causal loops called *Where the Past Belongs* featuring Angelica and Ash.

I haven't written more in this world yet but hope to get back to it one day and ride the causal loop roller coaster with the telepathic Angelica Huston once again.

PART 12

WHICH CAME FIRST: THE CHICKEN OR THE TIME TRAVELING EGG?

WHICH CAME FIRST: THE CHICKEN OR THE TIME TRAVELING EGG?

My Great Uncle Elias and I were standing near the chicken coop staring at an old white hen named Lucky.

The coop, like any chicken coop on basically any ranch, was modest. A ten-by-ten caged area and a covered roost made of scavenged wood for the chickens to go into at night that contained nests for them to lay their eggs in.

The roost was painted a cheery red about ten years ago and was now flaking and worn. It had rained recently, so the whole place smelled of ammonia.

As my great-uncle stared at Lucky, it was like he couldn't smell that terrible scent but had only eyes for the chicken.

Lucky was fifteen years old, ancient for a chicken, and a mess. Her feathers weren't all there anymore, skin showing under her neck, and she was too skinny, but she pranced around the coop like she owned the place and the other ten or so chickens seemed to agree.

"I tried to eat her once," Elias said. He was dressed in overalls and a white long-sleeved shirt. He had greying brown hair pulled back into a ponytail and was wearing his ever-present plain black baseball cap.

"This was about ten years back," he continued. "She wasn't laying anymore and it was time. Tripped while trying to grab her with a hatchet in my hand. Damn lucky I only broke my arm."

"But that doesn't..." I began.

Great-Uncle Elias lived on a ranch, so he did ranch stuff, but he was really a scientist, the kind that many would prepend the word "mad" in front of.

His area of focus? Time travel. For the last forty years.

The old horse barn was full of the kind of gear that Nikola Tesla would have been perfectly comfortable around, the kind that involves huge amounts of electricity and seems preposterously complicated.

During my teenage years, my folks shipped me out to the ranch during summers to help Great-Uncle Elias take care of things while he went about his science that seemed rather mad. They figured the fresh air and the hard work would be good for me.

"A week ago there were fifteen chickens in here," he continued. "A coyote came calling but Lucky survived. Again."

"But that doesn't..." I said, again.

"No matter what I do," he said, "something gets in here and has a nice meal once or twice a year. Coyotes. Foxes. A couple of snakes. Lucky always survives. And then there was the year they all got sick, every last one of them died, but not Lucky."

"But..." I said.

Elias looked at me, his face full of fine lines from the sun but the tan it had also given him made him seem healthy and hardy. "Lucky is in a causal loop," he said, his words quiet but the force of his confidence strong. "Lucky is protected by the fabric of reality itself. The Machine is close to working. I know it, but I'll only be able to send small things back in time.

Lucky has one last egg to lay which I will send back in time into this very coop and that egg will hatch and become Lucky."

He paused dramatically, put a strong calloused hand on my shoulder, and said, "It's so simple, Tim. Lucky can't die because Lucky is Lucky's own mother."

Great-Uncle Elias had this confidence that was hard to deny when you were in his presence, but his ideas were hard to believe when you weren't in his presence.

"Which came first?" I asked with a nervous grin. "The chicken or the egg?"

"Exactly!" he said with a big smile that made him seem much younger. "That's why I'm counting on you. Your one job this summer is to know when Lucky lays her last egg and bring it to me. That is when The Machine will be ready. That is when I will send her egg back in time"

***

GREAT-UNCLE ELIAS CALLED THE TESLA-LIKE contraption he was working on "The Machine." He never used the word time when referring to it, and I think that was a wise habit so as not to spook the neighbors when he spoke of it.

He lived and worked amongst the rolling hills of rural Vermont and they all talked about him a lot already. If they knew it was time travel he was working on, they might do more than talk.

That was another reason my parents sent me out to spend time with him. To keep an eye on him. To make sure he wasn't completely mad.

You see, Great-Uncle Elias had raised my father after his parents died in a car crash, so he was more like a father to him and a grandfather to me. My father had filled the role I had when he was younger and he didn't want Great-Uncle Elias to be alone all the time.

And that summer, my role was to know when an ancient chicken named Lucky laid an egg when it was clear she was way too old to do so.

So I did the only logical thing, I built a second chicken coop. Well... not a whole coop, just a second enclosed roost off the main area.

It was weird. Once I got it built up—it was not much more than a small box with mismatched shingles on the roof and a little ramp for the chickens to climb—Lucky seemed to know what to do.

This was Lucky's roost, and the first time she walked up the ramp, the ancient chicken strutted and clucked and fluffed up what remained of her feathers.

And the rest of the chickens let it be. I never had to chase Lucky into her coop or convince the other chickens not to go into it. They all knew it was for her. Everyone thinks chickens are dumb, but somehow they all knew.

Could Great-Uncle Elias be right about this?

I DIDN'T JUST RELY ON THE CHICKENS DOING THE RIGHT thing. I beefed up the farm's Wi-Fi, installed motion-sensor cameras, both visible and infrared, in both roosts, and reviewed the footage every morning.

With Lucky's missing feathers, she was easy to identify, even at night on the infrared cameras.

My great-uncle might be crazy, but it was still a "might" and, besides, I loved him and loved being on the ranch. I had responsibility and freedom, the kind I didn't get in San Francisco.

If Lucky was going to lay an egg, I was going to know about it.

And one day, as my great-uncle predicted, an egg showed up in Lucky's nest.

But it wasn't what I expected.

THE MORNING OF THE MIRACULOUS EGG, THE MORNING MY Great-Uncle Elias sent something living back in time, was pretty much like every morning. I ate my oatmeal and blueberries and reviewed last night's footage.

The farmhouse was old and drafty, but reassuringly comfortable since it had stood for over a hundred years. The kitchen was small with a potbelly stove that was still used for cooking in the winter.

Elias was already out in his barn workshop and I was eating, watching the footage from Lucky's roost at 10x speed and I almost missed it.

One minute Lucky was there sitting on her nest, the next she was gone and there was an egg, but the footage had flashed in between, so I wound it back and played it at normal speed.

Lucky untucked her neck, seemed to yawn, stretched out her feathers a bit, and walked away revealing an empty nest. But then the footage went white, jumped forward exactly two seconds, and then there was an egg sitting there.

I sat there, spoon halfway to my mouth, oatmeal dripping off and my jaw agape like I was some kind of idiot.

"What the hell," I said.

I checked the other footage, the camera in the other roost, the one out in the open area, and I saw nothing unusual except for the footage going white and missing two seconds.

My heart started beating hard and I felt sweat stinging the back of my neck.

An egg appeared out of nowhere, but it wasn't Lucky's.

WHEN I BROUGHT THE EGG TO GREAT-UNCLE ELIAS, HE was beaming. "I knew it!" he said. "I can feel it. I've been sending pebbles back in time all week but nothing organic has worked, but today is the day."

I opened my mouth to speak, to tell him the truth, but he started working on The Machine, the towering monstrosity of metal and wire, with gears, whirligigs, and old glass power transformers. It was tall enough to nearly reach the thirty-foot ceilings of this old red barn, and big enough to nearly fill it.

"I do feel bad for Lucky now, though," he said with a shake of his head. "The timeline won't protect her anymore, she can't possibly survive much longer, but all in the name of science."

When the prep was done, the lonely egg was sitting on a small metal plate in the middle of The Machine and Elias handed me some dark goggles which I put on.

He flipped a switch, one of those old-fashioned power breakers with a big handle, and The Machine came to life and started rotating around the lonely egg and the smell of ozone replaced the lingering hay and manure smell of the barn.

The Machine arced and sparked and spun and twirled until it was spinning so fast I couldn't see the mysterious egg, until it was a blur, until there was so much wind from The Machine it felt like I was in the middle of a thunderstorm.

And just when I thought The Machine was spinning so fast it was going to tear itself apart, there was a white flash and a loud popping sound and The Machine wound down to a groaning stop and the metal plate was empty.

And then Great-Uncle Elias was hugging me, slapping me on the back and saying, "We did it!" over and over again.

I didn't have the heart to tell him the truth.

THAT NIGHT WHEN GREAT-UNCLE ELIAS WAS TIPSY ON homemade wine and we were sitting in the kitchen, I got the laptop out and showed him the footage.

"I'm sorry I didn't tell you sooner," I said.

He stared at the screen blinking, so I wound it back and showed him again. "It goes white," I said, "two seconds are lost, and then the egg appeared."

"Well..." he finally said.

"I am so sorry," I said.

He shook his head, like he was trying to wake up or something. "No worries, boy," he said. "It happened exactly as it was supposed to."

"But..." I began.

He waved his hand, pushed the chair back, and got up. "It's a causal loop Lucky is in," he said. "Everything that happens ensures that causal loop's integrity. Even this. You'll see."

He walked out of the kitchen and turned around and added, "But your job is the same. Keep watching Lucky. Wait for her egg."

Three nights later a feral cat made it into the chicken coop and we lost two chickens, but Lucky was just fine. Again.

FOUR WEEKS AND THREE DAYS AFTER THE MYSTERIOUS EGG appeared in Lucky's nest, the old chicken finally laid an egg.

It was another moment where I was in the kitchen and

oatmeal was dripping off my spoon as I watched the footage, ran it back and forth, and made sure there weren't any seconds missing. But there wasn't. The old bird squawked and flapped her wings as if surprised, got up and there was an egg in her nest.

I switched to the coop camera and saw Lucky walk down into the open area, strut around for a bit, and fall over.

I left my breakfast and my laptop and ran out to the chicken coop, entered, and found that the proud old chicken was dead.

Lucky, the fifteen-year-old chicken had laid one last egg and had died. Great-Uncle Elias had to be right. The causal loop was complete and time itself was no longer protecting her.

Except where did that other egg come from? The one Great-Uncle Elias sent back in time to become Lucky?

AFTER REMOVING LUCKY FROM THE COOP—THINKING SHE deserves a proper burial—I took the egg to Great-Uncle Elias in the barn.

"Lucky is dead," I said, holding out the still-warm egg.

He blinked, pursed his lips, and nodded his head.

I don't know how long he had been waiting for this, how long he had hoped that Lucky would lay one more egg and prove his theory, but I have to imagine that he really cared for the old chicken. She was such a survivor.

"I know what to do," he said, taking the egg and placing it on the small metal plate in the middle of the dormant Machine.

He went to the control panel which was all analog dials and gauges and started mumbling to himself, looking at his watch a few times.

"What are you doing?" I asked.

"What must be done," he said, his voice hushed.

This went on for some minutes. At one point he got out a pad of paper and scribbled a bunch of numbers.

"What time did the egg appear last month?" he asked. "What time, exactly?"

I stood there blinking, my jaw moving, until I finally got it. This was Lucky's last egg and it had to be sent back in time into Lucky's new nest four weeks and three days ago so that I could find it, bring it here, and then Elias could send it back fifteen years to become Lucky.

I pulled out my phone, double-checked the time stamp on the video, and told him.

He fiddled with dials a little more, flipped the big breaker switch, and The Machine spun up and soon it was like we were in the middle of a thunderstorm with the sharp scent of ozone and small crackles of electricity hopping from point to point on the massive machine.

After a flash and a loud pop, The Machine wound down and the egg was gone off into the past so I would find it, so Great-Uncle Elias and I would do what was already done, so the causal loop would be fulfilled and Lucky would become her own mother.

***

Later that evening we were up on a hill as the sunset laid its golden light on the rolling Vermont hills. It was a cloudless sunset, warm and welcoming, making the world seem safe.

In front of Great-Uncle Elias and me was a fresh grave just big enough for a chicken. We had piled stones on top to keep the predators out and a few words had been spoken for the tough old time-traveling bird.

Great-Uncle Elias had even taken his black baseball cap off

—which he never did—when he spoke of Lucky the time-traveling chicken.

"Causal loops are confusing," I said after an appropriate amount of silence had passed. "I mean, it's like a circle, there is no beginning and no end. How does it start?"

Elias smiled and nodded and put his arm around me. "What you are asking is, which came first the chicken or the time-traveling egg?"

We both laughed and it felt good and then I said, "Yes. That is exactly what I am asking."

He nodded and we started walking back to the farmhouse in the quiet evening.

"Well, which is it?" I asked.

"Both, neither, I don't know," he said with a chuckle.

"So Lucky couldn't die until Lucky laid the egg that would be sent back in time twice and become Lucky," I said, mostly to hear myself say it.

"Yes," Elias answered. "Exactly."

"And once she had laid that egg, fulfilled her part in the causal loop, she died," I said.

"Yes."

"Because the... ahh... universe itself kept her alive because of..."

"Because of the causal loop," he said. "What was is dependent on what will be."

I thought about it for a moment, running it through my mind, trying to really understand it until a thought popped into my head. "So, that means most heroic fictional figures are time travelers," I said. "They are caught in causal loops."

"What do you mean?" he asked.

"Think about it," I said. "How many times should James Bond have died? Or Jason Bourne? Or Indiana Jones for that matter? No one is that lucky."

"Now you've got it," he said with an approving nod.

"But if they are like Lucky the chicken, that would mean that..." I began, but I couldn't continue.

"No, no," he said with a chuckle. "That wouldn't mean that James Bond is his own father. It would just mean that as an old man he goes back in time and does something that leads to his birth. That could be a very small thing, like delaying someone getting coffee. It could be anything, really, just as long as it directly leads to his subsequent birth."

That night, Great-Uncle Elias let me drink some of his homemade wine and we talked long into the night about the weirdness of causal loops until he finally said, "Now to make The Machine bigger."

"Bigger?" I asked. The wine had gone right to my head and I wasn't following him.

"Bigger," he said. "Big enough for a person. My mother once told the story of how she met my father. It involved her literally running into a tall, slim older man dressed in overalls with a long ponytail and a plain, black baseball cap."

My jaw just fell open.

He laughed, poured a splash more wine in my cup and said, "She also said that this older man looked strangely familiar."

I just stared at my great-uncle as he laughed, took another sip of wine, and said, "I've always known this time travel thing was going to work out for me. Always."

BACKSTORY—WHICH CAME FIRST: THE CHICKEN OR THE TIME TRAVELING EGG?

Genre: Science Fiction
Type of Time Travel: Backward only
Nature of Time Travel: Causal loop

A funny thing happened while I was putting this collection together. I started thinking about time travel, particularly causal loops. A lot. So much so that I had to start writing about them again.

In particular the "which came first: the chicken or the egg?" nature of causal loops where the timeline is inviolate kept spinning around my head.

I love a good causal loop story where everyone takes it very, very seriously and in the end, with great effort, and in the absolute nick of time, everything works out.

But what if you understood the nature of time travel? What if causal loops existed but nothing could really be changed in the end? Maybe it wouldn't be quite so breathless but it still might be interesting.

And that is where this brand-new story came from.

AFTERWORD

There's usually a single story that prompts me to put together a short story collection. In this case it was "The Pearce Shootout." I really like the rather challenging form of time travel in it, where you can only travel into the past and only with great cost and difficulty.

As I was putting together my publishing schedule for 2024, I really wanted to get that story out there again, and figured I could add a couple more time travel stories from my backlog to go along with it. I really didn't think there were that many of them.

At my wife's urging, I took a look at my short story catalog and found, to my delight, that I had written a lot of time travel stories.

I found time travel stories all over the place, written over many years. I guess this is what happens after writing about two hundred short stories, you can't remember all of them all of the time.

Wanting to get that one story out turned into hundreds of pages of them!

Funny thing is I am writing time travel stories again. "Which Came First: The Chicken or the Time Traveling Egg?" is brand new for this collection, written for this collection, and I've got another one in progress. I guess the focus on these stories has gotten my brain obsessed with them again (causal loops, in particular). So, who knows, there might be another collection of time travel stories from me in the future.

And speaking of the future, now for a note to my future self:

Dear Future Robert.

If in the future, time travel does happen to be invented, my advice is to stay away. Isn't life complicated enough already? And if it is invented, please feel free to send back a stock tip or two, but don't let me know how this writing adventure ends up turning out. I'm rather enjoying it and, as you know, I am not the type to read the last page of a book first.

And please, please DO NOT send me any stories that I wrote in the future. I don't care how good they are, if they got made into an award-winning streaming series, won an award or two, or made me a ton of money. I really would rather write these the old-fashioned way and not enter into some insane causal loop with you, my future self.

Sincerely,
Past Robert

ACKNOWLEDGMENTS

My biggest thank you for this collection has to go to Dean Wesley Smith. Not only has he taught me so very much about writing and publishing over the years, but three of these stories appeared in the magazine he edits, *Pulphouse Fiction Magazine*.

As of this writing, I've had stories in fifteen issues of the magazine and quite a few themed Pulphouse anthologies. Having someone say they like your story is awesome. Having someone like it enough to pay you for it and put it in a magazine with their name on it is very, very awesome! Thanks, Dean!

If I time traveled back and told myself when I was just starting to submit short stories to magazines that I'd have fifteen stories in a single magazine, I don't know whether I would have believed it.

I also need to thank those that spent their time to help me make this a better book. That would be my fabulous beta readers: Peter Klein, Roni Hornstein, and Eliot Schipper; my amazing proofreader Diana Cox; and my always encouraging, ever understanding about all the time this takes wife and first listener Aleia.

And thanks to you for taking your precious time and reading these stories.

ABOUT THE AUTHOR

Robert J. McCarter is the author of more than fifteen novels and over one hundred and fifty short stories. He is a regular contributor to *Pulphouse Fiction Magazine* and his short fiction has also appeared in *The Saturday Evening Post, Andromeda Spaceways Inflight Magazine, Everyday Fiction*, and numerous anthologies.

Robert writes in a variety of genres from contemporary fantasy to science fiction and just about everything in between. His diverse background–including a career in software engineering, growing up on a ranch riding horses, and acting–colors the stories he tells.

He lives in the mountains of Arizona with his amazing wife and his ridiculously adorable dogs.

Find out more at:
RobertJMcCarter.com

BOOKS BY ROBERT J. MCCARTER

Short Stores Collections

- Life After: Stories of Life, Death, and the Places in Between
- Anomalous Readings: Thirteen Curious and Confounding Tales
- Creatures Featured: Thirteen Stories of Monsters and Other Creatures
- Contemporary Musings: Sixteen Contemporary Stories from a Sci-Fi Writer
- Finding Time: 12 Meticulously Crafted Time Travel Stories

The Carterville Mystery Series

Find out more at CartervilleAZ.com

The Wood and June versus the Apocalypse Series

Find out more at WoodyAndJune.com

The Neutrinoman and Lightningirl Series

Find out more at Neutrinoman.com

Other Novels:

- Seeing Forever

- Where the Past Belongs: An Angelica and Ash Time Travel Adventure

For a complete list, go to RobertJMcCarter.com